FIGMENTS OF AN ARCHITECT

FIGMENTS OF AN ARCHITECT

BY H.G. LEWIS

Acknowledgements

Many thanks to the test readers: Harrie, Emily, Julie, Valerie and Ana who gave me much needed feedback and critique. Special mention to Valerie who was there to look through my first chapter from day one encouraging me along the way. Another special thanks to Adam, the cover illustrator, for a fantastic design and his accompanied feedback of the story as well. Again, thank you all so much.

PROLOGUE

"This is as far as I can drive us," Rob said halting the car in front of an iron bar gate. A sign which hung over the top of it left no room to interpretation by reading 'Private Property, No Trespassing.' It was left illuminated by the headlights of the car until Rob turned the ignition and the lights died down. Rob then pulled up the handbrake and glanced over to his passenger.

"Well the rest of the way we'll just go on foot then. It's not like we did not expect this," Katie replied, twirling one of her hair bangs absentmindedly.

Rob's face drew a mixture of trepidation and exasperation. "Are you sure you want to do this?"

Katie rolled her eyes having heard that sentence multiple times on the drive up here. She turned to look at her partner in crime. He was not bad looking, a baseball cap held up his long blonde hair which he had neglected to wash today. He had broad shoulders and was dressed in a denim jacket and jeans. On first appearances he may look like the quite typical jock but looks can be deceiving. He was her boyfriend or at least her friend with benefits. He was great to look at but otherwise had little depth to him. Her friends often mentioned how sweet and kind he was, but at the same time how boring he was. He was marriage material, not sex material Katie often said to herself but weirdly she kept him around, partly because he was so infatuated with her, so he obeyed her without complaint. Tonight though seemed to be a different story.

"What's the matter Rob? Don't tell me you're scared of some abandoned manor?" Katie goaded knowing it would get to him. Katie herself was eager to get inside and explore the place. She had been bored senseless writing articles for a newspaper in a town where the most exciting story would be a missing cat. She wanted nothing more than to escape Aberstahl, the sheltered town that it was, bustling with students who would always remind of her of her uni days and its picturesque hills surrounding it symbolising the prison it has become. Before Rob could reply hotly to her jeering Katie opened the car door to step out into the cool autumn air.

Rob had quickly followed suit locking his car as he went. Katie had her excited eyes fixed on the derelict manor in front of them. It was in relatively good condition for its years rumoured to have been built in the 16th century. It was the old residence of the Hinderwell family, a family line which can no longer be traced as the last owner in a spurt of madness killed himself in 1890, leaving no heirs. It was always a surprise to the townsfolk as to why it hasn't been utilised by some business at this point. Rumours circulated that it is cursed but Katie often dismissed such nonsense. The Hinderwell family were known to be obscene in their power trips having built the manor on a hill which had perfect view of Aberstahl below. This was the earliest version of big brother that Katie had come across. The manor itself was square in shape and had many painted windows typical of the time it was made, it was designed partly as a fort having one or two defensive spires and a drained moat all around it. This is the place! Katie thought this is the place where I'm sure to get a lot of views!

"It's not the manor that scares me, it's the fact we will be trespassing. A huge fine if we are caught. I don't fancy paying that." Katie was rudely awoken from her internal reverie to glance over at her whinging partner.

"Where are your balls Rob? This is owned by the council. They don't give a toss about the place. I hear students venture up here all the time and use it as their drug den. If they haven't been dealt with I don't think we will be."

"Clearly non-existent which is what my wallet will be if we are caught," Rob grumbled but offered no other complaint. It was good that he realised he would be paying the fine and not her, Katie secretly acknowledged; he came from a rich family which obviously helped this thing to continue longer than she had planned.

"C'mon then. Have you still got the camera? We have a lot to do and it's cold out." Katie beckoned a resisting Rob to the gate. He had in his hands a video camera bag. Her camera. It was costly, but she felt to do this right she must have a good quality camera. Katie approached the gate and with not an ounce of hesitation climbed the rungs and leapt neatly over to the other side. She was now trespassing not that it bothered her. Rob approached the gate and unlike her hesitated.

"What is it now?" Katie sounded over to him tetchily. Like it or not she needed him for this. She could not do this on her own. She did need her camera man after all.

"Just figuring how to get over it without damaging the camera," he answered.

"It's in a bag, that's supposed to protect it," Katie shouted back with a hint of condescension in her voice.

"Even so, it's expensive, I don't want to risk it."

Katie clicked her tongue in annoyance and walked back to the gate. As much as it was well intentioned it was making her impatient. "Here," she said holding out her arms, "pass it to me before you jump over." Really, they should have thought of this sooner Katie privately admitted but she was in an excited rush.

Convinced, Rob started to clamber up the gate. It creaked eerily under his weight and in a quiet, dark place like this the noise was definitely louder than it should be. Even Katie gave a nervous glance over her shoulder. Having placed the bag in Katie's waiting arms Rob attempted to clamber over. Either it was his weight or his innate clumsiness but as he jumped over his foot caught the top rung.

"Oh shit!" Rob cursed as he sprawled forwards smacking into the wet grass below.

Katie couldn't help but burst into laughter, "are you alright?" she managed through a fit of giggles.

Rob got to his feet red in the face. He said nothing as he laid his hand out to silently ask for the return of the bag. Katie handed it over still giggling at him. "Let's go," he muttered sheepishly as it was this time that Rob led the walk to the manor.

Katie who had finally calmed her laughter down followed him on the uphill walk closer to the manor. The walk was made in an awkward silence, in the dark it was hard to see but Katie got her pocket torch to help illuminate the way. Thankfully it was a clear sky, so the moonlight certainly helped. As they reached flatter ground Katie realised they were now on the edge of the moat. It was covered in grass and just looked like a big trench had been dug all the way around the building. There was thankfully an old wooden bridge which led to the front entrance of the building.

"Okay here looks good to start filming." Katie pointed to right in front of the ageing bridge.

Rob followed her gaze and agreed, "okay let me get the camera set up."

Katie trotted over to her spot mulling over in head what she planned to say. They would do many takes but what Katie ideally wanted was a lot of footage, so she could edit it later. It was a recent dream of hers to make it big on the internet seeing many people her age gain a lot of money simply by recording their daily lives. Katie had a bolder strategy and that is to explore ruins such as this manor and perhaps dramatise it a bit. TV shows have done it but barely any vloggers have, she hoped that would be the key to her rising stardom. She glanced at Rob and realised he had nearly set up the camera. She could trust his pair of steady hands to get a good piece of film. What is more he has admitted he has handled video cameras in the past which made him more than ideal.

"How do I look?" Katie asked seductively giving herself an exaggerated twirl around.

"Beautiful," Rob answered without zero hesitation. Katie actually felt herself blush slightly. Well he was good at compliments she admitted in her head. Katie had opted for a more practical wear for this night's venture, wearing hiking trousers and boots along with a waterproof coat with a furry hood. They were bright coloured in an obnoxiously light blue which would help her appear on film. Despite her practical wear Katie still thought it wise to glam herself up with makeup as she was planning to distribute this on to the internet. People often praised her makeup skills as she wore an almost gothic eyeshadow along with a navy-blue lipstick. Her hair had pink highlights amongst the naturally coloured brown, she often changed her hair colour never satisfied with the results.

"Are you happy for me to start recording?" Rob pressed now holding the camera to his face looking through it. This camera had come with a torch which helped illuminate her for the shot. It did come with a night mode, but she opted to save that for when they were inside the building.

"Just a sec!" Katie checked herself on her camera phone to ensure there was nothing wrong or embarrassing on film. "Yep go ahead!"

Rob held up his spare hand reducing it a finger a second to signal a countdown. When he gave the thumbs up Katie began.

"Hi everyone! It's your favourite vlogger Katie doing an extra special episode tonight. Right behind me is the not well known but definitely spooky Aberstahl Manor! Tonight, me and Rob the camera man are going to explore the inside of the manor and see what we find!" Rob showed his hand in front of the camera to give a little wave. This irritated Katie, but she decided to let it slide as she was still being recorded. "We have no idea what we will find, but let's hope it is a mystery of some kind!" Katie then started to beckon Rob to walk with her as she turned her back to the camera and proceeded to walk across the bridge. It looked stable, but she couldn't help but look down to check her footing. She continued talking to the camera glancing back at it every so often. "For a bit of backstory Aberstahl Manor is nicknamed Wood Makers Lodge as the final living resident George Hinderwell was an accomplished mannequin and doll maker. In 1883 he lost his wife of three years to Tuberculosis making him go into a mad depression. It was told that in the last seven years of his life he dedicated his time to making dolls exactly in her image in the hope she may return."

"Erm is that actually true?" Rob interjected.

Katie who had by now crossed the bridge seethed with annoyance at him interrupting her, she therefore rounded on him, "whether it is true or not Rob, what is definitely true is the manor is abandoned and apparently has a shit tonne of mannequins and dolls left lying around. And keep talking on camera to a minimal! It is my show not yours." Katie sighed as she reached the front entrance, "I'm going to have to edit that out," she muttered to herself.

"I was just thinking of the audience that's all. We don't want them scared away with some stupid campfire tale," Rob reasoned behind the camera most likely still recording this exchange.

"People dig horror films for a reason Rob!" Katie exasperated, "some people love to be on edge I was just helping to build that up. Something, you may have well ruined!"

Rob looked apologetic behind the camera, "I'm sorry Kate."

"Well whatever. Now it is time we go inside." Katie attempted to push against the front entrance, but it did not budge.

"It is probably locked Kate," Rob sounded behind her.

It took all of Katie's self-restraint not to bite Captain Obvious' head off in retaliation. She huffed as she gave up trying to open it further. "Students have definitely gotten in here we just have to find the entrance they use." With that Katie began to walk along the side of the manor. However, since a moat covered all the way around the edges, the strip of flat land was slim. "Be careful not to lose your footing, then we can kiss my £800 camera goodbye," Katie shouted back to a much more cautious Rob.

"Thanks for worrying about the camera!" Rob quipped back with a hint of annoyance in his otherwise inexpressive tone.

Katie ignored this retort as she shimmied, torch helping illuminate the way. This awkward exercise persisted for two minutes with no sign of any other entrance; that was until Katie spotted a strange concrete jutting ahead. It was at floor level and as they drew near Katie recognised it as a cellar entrance. Realising this Katie sped up her movement until she was right in front of it, Rob who was holding a heavy camera took another minute to reach it. Katie gingerly clasped her hand on the handle to metal door and pulled on it. The door gave way and with a creek the entrance was laid bare to them. Katie gave a triumphant glance to Rob who merely shrugged.

"It seems a bit out of place this door way don't you think?" Rob asked crouching down and attempting to see the bottom of the staircase leading down.

Katie wasn't about to question her luck. "The council probably added this later on. No way this was around four centuries ago." She shone her torch down the entrance way to show a concrete floor. It was shallower than she expected. "We'll get the next session when we are inside, c'mon!" Katie began stepping down the narrow steps into the dark cellar. Katie heard the heavier foot falls of Rob who followed suit.

Katie was able to stand upright once she got to the bottom. Using the torch light, she surveyed the room. The cellar was unremarkable, grey concrete lined the walls and floor. There were piles of wood placed along an entire side of the room. It looked like old tree logs which have been cut and just left there. Otherwise another staircase opposite most probably led into the actual manor.

"Shit!" Rob shouted in surprise behind her. Katie glanced at him curiously as he stooped down to pick something off the floor. In his hand was a plastic syringe. "Some students have been doing the big nasty here," Rob deduced fiddling with the syringe in his hands.

"If you don't want aids I suggest you leave that on the floor," Katie replied bemused as Rob hurriedly dropped it to the floor.

"Have you ever done heroin Kate?"

"You're asking me that on camera?!" Katie thundered as they approached the other staircase leading up.

"You said before you would probably edit it out anyway," Rob reasoned still keeping the camera on her.

"Yes, but I'd rather not add to my workload with you asking stupid questions. Moron."

"I was just making conversation."

"By asking me if I took an illegal substance?"

"Have you?"

"Anyway, viewers here is the entrance to the manor we managed to find," Katie said keen to move the topic away from drugs. Rob merely smiled as he allowed her to address the camera. "As you can maybe tell we haven't been the first to use this entrance, but regardless we doubt they will coming here tonight. I wonder what we will find?"

Katie left that question hanging as she started climbing the stairs up into the manor. She gingerly pushed on the hatch door above as it easily gave way. Climbing up and out the hatch way Katie gave a happy gasp as she started taking in her surroundings. It looked like they had come out and into a servant's kitchen. The room was large and had decaying furniture all around. A black iron stove was left unused along with long wooden tables clearly to be used for preparing the master's dinner. Everywhere was covered in dust and all the colour had faded. Curtains were moth eaten but allowed moonlight to trickle in to help with visibility.

As Rob got up and out grunting with difficultly Katie directed to him, "make sure you get a good panning shot of this place Rob." Rob complied as Katie began exploring the room. She lightly touched places with her fingers as she marvelled at the place. Weirdly the place was quite cluttered, rusted knives, spoons and other kitchen utensils have been left on the surface. It is as if no one has bothered to clean the place up at all. Was this the students messing around? Katie wondered.

"Rob how is the picture? Do we need night vision on?" Katie asked as she prepared to leave the kitchen.

"Pictures good Kate. At least from what I can tell."

"Okay let's move on, I wanna find a doll somewhere for the next bit."

Katie opened the door in front of her. As she did a creaking floor board sounded above them. Rob and Katie exchanged worried glances. "Rats," Rob explained more to himself than to Katie but she too accepted that explanation. Or at least, tried to.

As they left the servants kitchen they found themselves in a narrow corridor. It was also faded beyond repair. Doors littered the walls as Katie struggled to decide where to go. Noticing to her immediate left a door was ajar, Katie peered through it. It was a small unremarkable bedroom. A servant's bedroom. Katie realised this whole corridor was just the servants' quarters. Beckoning for Rob to follow her Katie began a purposeful march to the other end of the corridor. As they both walked floor boards creaked under their weight. Katie nervously winced when there was a particularly bad creak glancing to the ceiling to make sure it was not above them where that sound was coming from.

Katie opened the door cautiously as they left the corridor. She clapped her hands together as her guess was right. They had made it to the front entrance hallway. This was by far the largest room yet.

Rob let out a low whistle which carried around the whole room. A large staircase was to their immediate left. It was more like two staircases as it snaked around an archway leading directly into the heart of the building. The staircase was made of wood and had an extremely faded red rug covering most the steps. To their right were two large windows which made the torch Katie had in her hand almost obsolete. What got Katie's attention the most was a figure on a plinth right next to the stairs. As she approached it she realised it was what she was looking for. A wooden sculpture of a woman. It wasn't a doll as it was life sized. It was obviously incomplete and faceless.

"Here is good," Katie said to Rob as he got her in line with the wooden sculpture. "As we have made it to the front entrance we have found the first evidence of George Hinderwell's works. A sculpture of a woman whom I suspect to be his wife. This must be one of his earlier works as it is clearly unfinished. Notice that the face has been totally left alone. Either he couldn't bring, himself to sculpt her face or he had already forgotten what she had looked like. Hopefully we will find more attempts in his workshop." Katie nodded at Rob to indicate her part to the camera was more or less done. As she prepared to head upstairs to where she suspected his workshop would be. Rob sounded off.

"Say this George bloke, you said he went mad right?"

"Right, killed himself after seven years of madness."

"And used that time to try and sculpt his much-missed wife?"

"What are you getting at Rob?"

Rob shrugged moving closer to inspect the sculpture. "I'd just thought he might be better than this."

Katie looked more closely at the sculpture. Rob did have a point. It was poorly made, even amongst their untrained eyes. There was gashes of wood missing in areas and the wood itself was frayed in most places. "Even a good artist can make a bad painting every so often I guess," Katie dismissed.

Rob nodded in agreement as he tore his eyes and camera away from the wooden figure. "Explains why I've never seen his stuff in a museum as well," he chuckled lightly to himself.

Katie silently agreed with Rob as they ascended the stairs. As they got close a door somewhere out of their sight and in the building swung loudly and shut with a slam. Katie and Rob froze in unison at a sound they both knew they could not dismiss as rats.

"Say, perhaps we should call it a night Kate?" Rob asked hopefully clearly spooked by the sound.

Katie steeled herself as well but reasoned as, "wind."

"What?"

"That was just wind. A place like this I wouldn't be surprised if a window had shattered somewhere."

"Kate, I'm not so sure…"

"Where are your balls Rob? Did you leave them outside? Or perhaps in the car?" Katie jeered cruelly. She knew it was too harsh considering what she had asked of him to do for her. But they were so close. She was not going to get spooked now.

"Fine! Fine! Let's hurry it up at the very least!" Rob said angrily. He had lost his patience, something Katie had not seen before.

As they reached the second floor, Katie glanced left and right. Which was the best way now? She pondered. She noticed a humanoid outline to her right. Clearly another wooden sculpture. "This way Rob," Katie pointed as she began walking to the room ahead of her. As they got halfway Katie froze. The human outline had gone.

"What is it Kate? Having second thoughts?" Rob asked hopefully behind her.

Katie licked her rapidly drying lips tasting her own lipstick. "It's nothing," she muttered as they continued walking forward. She could now clearly see wooden sculptures ahead, but she swore they were not in the place she saw the other sculpture. Perhaps Rob's nerves were rubbing off on her. They were passing multiple empty rooms now not giving so much as a glance as Katie beelined towards the room which had loads of sculptures in.

Both of them hurried inside. Neither wishing to admit to the other they were now spooked.

"Okay, there are plenty to choose from in here. Our Mr Hinderwell was a busy man!" Katie said out loud as to stop the oppressively quiet silence.

The room itself was spacious. All around them were wooden, humanoid mannequins, all life sized and all in varying states. Some had white sheets over them covering them from view. In the centre was a wooden stool in front of it was another sculpture. At least Katie hoped it was. It was also covered in a white sheet. This might be his final work Katie thought to herself approaching it slowly.

There was a scared gasp behind her which made Katie glance back at a pale faced Rob.

"What the hell is it Rob?" Katie asked tetchily with her coward of a boyfriend.

He looked at her with abject fear on his face. One that made Katie's skin crawl instinctively, it was another reaction from him Katie had never seen before. "Listen closely Katie, I swear I am not going crazy, but I saw one of those wooden things move."

"What?" Katie said stifling a giggle, "which one?"

Rob pointed to one in the corner with a sheet over it. Katie stared at it for a good ten seconds. It remained frozen in place. As she expected. "It's the moon light, the shadows can cause illusions. Now calm down!" Katie commanded on a pale and sweaty Rob.

He nodded composing himself, "sorry Kate, don't know what came over me."

"It's fine. Say after this part is done we'll head back okay?" Katie started taking pity on Rob. For all his faults she did not want to see him scared out of his wits for fun. Rob nodded encouragingly hoisting the camera to focus back onto her.

Katie was now right next to the central sculpture. Bracing herself she touched the sheet covering it. It fluttered lightly at her touch. Feeling emboldened Katie pulled the sheet off. In front of them both was clearly George Hinderwell's master work. Far better than the joke of a sculpture down stairs. It was smooth and well kept. The sheet must have preserved it all this time. It was clearly his wife. The shape was humanly perfect, with wide hips and large bumps for breasts. It was clearly meant to be naked. The face was also well sculpted, the expression difficult to tell. It looked solemn? Lonely? Katie wasn't quite sure.

Katie took her eyes off the sculpture to look at Rob who was looking at her through the camera again. "Make sure you zoom in on the face okay?" Katie instructed but Rob wasn't listening he instead changed his face into one of terror.

"Katie that one moved as well, I swear it did!"

Katie turned around to glance at the sculpture. It was fixed in place, unmoving, however Katie realised the facial expression had changed. Was it always that menacing looking? Katie wondered, or had she simply misread the facial features? "I think it looks the same?" she said unsure of herself.

"Katie, I need you to back away from it slowly. Something clearly wrong is going on," Rob pleaded with her.

"It's not a tiger Rob," Katie laughed as she turned to look at him. As soon as she did that Katie inside knew she had made a terrible mistake.

"Katie!" no sooner as she had turned to face Rob, Rob had charged at her with all his might. He dropped the camera and shoved her hard away and across the floor. Katie yelped as she landed painfully on the wooden floor.

"Hey what the fuck was that for?!" Katie shouted indignantly but faltered immediately at the sight in front of her. Rob was struggling to move as a wooden arm had clasped itself around his neck. Right where her neck used to be. The sculpture had moved. Rob was going slightly blue in the face as he attempted vainly to wrestle the wooden vice off his neck. Katie slowly raised her eyes to see the wooden sculpture smiling wickedly as it applied pressure to Rob's neck. It got off the plinth slowly and pulled Rob closer as he was clearly overpowered. It clasped its spare hand to now fully envelope his neck. It was killing him.

Katie screamed in terror frozen to the spot on the floor as Rob's eyes bulged. He drew painful gasps and in a desperate act used all his strength to fling the wooden monster off him. His resistance forced the doll into the wall smashing over another doll to the ground. Rob clawed his hands against the gleeful dolls face seemingly unperturbed by his fighting strength. Rob began repeatedly smashing it against the wall using his strength to hopefully cause it to loosen its grip. The smashing was ferocious, and it looked like the wooden doll was struggling to maintain its grip. Could Rob beat it? Katie wondered.

Coming to her senses she got to her feet in preparation to help Rob dislodge whatever was attacking him. However, she froze again as she saw another moving doll creep up behind the animalistic Rob. This one was also beautifully made in the shape of a woman. Its graceful look was taken away as it raised a wooden leg high and brought it crashing down onto Rob's back leg.

The blow issued a sickening cracking sound as Rob's leg gave way. The monster had snapped it in half. Rob's blue face contorted in agony as all he could do was silently scream. He collapsed onto his knees as the wooden doll which was strangling him applied the final pressure.

He glanced over to a terrified Katie tears billowing out his bulging eyes. Their eyes met his dying glassy ones with Katie's fear struck ones. He mouthed a word at her one that Katie read as: Run.

"ROB!!" Katie yelled as she heard a final snap from the neck and his body went limp. They killed him. They murdered him with etched glee on their faces and now the pair of dolls turned their gleeful looks to Katie.

Katie took a second to react as she was still crying over at the crumpled man who she had called her lover. She had brought him here. She forced him to save her. She made him sacrifice himself for her. The dolls began advancing on her and Katie willed her legs to motion she turned and began sprinting away.

Tearing out of the room Katie did not check behind her if her assailants were following her. Yet, as soon as she had started sprinting away from the horrors she had to stop again. Her exit to the stairs were blocked as more wooden dolls had appeared. They were all female in shape and looked at her with that terrifying gleeful face. Was she going to die here?

Katie ran the other way deeper into the manor. She was hearing many footsteps behind her. A small swarm of murderous wooden women were now pursuing her. Katie wailed in anguish as she ran left and right in an attempt to shake off her fate.

Katie thought of jumping through a window but there was no guarantee she would survive the fall. "Stay away!! Don't come near me!" she shrieked. Katie was running out of corridor. As she drew closer Katie could see another humanoid figure at the end of it. She was trapped.

Slowing her pace down Katie drew a whimper as she glanced over her shoulder to six wooden dolls closing in on her. Was this how she would die? Being torn, beaten and strangled by unexplainable, murderous wooden creatures? This is not how she planned to go. Katie glanced back at the figure trapping her and noticed it was different. It had a thicker frame than the rest and was doing a casual walk forward. In the dark and without her torch Katie could not identify what it was. Suddenly a bloom of smoke came from where the mouth was. A light of the end of a cigarette could now be seen. Was this a person? Katie hoped so.

"Help me please!! They are going to kill me!" Katie implored taking her chances with the lone figure.

Katie heard a clicking noise as the figure illuminated itself with a lighter. It was a man. Dressed in a smart black suit with a dark red tie. He was the same height as Katie but with wider shoulders. He had icy blue eyes with a smart short brown hairstyle. He fixed her with a piercing glare. An annoyed glare. One which saw her as a hindrance. "Understood."

The man leapt forward roughly shoving Katie out of the way as he placed himself in-between Katie and the wooden monsters. They did not stop moving forwards unperturbed by this man's appearance. As they reached within arm's length the man acted. He swiped forwards and a blaze of flame struck across the first doll. The blaze made the doll split in half as it crumpled to the floor. The second leapt over its deceased sister reaching out to seize the man, but before it could grab him the man swung again decapitating the beast. Katie realised in his hands was a sword. A sword which was on fire. What? Where did the sword come from? He wasn't holding it a second ago. Katie was left gobsmacked as the man swung through the dolls like a hot knife through butter. They all were powerless against his onslaught as he nimbly swished in the narrow corridor through all six of them.

No soon as the man had struck down the first wooden creature had he quickly dispensed with all of them. A lot of them were now on the ground in a smouldering heap charred by the flame on the sword. Katie glanced back up at her saviour and noticed the sword had now disappeared again. Where did he put it? He had a ruck sack on his back with the zip open, but it was far too small to store that sword. He had no scabbard on his waist either. This was too much for Katie to process. She slumped against the wall in absolute shock.

"Central, I have a lone female witness on site, please advise."

Katie glanced at the man in the suit, he was looking at her with a neutral expression. He was very calm, but the eyes betrayed him. They looked fierce and angry, glaring right at her. He was talking into his wrist as Katie later realised he had an ear piece. Was this guy some kind of Special Forces? Katie speculated.

"No, I am uncertain. They could have been activated because I entered their territory. Therefore, it is inconclusive as to whether she is an architect or not."

Katie felt more questions spur into her head, but she was too in shock to really engage with them.

"She is in shock. Yes, I am happy to deal with it. Again, I am unsure, I'll ask now." The man stopped speaking into his wrist to directly acknowledge her presence, "are you alone?"

Katie glanced at the man feebly, "I am now," she muttered.

"You had an accomplice? Where are they now?" the man pressed sharply.

Tears welled in Katie's eyes as she pointed back the way she came. Not saying anything this was enough for the man to understand the situation.

"Central I believe we have a casualty. Yes, I'll contain it." The man gave an annoyed huff, "please standby for further updates." He proceeded to look down at Katie, not an ounce of sympathy in his gaze. "Stand up!" he barked, "take me to where your companion fell immediately."

Katie issued no complaint as she got to her feet and shuffled forwards. The walk back the way she had fled was haunting. Yet her saviour, the well-dressed and dangerous man, was not to be crossed. Katie could tell on an instinctive level.

Before long Katie had reached the room where the dolls had come to life. She shuddered as she passed the threshold and even more so when she saw the body strewn before her. Katie collapsed to her knees and howled in grief. She could not bring herself to get closer to see the facial expression of her lover.

The man passed her now inspecting the scene. He noticed the camera on the floor tutting in annoyance he brought his foot down forcefully onto the camera smashing it beyond repair. This action brought Katie to her senses, "what are you doing?!"

He looked at Katie. "Containing the situation." He made an expression as if to challenge her to complain but Katie was too weak-willed at this point. He moved to the body looking over it his expression softened slightly. "Central, I have visual confirmation of a deceased citizen, young white male death by asphyxiation. His name?"

Katie realised the man had asked her. "Robert Shaw," she managed feebly not daring herself to come closer.

"Robert Shaw. Yes. Yes. Ok I'll do that." He looked at Katie with a mixture of disdain and pity. "The body cannot leave this place."

"W-what?"

"Under protocol what happened here must be contained. That includes the circumstances of his death."

"What are you-?"

The man reaching into his open rucksack and withdrew a plastic bottle. It was full to the brim with a purple liquid. He began pouring it all over Rob's body. Katie was beginning to realise what he was preparing to do.

"You can't!" she said forcefully earning his steely glare.

"Then come here to try and stop me."

Katie faltered at his challenge looking miserably at the corpse by his feet. This man was scary. Too scary. Not only an enigma but deep down a violent person she could tell from his demeanour. He had a calm and collected expression but again those eyes betrayed his whole persona. He was not an ally. Katie decided that, he was not here to really help her.

He lit a cigarette taking a puff before dropping it onto the corpse. Instantly the corpse ignited. The fire started spreading as the man watched on placidly. "Robert Shaw died in an arson attempt he himself instigated on Aberstahl Manor. A tragedy indeed. This is what happened here."

He was covering it up. The bastard was using Robert's sacrifice and turning his name into a criminal one, Katie felt herself seethe with rage. "You're responsible for what happened here aren't you?!"

The man gave Katie a measured look moving over to her. "Possibly, however I am not responsible for your decision to be here. This is private property. Your timing here was… ill-made."

"What the hell happened here?!" Katie thundered finding her backbone. The man kept his neutral expression as the fire began to heat the room. It started trickling to the walls now.

"This building is scheduled to be demolished I am here to survey that it is fit for demolishing."

"Don't fuck with me!" Katie accused.

The man for the first time gave a small smile. It was cruel and not heart-warming in the slightest. "You need not believe my word now. You do not need to believe my intent either. However, I am keeping my word about saving you. I do not go back on promises like that. Now come we must leave."

Katie was about to retort when she heard a door open in the distance. "More of them?" she whispered out loud.

The man glanced over to where the sound came from. "Almost certainly, George Hinderwell was a busy man. Now come."

The man swiftly departed from the room, Katie hesitated glancing over at the fire. The corpse of Rob was barely seen now as the fire began raging in earnest. Katie tore herself from the sight and hurried up to catch up with the man in black. They reached the staircase before Katie called after him, "What are those things? Why did they kill Rob and try to kill me?"

"Figments," the man answered not stopping to talk as he descended the stairs. "More succinctly put, spectre class figments made by George Hinderwell. They'll attack anyone in sight if an architect is in their territory."

"Figments? Architects? What does any of that mean?!" Katie pressed hurrying to catch up with as she saw a wooden face emerge from a doorway not far away.

The man unhelpfully stopped at the bottom of the stairs to look up at her. "Your comprehension of the situation is not necessary for your survival. Now get behind me we have company."

Katie complied knowing that behind her, descending the stairs, were more wooden dolls. Each with that sickening gleeful expression on their faces. Katie Stood behind the man as he watched patiently, the wooden dolls started appearing in number. Smoke was billowing from the corridor they had just left. The wooden women seemed uninterested or simply unaware a fire was now raging heavily. There were at least ten of these creatures all of whom bee lining for the pair of them. The man brought his arm back and into his ruck sack. Katie saw him reach into it seizing onto something Katie then realised it was the hilt of a sword. Pulling it gently out of the ruck sack the same sword Katie had witnessed earlier was in his right hand. It could not have been in that ruck sack the whole time?! Katie thought incredulously. It was simply too small of a ruck sack. The man reaching again into his bag with his spare hand with drew a purple bottle. It was jewel encrusted and full of liquid, a rag stuffed into the bottle mouth. The man swiped confidently across the top of the bottle with his sword to set the rag aflame.

"Now, burn you fake abominations," the man said in a theatre like proclamation before throwing the bottle over the closest doll. Immediately setting the closest trio a light in flame. The trio collapsed quickly under the amount of fire produced from the Molotov cocktail the man had thrown. He repeated the process again, withdrawing a virtually identical bottle from his bag and throwing it at more of them. Soon his pyromania was setting the whole manor ablaze in front of them. Katie started coughing from the amount of smoke being produced. She looked at the scene in front of her watching this man methodically destroy these things with ease. From the way they acted Katie could tell they were not alive. They were not intelligent. They were just like puppets driven by a single sinister purpose. Some just walked into the flame only to keel over into burning wrecks. Katie glanced towards the pyromaniac as he swung his sword across a doll that managed to get too close. The doll collapsed in a smouldering heap as he smiled wickedly. With the light of the blaze in front of him reflecting off his eyes Katie noticed he looked almost demonic. His face etched in a very similar gleeful expression to the dolls that had murdered Rob. He was enjoying this. Soon the smoke started to prove too much for Katie and the man. He gestured with his hand to follow with a rag over his mouth.

Reaching the front entrance Katie was all too reminded of her futility of not being able to open it when trying to get inside. The man was unperturbed by this however striking on the door lock with his foot smashing it open with ease. Katie saw her opening, she along with her saviour, bolted out of the manor and into the fresh autumn air.

Katie took several strides more than the mysterious man collapsing once she reached the other side of the wooden bridge. She coughed and spluttered as she attempted to breathe thankful there was no more smoke clogging her lungs. Footsteps behind her indicated the man had got off a lot more unscathed and was standing behind her.

"I have kept my word," he said as if to make the point.

Still coughing and spluttering Katie massaged her throat still in slight disbelief that she was alive. "Thank you," she rasped, "please, can you honour Rob more? He doesn't deserve being blamed for all of this, I do. Not him. He saved me, if not for his actions it would be my body being burned right now."

"I cannot alter what those above me decide what is best. That is the chain of command. However, he has my personal respect. Any individual who stands up to those monstrosities deserve a hero's burial. I am personally sorry that the circumstances could not permit that."

Katie let those words sink in. He really was an enigma. This man she could not get a read on shows up at the right moment to save her and in a trivial attempt to console her praises her boyfriend's valour. Oh Rob, she thought to herself, how I will hate myself for the rest of my life, if only I could bury it forever. Coming to her senses she began to turn and face her hero of the hour, "by the way I never caught your name Mr er?"

As she turned to face him. Katie's eyes started to become unfocused. She heard a jangling of metal and feel an immense sense of fatigue wash over her. Was she just tired? She wondered, or was it all just a dream? Yes, perhaps it would be best just to consider this whole thing as just a dream. It is easier that way.

As Katie plunged into unconsciousness she heard her saviour say one last thing.

"Squire. Mr Squire."

CHAPTER 1

The bus driver squinted at Lucy's scrunched, barely looked after bus pass; seeing as she kept it in her back pocket and always forgot to take it out before seeing it swim in the washing machine, she could not blame him for taking a second look.

But really? To take this long? She could feel the angry stares of her fellow 8am commuters drill into the back of her skull. It was raining, some girls had forgot their umbrellas. The old man behind the wheel grunted as to suggest he was satisfied allowing her to board. After what felt like a Mexican to an American border interview Lucy quickly pelted up to the second deck to get a window seat. She found a double seat near the back free, beelining for it she made no waste to lay claim. Thrusting her sports bag onto the plastic seat she sighed in relief and laid her cheek against the cool window. The window was fogged with condensation as the wet autumn morning made its daily rounds. She brushed her short, black, wet hair out of her eyes moving her hair band to catch her fringe.

Finally, peace. It was another restless night, another nightmare. She sighed and closed her eyes trying not to think why she had to get up so early. Flashing her eyes open Lucy sought to untangle her headphones cursing the level of difficulty this knot had for her. Plugged in, she played it on shuffle waiting for what surprised her. Soon a lurch on the bus showed it had moved from the bus stop and was on its way. Opening her eyes again she examined herself in the window's reflection.

Yep, still look like death she lamented in her thoughts. The bags under her eyes could carry a full Tesco's shop. Other than that, a plain, grumpy 8am face greeted her. Lucy never thought to hide her face behind a wall of make-up she found it intoxicating, caging.

The bus came to a halt, another bus stop. Lucy checked her watch, she had plenty of time before her 9am lecture yet she still felt paranoid that getting on a bus less than an hour before the lecture was too risky. The town of Aberstahl proved to disrupt any journey with its tight street corners and horrendously over populated roads. It was either the bus or cycle and, in this weather, it was bus, every time.

The bus lurched off again as Lucy tried to focus her thoughts on nothing. To be in the Zen, to meditate all the reality to the back of the mind. The bus was filling up, she noticed the second deck was nearly full.

This was a cause of great concern for Lucy she hated anyone sitting next to her on the bus. It was her time of self-reflection, her Zen, not for someone to laugh at a meme next to her out loud or for someone with just a mutant shoulder range to pin her against the window against her will. She started eyeing the trickle of passengers coming on now putting her left hand firmly over her bag claiming the seat next to her. She hoped this was signal enough to suggest you are not welcome here.

"Excuse me, is this seat taken?"

Oh, fuck. A guy, a student no doubt Lucy observed, he had pushed his headphones around his neck to ask the question he already knew the answer to.

"No fuck off and stand downstairs!" is what Lucy wanted to say.

"No, it's not taken," she said smiling politely and moving the bag between her feet is what she did. He naturally sat down making her morning ruined. He looked fine enough, smartly dressed with fogged glasses but with a long black trench coat to go with the white shirt. Her interest in him quickly dissipated after that observation. She turned to look out at the window again to see the rain hammer its way through everyone's Monday blues.

The man started laughing next to her. A disgusting laugh. Loud and inconsiderate of everyone around him. She glanced at his phone in his hands, a YouTube video, looks like a vlogger of some kind. She turned away only for him to start laughing even more. Lucy's eyebrow's twitched, anyone who knew her knows when she is angry, her right eyebrow starts twitching. She glanced at him this time for longer, hoping he may get the vibe she was trying telepathically to send to his brain. "It's 8am! Take your energy and your laugh out of my Zen please." She thought this message if sent telepathically would reenergise his sense of awareness.

Amazingly, he saw her looking at him. Taking his head phones off Lucy was expecting the inevitable apology.

"Can you turn your music down? It's really loud and inconsiderate. Thanks!" he then turned back to the video.

Lucy seethed with rage her face contorted into the worst abomination a Monday could muster. She wanted to hit him. Break his glasses and break his phone in half over her knee. She unfortunately was not that type of person. Leaning back to the window she lowered the volume on her music, leaving him to his chuckling and with her attempting to get to her Zen again.

8:34am, the bus made a halt at the University. In all its grandeur the rain made it look a dismal prospect.

She again cursed herself for wearing converse trainers, the notoriously non-waterproof footwear. The trickle of students leaving the bus was slow, not much enthusiasm. The boy that she had sat next to had raced ahead and was already gone from view. Lucy was in no rush. She waited in her seat until the pushing and the mock apologies had gone.

Thanking the bus driver, she got off the bus and began a brisk walk in the cold and wet. The psychology department was not far but required some steps up the slope in the centre of campus to reach it.

Several people rushed past her fearful of the prolonged exposure to the elements. Lucy still took her, in comparison, leisurely stroll to the Brisbane building home to her first lecture of the day. As she got in and shook her hair like a dog her phone vibrated in her trackie pockets. She checked it knowing who it was.

"Did you get enough sleep last night?"

Moving towards the lecture hall Lucy replied, "no."

"Did you leave the light on like I suggested?!"

Feeling like she was getting two lectures at once Lucy was curt, "I did, didn't help much."

Getting into the theatre Lucy decided to go middle ground. By being at the back there was the biggest chance to get picked on and by being at the front there was a high-risk chance to be found out on your phone during the lecture.

Finding a seat in the relatively empty theatre Lucy proceeded to check her phone again.

The reply was more sympathetic this time, "it's only for a couple more days and I'll be back real soon."

Lucy feigned ease by sending back, "I know ☺ I hope everything is alright back home."

"Morning Lucy!" a girl plopped herself down in the seat next to her. Looking up from her phone she saw it was April one the girls she met at the netball try outs. She wore a bright yellow bandanna and gold hoop earrings. April was loud and energetic typical of her birthplace which was the United States.

"Morning," Lucy replied notably less energetic.

"Man you look like shit!" April was one of those whose speech was faster than their thinking.

Wincing while stretching Lucy merely grimaced in response not keen to keep a long conversation flowing. April would gnaw her ear off.

The lecture hall gradually filled up with three minutes to spare, April thankfully was chatting to someone on her other side giving Lucy some peace and quiet. She kept her eye on the door Wentworth usually comes through.

With the four lectures she has already had with him he has never been late and always arrived exactly at the 9am chime. It's like he waits outside until that very moment to enter. Wentworth was a frail man, who even with a microphone was hard to be engaging with. His module which was compulsory for all 'Social Psychology' was a nice break in module for the rest of the degree. The terms were not complex and it felt like A-level revision, still Lucy planned to turn up to all of them. Three weeks in and she can see the lecture dimming down in size. Wentworth made no comment on it, for all his faults the cheery old man smiled with a cup in tea in hand indicated he was content nonetheless. The dullness of his lectures earned the motto, 'you Went to the lecture but did not get the Worth.'

It was now 9am. Wentworth had still not appeared. Lucy checked to see if her watch was wrong comparing it with her phone. Both said 9am.

Turning to April Lucy asked, "say, we didn't get an email to say this lecture was cancelled, did we?" Lucy knew she was poor with emails the 999 emails she had yet to read in her inbox was indicative of that.

April snorted in response, "I wish."

"So how come Wentworth is not here yet?"

Realising this as well April scanned the lecture hall. Her eyes narrowing and looking at her phone time which now read 9:02am. "It's probably the traffic, or the rain, who knows?" she dismissed.

"He lives on campus."

"How do you know that? You don't stalk that old bastard, do you?" April laughed.

"No, he said it in passing, in one of his lectures, you know like the third one or something?"

April stared at Lucy in amazement. "You must have been the only one to have been listening to him that whole time. I was instead contemplating hanging myself." Ignoring April's tendency to over-dramatise Lucy accepted nothing more was to be gained by asking her.

It was now 9:05am some students were getting restless. Every first year was familiar with the rule that they were permitted to leave the lecture if no lecturer turns up within ten minutes. Lucy disliked this attitude finding her entire ordeal on the bus this morning pointless if her lecture was cancelled now.

9:08am still nothing. Lucy was grinding her teeth; the lecture had better not be cancelled, all this lost sleep! She cursed in her head. Two students got up the clearly bravest and pioneers of the generation, started walking towards the exit. They were a couple holding hands, boy and girl. Typical, just probably wanted to go back for the morning shag Lucy thought.

Suddenly the door finally opened and everyone started groaning. It was not Wentworth who came through those double doors however. A man walked through looking a lot younger than Wentworth. At first Lucy thought he was a student that was late. On further examination, the man carried with him a wad of paper which he slung onto the desk with a heavy thump just next to the blackboard. He then proceeded to take off his long brown trench coat and slung it over the chair which the lecturer usually sat on.

Rounding on the crowd in front of him he raised an eyebrow at the opportunist couple about to leave.

"Off on a romantic skive?" he asked folding his arms. He was thin with an unremarkable height probably meeting the same height as the average student. His youthful features were the complete opposite to what he was wearing. He had a white shirt with what looked like coffee stains on his sleeves which he started rolling up. He had a manure brown waistcoat on, that looked like it belonged in an old person's wardrobe, to top it off a tie that was a bright industrial blue, it was ill-matched with the waist coat. The tie itself literally hurt Lucy's eyes to glance at it long enough. His hair was brown and matted but looked dry, his ears were obscured from view and his fringe had to be pushed aside for the fear that it might actually engulf his eyes.

There were several sniggers echoing around the hallway and April whispered in disbelief, "oh wow." From her tone, it was not complimentary.

The couple that was too stunned to speak made the man lose interest. He whisked them away with his hand making them sit down still unsure about it all.

"Apologies about the lateness," he began using his voice alone to address the crowd without a microphone. His voice did carry despite his weedy appearance. "Well I'm not really sorry, I am only saying it as it is a routine thing to do," he finished turning to his big pile of paper on the desk.

"The 1940s called, they want their clothes back!" someone catcalled to a raucous outburst of laughter from the students in the theatre. Lucy did not join in but April happily sniggered away. Glancing over it did not surprise her that Thomas Stockton the boy who had to assert himself as the alpha male revelled in the other student's appreciation of his joke at the lecturer's expense.

The lecturer turned around to look at Thomas Stockton sizing him up. The look was worrying, it was not anger or disappointment it was condescension, it was pity. Leaning against the desk the lecturer replied, "the 1990s called, they wanted their accident back."

Lucy practically snorted like a choking pig but most of the student theatre fell eerily silent. Many faces were utterly aghast, Thomas Stockton's face had completely drained of colour. Did this lecturer hit the nail on the head? Did he know Thomas Stockton? Lucy wondered.

"You can't say that! I'll have you reported for that!" Thomas yelled back his face returning to a ruby hue.

This time it was the lecturer that laughed, it was harsh almost cruel. He looked at a piece of paper then back at Thomas, "Thomas Stockton, is it? Yes, I've been told about you, an outstanding debut, ten out of ten," he jeered. "Tell me Mr Stockton are your insecurities that bad that it requires to validate your masculinity and your existence to a hall of 300 or more people?" Thomas said nothing nervously glancing at his friends sitting next to him hoping for some shining knight to rescue him. They were avoiding his eye contact.

"Mr Stockton what possessed you to target a lecturer with barely three weeks of uni experience? Did you think three weeks of banter with what I am presuming your rugby chums and the towel whipping made you macho enough to attack me?" The lecturer doubled over, he was enjoying this.

"I was hoping to find a punch bag in this lame bunch, but I did not expect to get any volunteers!" he grinned showing surprisingly white teeth, the hall listened on his every word, was this fear? Lucy thought.

Thomas finally had the courage to speak up, "you are so done for! I am recording this lecture! I am going straight to the dean of studies you will be fired!" he retorted almost spitting in hot anger.

The lecturer's eyes practically sparkled at this as he started walking up the steps towards Thomas; everyone silently watching him as he went. He started chuckling, "why bother going yourself? I'll give the email address to the head of the department; everyone get out your notes and pens! It is very important to write this down!" Instantly everyone complied those who did not intend to write notes suddenly did. Those with laptops waited on baited breath.

"www.c.p.harkin@aberstahl.ac.uk, I am not going to repeat that to everyone, I will write it down on the blackboard but first I've got to deal with an annoying little prick I have discovered this morning." He was just next to Thomas now standing over him as the guy paled at his glare.

The lecturer leaned in to whisper but since Lucy was only two rows below she could just about hear him, "let's end this here shall we? Unless you prefer me to go into detail as to how I was able to tell, with just one glance, that you were a product of poor sexual education. By all means report this to the department you can join the frigging queue but let this be a lesson to you. There are bigger and far meaner people in this world than you would like to project yourself as, bear that in mind the next time you put your face above the parapet." With that the lecturer stood back up giving Thomas a patronising double tap on the shoulder before walking back down the stairs towards the black board.

He looked at everyone feigning ignorance to their horrified faces saying, "okay, shall we get this ball rolling?"

He turned to look at the black board and started writing on it fluidly, professionally without hesitation he wrote a name. It read Professor Arthur S. Squire, that young guy is a professor? Lucy scanned him intently he could only have five years on her if that. Her phone vibrated intensely indicating another text but for the first time ever in a lecture Lucy was too engaged for her to check it.

Professor Squire plopped his bum on the desk twizzling the piece of chalk he used to write in his hands. "Apologies for the hand writing, but my name is Arthur Squire. You can ditch the professor title; I care little for it. Also Arthur is fine, no cute nicknames though, I hate cute things." It was now 9:30am and Lucy never felt so awake in her life. She also suspected no one would dare give him a cute nickname.

"You are all probably wondering why I am here and not Wentworth? Raise your hand if you are."

Lucy looked around as she raised her hand nearly everyone did. Arthur's eyes sparkled again, they were full of life nothing like Wentworth's.

"Good, glad to see everyone is engaged. I'm afraid Wentworth is ill he has cancer and wants to spend time with his family. Or did he have a stroke?" the last question looked like he posed it to himself as many people gasped. He shrugged as if to say it was not that important. He then moved back to the black board and started writing a word. He circled the word as if to make it look like it was the centre of a spider diagram.

The word was: Belief.

"The plan was for me to take over a lecture near the end of term, but life has ways to mess up these plans. As you all know, this module is meant to break in and gently settle you all into the most basic concepts of psychology." Arthur snorted, "social psychology? This is not social psychology; this is psychology for Neanderthals. I have little interest in coddling freshers, fresh off their mother's breasts and guide them through the shallow end." Lucy at this point was wondering if this guy actually wanted himself fired. "Wentworth may have given you the armbands but we will be wasting time if we did his approach. Social Psychology is us, all of us what our minds make us do. What makes our minds all behave differently?"

He obviously did not expect an answer as he placed his hand dramatically on the black board next to his written word: Belief

"Belief, what is it?" he looked patiently at his students. No one raised their hand. He said nothing just patiently watching all of us. It was infuriating. Lucy wanted to answer but was she brave enough?

Someone came to save the day raising their hand sheepishly. Arthur pounced on it like a leopard nodded encouragingly. "I dunno, like what we think is true?"

Arthur becomes unreadable writing her exact wording on the black board even the, 'I dunno' part of her answer, in response some students chuckled faintly.

Another raised their hand, "from what perception we view from reality?" Again, unreadable Arthur writes it word for word.

More people start raising their hands and Arthur writes down all their suggestions without questioning them.

Lucy raises her hand thinking everyone else's answers being too bland. Arthur took two more suggestions until rounding onto Lucy; their eyes meeting Lucy said, "it's the most powerful tool for control. It's what separates anyone from becoming everyone." Lucy definitely said this to impress Arthur but he fixed her with an unreadable stare one that was longer than normal before writing it on the board with no comment to add.

A polite knocking from the door indicated the next lecturer wanted in, the time had just turned 10am.

Suddenly many students started getting up to pack up and a murmur started getting louder as people were itching to leave.

"I'm sorry did I say class dismissed?" Arthur said raising an eyebrow fixing them all with a haughty stare.

Sure enough students sat down and the murmur disappeared. "What you all suggested to me there, is what you know belief as. You all seem to be forgetting something. That is above all else it has the ability to create, to bring ideas to life, sometimes literally. This comes from inside your brain and nothing else on the planet can do that, can create like we can." Another polite knock on the door this time more forceful than the last, that kind of knock if you felt your last one was too passive. Arthur showed no indication that it bothered him.

"Assignment time for next weeks' lecture!" everyone groaned at this, "what? You didn't think I would be that cool guy who does not give out assignments? Think again." Arthur hands the sheets he had in a flurry asking for those at the front to pass it back. Lucy got a copy of April she looked unhappy at having work set so soon.

Lucy read what was on the sheet: 'Write about something you believe in that others, you think, normally would not. Justify or explain why you believe in it'. This seemed to Lucy like something you may set a year 7 but not a 1st year at university.

"Another thing! It has to be hand written." More groaning especially from those using laptops, "if I see a typed copy handed to me next week I will shred it with relish and mark you absent for every lecture that you do not provide me a written copy. Seriously this generation," he huffed. "Trust me your handwriting reveals to me more than any typed copy, even if your hand writing is crap I'll still read all of them. No excuses."

"What if you don't have hands?" someone protested showing his prosthetic arm.

Not perturbed Arthur retorted, "then use your teeth, you have already proven to me that you still have a mouth."

The knocking on the door was loud and aggressive now as Arthur proclaimed, "class is now dismissed, make sure you do what it says on the paper you will regret it otherwise!"

The door flies open and a red-faced man stood their looking thoroughly displeased. "Arthur!" he growled, "I should have known."

Lucy checked her watch it was 10:10am no wonder he'd be pissed as she collected her pens and paper she noticed she made barely any notes or learnt anything in today's lecture. From around her, people were making the same observations.

Down below Arthur got his belongings going to the door he passed the red-faced lecturer. In keeping no effort to keep his voice down Arthur said, "Rhys! You should have knocked I didn't know you were outside!" with that he left the room to an infuriated man giving Arthur the birdie as he left the room.

Lucy smiled to herself, while finding his obscene and blunt personality refreshing she thought it best not to get involved with him. Moving down and out of the lecture theatre she was yet to realise how her thoughts often betrayed her.

CHAPTER 2

10:30am, Lucy had decided to get a coffee, needing that caffeine boost to get her through the rest of the day. Her next timetabled hour was not until 2pm. She was at the back of the queue with every student before her doing the exact same thing. Caffeine just seemed like a must in a university life. She never drank coffee normally but felt like it was a must have to assist with any long days or early mornings. The baristas were fiddling with knobs, dials, types of milk and cutting the crust off the sandwiches for a pedantic woman at the front.

The service industry was ruined Lucy observed, the poor guys behind the counter having to accept the customers every whim, the power play was all too clear to see. This empathy from Lucy was of her experiences of being a waiter back when she was 16, slavery without the chains.

Deciding not to depress herself further, Lucy got out her phone.

"Oh dear," she whispered to herself, four messages all from the same person. She is probably pissed she has not replied within the hour. Looks like only a call could fix this probably best to wait until she had ordered her coffee first, weather the storm later. Thankfully the storm outside had gone leaving just an overcast grey sky, still, it was an improvement.

"Can I take your order?" the barista looked disgruntled but still attempted a welcoming smile.

"Can I just have a coffee please?" Lucy ordered moving to get her wallet out of her sports bag.

"Cappuccino? Americano? Mocha? Latte? Espresso?" the barista listed professionally as Lucy fumbled with her bag pockets.

"What? No, just a coffee none of them please." Lucy finally procured her wallet from her bag, the barista just stared blankly at her.

"Sorry, we don't do 'just coffee' here, would you like something else?" she was getting slightly impatient.

"You're kidding me? You have all that fancy stuff with pointless chocolate shavings and foam yet don't have a coffee? A normal coffee?" Lucy said surprised, there was a curt cough behind her which she ignored. "Fine. Can I have a tea please?" Lucy sighed defeated.

"Which one? We have earl grey, herbal tea, lemon-"

"Just a goddamn normal tea!" Lucy snapped which made the barista scowl and moved to get it prepped. Lucy through her head back in exasperation she had just done what she hated, the bitchy customer. Feeling guilty Lucy kept very mute for the rest of the experience as she got her tea served and moved away.

Taking it to the stall she added milk and left the tea bag swimming. She added one, two, three, four, five scoops of sugar mixing it all in. Scooping out the tea bag and flinging it into the bin she was now prepared for the outdoors. Tea was not her first choice, but she knew it had some caffeine in it and that was something. If things got worse she could get a normal coffee from the psychology common room. That room was always full however and she was not fond of crowds.

Taking gentle sips from her cup Lucy felt her phone vibrate. Moving outside to face the brisk air she swiped right on the screen to answer it.

"I was just about to call you."

The voice on the phone snorted, "yeah right."

"Sorry I was not responding; the lecture today was… different." Lucy had crossed the road by now sipping her tea carefully.

"All the lectures are supposed to be different, that's the point of them Lucy," the voice jeered.

"Funny," Lucy replied not troubling to hide her sarcasm. "No, different as in Wentworth was not there. Remember? That cute old guy I had mentioned."

"What? So, the lecture was cancelled?"

"No some guy I had not seen before called Arthur Squire took over. He was quite the character. Ever heard of him?" Lucy came to a crossroads one way was to the library, a short cut but required going around behind the arts department, its obnoxious frame casting shadow making it look quite dark even at this time. The other route was a stroll through the campus park it would definitely take longer that way.

"Nope, I don't really pay attention to guys! Sounds like you liked him though," the phone accused.

"Haha, you of all people must know that is not true," Lucy flirted as she decided to take the shortcut.

"When I am back, you're going to have to make me believe in that," the voice whispered coyly back.

Belief. Lucy came to a sudden halt. She instantly felt incredibly ill. Some words popped into her head that she had heard somewhere before, "belief is creation."

"Lucy?" the voice asked sounding hurt at not getting a reply. The world felt eerily silent except for what was coming from behind her.

A gargling. A strange wetness. The sound of rotten chains slid against concrete. A moaning.

"Lucy! You there? You listening?!" the phone sounded alien to its surroundings. Lucy felt that awful gargling noise get closer. She felt rooted to the spot not daring to move. Her hands were trembling the phone was getting louder, Lucy hung up she did not know what was going on. It felt so real but how could it be?

Coughing, wheezing, choking something was lumbering to her, getting closer. She could smell the all too familiar rotting corpse. Its pungent waft wrinkling her nose. She whimpered. Go away! She thought, go away!

The creature halted but it felt close. Lucy could not bring herself to turn around to see her nightmare. She knew what it was. She did not want to see it again.

"Please leave," she pleaded with the creature through barely contained tears. Hallowed retching is all she got in response. No one else was around her. No one. The campus was deserted this early no one comes down here. She was alone.

Suddenly a hand clasped her shoulder. Lucy gave a petrified squeak but remained still as possible. If I do not provoke it, it will go away Lucy reassured herself. If I do not provoke it, it will go away! She repeated in her head. She glanced at the hand, it was a sickly green, the veins were protruding and blue. They were still, no blood pumped through them veins. It tightened its grip Lucy tried her best not to react. She wanted so desperately to run! But the hand had prevented her from escaping.

Another retching sound and green bile landed on her shoulder it stunk, rotten and foul. Lucy started to openly cry now silently pleading for her ordeal to be over. The breath of this creature felt ragged on her neck, it caused goose bumps all over her body. The hand moved sliding from her shoulder up her neck. Creeping, crawling, edging up her body.

It cupped her cheek, resting there. Not wanting to stop its gnarled fingers moved to her lips. They rubbed her lips leaving a rotten feeling over Lucy she was tearing up, shaking terrified. The fingers suddenly forced their way into her mouth.

Lucy screamed but it was muffled but it made her spring to life. She elbowed, with as much force as she could muster, her assailant in the ribs. It wheezed in pain keeling over as Lucy sprinted for her life down the path.

She did not stop to look back, she did not want to, behind her was the stuff of nightmares. What she saw in her nightmares.

Lucy sprinted out from around the arts building, up some stairs barely containing her tears. Without decelerating she pelted up a pathway until she almost collided with a woman walking towards her.

"Lucy?!" the woman exclaimed as Lucy in her attempt to slow down tripped landing hard and face first onto the concrete, luckily, she had enough time to shield her face from impact. "Lucy? Are you alright? Have you been crying?" the woman mithered kneeling down to help her up. Lucy took the hand gingerly being lifted to her feet. Her knee caps with grazed one of them was bleeding. Lucy was still panting she felt clammed up her distress evident. "You poor thing, do you want to sit down?" Lucy shook her head in response still catching her breath.

Lucy finally took a full glance at the motherly figure in front of her. It was Caitlin Harkin head of psychology at Aberstahl University and her personal tutor. This was some coincidence. She was in her mid-forties dressed plainly in a green rain coat and had her wispy brown hair tied up in a bun behind her head. She looked like she was dressed to be on country file.

Lucy remembered the first meeting she had with her, as her PT, a truly kind woman who seemed trying too hard to be a maternal figure. She was renowned in the department with her research into the child psychosis and development, like many academics she was still an extremely quirky character.

Handing Lucy a tissue Mrs Harkin gave Lucy her full attention. There were other passers-by now, eyeing the scene with curiosity. Lucy wiped her eyes managing a, "thank you." Harkin smiled encouragingly. She noticed the stares from the other students and staff.

"Let's get you cleaned up, good thing you bumped into me! I'll take you back to my office. I was on my way there now in fact after my seminar, would you like a coffee and a catch up?"

Was this lady an angel? Lucy realised part of her dilemma this morning was not getting a coffee. The tea she spilled she would have to be left behind no way was she getting it back. She momentarily panicked, her phone?! Did she drop it?

"Is this yours?" a man asked tentatively. He held out a smart phone that had a smashed screen. Lucy felt crest-fallen at the sight. She nodded meekly taking it out of his hands.

Harkin watched the exchange patiently as Lucy examined her already beyond repair phone. Not smart enough to survive a fall it seems Lucy lamented internally.

"Did you.. um did you? You know, find it back there?" Lucy asked trying not to sound weird.

The student glanced back from where he came and pointed, "yeah down there, behind the arts building." He looked quizzical now.

"Did you see anything weird?" she pressed more resolutely this time.

His eyebrows raised he replied, "does spilt tea count?"

"Okay let's move along now Lucy, no point wasting time here," Harkin interjected swooping Lucy up and taking her to the psychology building. At this point Lucy avoided eye contact with anyone. Usually, Lucy would not like anyone worrying over her or caring for her but this time was a special case and she was grateful for Mrs Harkin's intervention.

Coming back to her senses Lucy realised they were now in the psychology building reception. Mrs Harkin gently let go of Lucy and moved to the desk.

A black woman Lucy recognised known as Laura caught Harkin's attention. Laura wore bright clothes with a yellow sweater and dreadlocked hair, she clearly took advantage of the relaxed uniform policy at the university.

The psychology department offices were cramped however being in a single floor building is nothing grandiose like the maths departments offices. In fact, the psychology building had to be shared with Sociology, Aberstahl while being a good university was not exactly a large one.

"Caitlin, we have some students who would like to see you," Laura said not looking up from her computer. Lucy realised that her nails were ridiculously long she would not be surprised if she impaled the keyboard when she typed.

"Tell them they will have to wait," Caitlin interjected nodding to Lucy. Laura took a glance at Lucy.

"Hello love! Oh my, what's wrong?" Laura was super friendly with all the students.

"Laura she's fine, just needs less people inquiring," Mrs Harkin responded coolly. Laura got the message.

"What shall I tell the students? I said you'd be available after your seminar. They wanted to complain about a member of staff."

Mrs Harkin not bothering to stick around walked past the desk beckoning Lucy to follow. She managed to reply before leaving the room, "tell them to fill out the Arthur forms." Mrs Harkin was sharper than she presented herself, or rather, probably knew Arthur to be the cause of many of her woes. Lucy could believe either.

Ushering Lucy into her office Mrs Harkin closed the door behind her. Harkin's room was cluttered, if a bit dirty. Books laid sprawled everywhere some half open. This required Harkin to grunt with effort as she moved some off the guest seat in the office. For the head of the department this office was not very big. Lucy noticed several crayon drawings pinned up around the room often depicting 'mommy'. The desk was piled with dirty bowls and mugs, even some teabags seemed melded to her desk with age.

"Ah pity, I forgot I have not washed my mugs yet, a disposable cup alright?"

As Lucy sat down on the quite comfy chair she nodded. It was normal coffee she was not going to say no. Sitting down herself and flicking the kettle on Mrs Harkin rummaged in her hand bag and withdrew a plastic bag full of disposable cups. Mrs Harkin seemed just like a student avoiding her washing up at all costs.

"Any sugar?" Mrs Harkin asked.

Lucy smiled faintly. "Lot's please, Mrs Harkin… Thank you." Lucy again failed at not coming across as awkward.

Mrs Harkin smiled sweetly. "Call me Caitlin, you first years treat us academics like your old teachers, we are nothing like them!" Caitlin chuckled to herself, adding, "evidently." She pointed to the mess around her room, "why, you might not think it, but we have more in common with our students than you realise!"

Lucy took the coffee off Caitlin blowing on it gently. Caitlin realising Lucy was not going to start the conversation asked, "so what happened? You looked like you saw a ghost!"

Lucy winced at that horrendous cliché, she was not exactly wrong either. How could she tell her PT this? Something in her dreams came out and assaulted her? Has been doing so repeatedly for the last few months. That is why she cannot sleep, that is why her university experience has been hell. Her freshers' week wasted whimpering indoors as everyone else partied in the night. Where would she begin? How could she make Caitlin believe her? She was a psychologist; she would probably think Lucy was insane or at least had some sort of condition Lucy knew she was not. She could not be insane.

After an incredibly long pause as Caitlin watched Lucy thoughtfully Lucy finally mustered a reply, "I'd rather not say…" She trailed off clearly agitated.

Caitlin's eyes widened as something like realisation swept across her face. This realisation turned to barely contained anger. Lucy wasn't certain they were on the same page with this reaction, "Arthur!" she hissed under her breath. Caitlin looked and Lucy could see the cogs moving as Caitlin was deciding how to respond. "I'm so sorry Lucy!" she began, "he's an utter arsehole, a complete dick and one that if circumstances were different I would have cut him loose months ago!" Caitlin snarled she got up and started pacing.

Lucy alarmed tried to interject, "I think you have it wrong he-"

"Now, now I know students try and downplay their complaint for fear of being a grasser or a snitch or whatever," Caitlin cut off yet seemed trailing off into her own rant. "He has gone too far!" she snapped to herself, "to make a first-year girl cry! What is he playing at? He wanted to teach them so what?! So he could bully them!" Caitlin thundered.

"It has nothing to do with Arthur!" Lucy yelled over Caitlin which made her stop in her tracks. Toning her voice down Lucy reiterated, "it has nothing to do with Arthur."

"Oh," Caitlin said looking momentarily embarrassed. She sat down rubbing her eyes, "I'm sorry things have been stressful, you can probably guess he does not help anything on my end."

Lucy saw on opportunity for a divergence of conversation, "why don't you fire him?"

Caitlin gave Lucy a withering look, "if I had a pound coin for every time someone said that to me I'd be living in Barbados. No, my dear I won't fire him, for all his faults he has plenty of benefits too. Besides if I fired him I'd be giving him exactly what he wants. I am planning to never do as he wants," she huffed sounding proud.

Lucy pressed further partly out of her own curiosity partly so she could avoid the drilling of what happened half an hour ago. "He wants to be fired? But why? Can't he just leave if he wanted to?"

"He doesn't want to leave, he wants to be fired there is a difference," Caitlin explained.

"Is that why he is deliberately mean to everyone?"

Caitlin laughed at that, "he tries to be, you see, I would call him mischievous and daring not necessarily mean. It can come across as that but trust me when I tell you he is actually quite sensitive." It sounded like Caitlin was talking about her eldest son rather than a co-worker. "Why barely two weeks ago when he got his new office some of the staff played a prank on him," she giggled.

"What was the prank?" Lucy asked leaning in.

"Arthur's office is usually pristine and ordered, so several staff members moved his stuff around. Only slightly. For example, his potted plant was rotated 45 degrees, his chair was lowered. His collection of books were put in a non-alphabetical order etc." Caitlin started laughing to herself, "his reactions was priceless! He thought he was going mad!"

Caitlin started laughing more obscenely this time obviously recalling the memory in her head. Lucy tried to meekly laugh with her but with the mention of someone's mental well-being did she wince again. Caitlin picked up on this she stopped laughing abruptly as her demeanour changed, it became more serious.

"W-what?" Lucy asked she felt like she was being drilled into. Was all of this before just an act?

"Lucy, do you really think you could distract me with staff gossip?" Caitlin whispered. "What happened back there? Someone attack you? You need to tell me as it happened on here campus."

Lucy nervously chewed her bottom lip, finding it very hard to make continued eye contact with Caitlin's intrusive stare. "No person attacked me," Lucy insisted careful with her word choice.

Caitlin scanned Lucy in attempt to catch out a lie. "Then what am I supposed to believe? You ran from a squirrel? You terrified of squirrels Lucy? Because what I saw was a terrified girl run for her life. You smell of vomit, look pale and cut open your knee cap when I found you. What am I supposed to infer from that?"

Lucy consciously touched her shoulder. It was wet and still warm. A physical reminder of her experience moments before. Could Lucy say there was a dangerous person on campus? Just to avoid the truth? The truth, at least to her, she did not expect anyone else to believe. Yet, Lucy could not bring herself to lie and conjure up a fake rapist or criminal on campus just to avoid the truth. "This not my sick," Lucy began cautiously, "I was running from something; but you wouldn't believe me if I told you."

Caitlin leaned back in her chair, her face still deadly serious. "Try me," she dared.

Well here it goes Lucy thought to herself. "It- erm, it appears out of nowhere and gropes me. It's like a ghost but it can touch me. It haunts me. I swear it is not a hallucination and I am not going mad. Other people have seen it!!"

Caitlin's facial expression finally changed but not the way Lucy anticipated. It looked nervous and uncertain, not the usual condescension and disbelief Lucy usually expects. She took a nervous sip of her own coffee and massaged her eyes. "It's one of 'them' huh?" Caitlin looked deeply concerned.

"You believe me?!" Lucy asked aghast at how easy that was.

"I do, I've seen this sort of thing before. More accurately put I have to deal with it on an uncomfortably frequent basis. Answer me this Lucy. Does it appear at the worst times and others definitely have verified its existence?"

Lucy nodded with no hesitation in a hope to convince a woman she never thought would believe her.

"I see," Caitlin quipped looking very sympathetic. "You poor thing, this is a terrible situation I do not wish on anyone."

Lucy could not believe her ears someone understood her problem? "Can you help me?" Lucy pleaded fighting back her raw emotion.

Caitlin reached out and held Lucy's hands gently and lovingly, this broke down Lucy's defences. She cried. She held onto the second human who believed in her and cried. She shivered uncontrollably as she let the damn burst. Emotion came through wave after wave after wave.

After what appeared an age Lucy started calming down. "All better?" Caitlin asked.

"Somewhat," Lucy sniffed, "but you never answered my question? You've seen these ghosts, haven't you? How do I get rid of them? How do I stop becoming afraid of them? When will they stop controlling my life?!" Lucy had never exclaimed as much as she did then. Caitlin seemed startled.

She looked thoughtful as she mulled how to respond. "You call it a ghost hm? Sorry, but I don't think I can help you," she said flatly.

"What! But Caitlin, Mrs Harkin please you believe in me! Not many people do! You're a psychologist am I sick? There must be something you can do!" Lucy was practically begging at this point holding onto Caitlin's hand tightly.

"If you let me finish Lucy," she soothed, "I would not refuse a pleading student besides if they wanted their marks raised." She took a long deep breath, "believing in you is different from being able to help you my dear. You're not the only one in the world with this," she paused, "peculiarity," she managed eventually looking unsure of herself.

"Then what should I do?" Lucy pressed.

Caitlin pulled several expressions, it seems she had an internal conflict in her head. It went from sympathy to worry to concern, finally it rested on conviction. "You had some homework to do I suggest you do it as soon as you get home." Caitlin said to the surprise of Lucy she turned on her seat to look at her computer typing notes on it.

Lucy's eyes narrowed, "this is not going on record, is it? And why would that homework help?"

Caitlin snorted, "I'm afraid saying student was distressed from seeing a ghost on paper docs not look very professional. I am instead saying you're having difficulty acclimatising to university life which is a half-truth." Caitlin suddenly leaned very closely locking eyes with Lucy. She was so close Lucy could count the wrinkles on her face. "What you are dealing with is quite possibly very dangerous. You need to take me at the utmost very seriously. Do your homework tonight and hand it first thing in tomorrow morning, I'd recommend you do it in person." With that she leaned back as Lucy tried to find words.

"Arthur's homework?"

"The very same."

"Can Arthur help me?" Lucy stood up now slinging her bag back around her shoulder sensing finality in the matter.

Caitlin again took another characteristic long pause. She seemed like she was having another internal dilemma. "He can help you, in fact he'll probably save you." Why did that take so much time to say? Lucy wondered. This was not a vote of absolute confidence coming from the head of department. Caitlin was also being very calculating, she was choosing her words carefully.

Lucy thanked Caitlin for her time and prepared to leave. Upon opening the door Caitlin managed a get one more remark before Lucy left.

"Don't blame me too much for what happens next," Caitlin pleaded. "There will be no going back, your life will never be the same again." So this was Caitlin's dilemma and concern for Lucy?

"Don't worry Caitlin, where I go from here if what you say is true, will be better than where I am now." With that Lucy left the building to head to the seminar she had not prepared for.

All the while along her journey she felt continually watched. Like what was haunting her was getting more and more ambitious.

CHAPTER 3

Lucy's head was pounding. The lack of sleep was clearly getting to her as she rested her head against the cool glass of the bus window. She watched wearily as the rain droplets trickled down out of sight. She was glad she was dry, there was a weird comfort watching the rain behind a glass window. It was therapeutic, therapy is what she needed.

Lucy had evidently disappointed her seminar tutor in the afternoon. She had not done the reading and when he looked at her to save the seminar she said bluntly she had not done the work. It was one of the longest hours she endured, all she could do was make that hollow promise of catching up.

Lucy moaned in frustration slapping the side of her face. How could she have got behind? It was only four weeks into university and she had already slipped behind. Her anger mounted. Her baggage from before university was still haunting her, literally.

She was still unsure on Caitlin's advice, to do this homework? And what? Hand it in to what she suspects was a woefully insensitive and apathetic man. A man. They are not always known for the kindness and understanding that Caitlin exhibited. As if she was on some endeavour to make her mood fouler Lucy then realised she had no phone. Lucy was normally extremely protective of her phone being one of those younger generations who treated it like it was precious, a fundamental organ to her existence. She fumbled with it in her track suit pocket feeling the cracked glass tentatively. She could only fear the backlash of those unread messages.

The bus came to a slippery halt as the rain picked up in pace. Many of the dead occupants in the bus rose to life as this bus stop was right outside some student accommodation. Lucy got off here as well but her accommodation was another ten minute walk.

Trudging out into the wet, she resigned herself to the swim home. Times like these made her realise why people had umbrellas. Lucy parted from her fellow students to carry on walking up the street then taking a sharp left down an alley way. It was a shortcut not many of her flatmates realised. She was always an exceptional runner and coupled with her keen sense of directions she nearly mapped out the sizeable town of Aberstahl in her head, not that she ventured much around it. Her walk turned into a brisk jog, huffing, with her sports bag slung behind her shoulder.

Her muscles were sluggish and painful; the lack of sleep did not give her much energy. She called off attending netball training but without a phone had no way to inform the captain. She planned to message her through her laptop when she could.

Soon enough, the tower block that she lived in loomed into view. It was easily one of the tallest buildings in Aberstahl but was an ugly concrete leviathan compared to the rest of the town's picturesque landscape. This earned the building the nickname 'Sky's Razor'.

Going through the front entrance Lucy sighed in relief shaking her hair like a wet dog to help dry herself. In the foyer many students mingled, to her left was the games room which had a couple of pool tables and video games consoles; to her right was the common room having sofa's and tables for any flats who like to come together to have indoor parties. Right now, it was locked with an angry cleaner notice attached to the door. In front of her was a staircase leading up, each side of that was an elevator. Lucy proceeded to climb the stairs, her floor was only up three levels.

She ignored the energetic and excited faces that flew past her. The time must have been around 4pm meaning people are having food and are getting ready to pre-drink. Lucy found the whole exercise of pre-drinking smart but exhausting. She never drank much and her patience often wears thin as everyone happily gets drunk around her.

At the third floor, she moved tiredly to the door to her flat: 3b. Once inside she moved straight to her door which was down the end of a narrow corridor. Her room was adjacent to the kitchen which she could hear chatter from. Before deciding to go into her room Lucy poked her head around the kitchen door.

Two boys were sat down at the table watching a video on a laptop. Lucy identified them as Brent and Adam.

Brent was a short and loud Scotsman whose accent was so thick he could have been in William Wallace's army. He was currently dressed in some thin shorts with a plain blue shirt with stains all over it. He had a buzz cut which exposed his small ears which he was sensitive of.

Sitting next to him was Adam who was the tallest in the flat his lanky form made them look perfect for a Laurel and Hardy routine. Adam was a lot more smartly dressed coming from London, he was wearing a white button up shirt with a loose tie slung around his collar. His wispy styled ginger hair looked thoroughly waxed in place. It was him who turned around to the kitchen door creaking.

"Lucy! Welcome home, good day on campus?" he inquired adjusting his glasses which were escaping down his nose.

Brent glanced Lucy's way and in a lot more of a grumpy fashion said, "you look like shite Lucy."

Lucy could not help but smile at the pair. They were perhaps the closest boys that she had as friends at university. Brent was a swimmer and Adam a hockey player. She needed cheering up and these two, when bickering, did just that.

"Hey guys, what you watching?" Lucy asked as she dropped her bag by the door and moved to sit next to Brent. He shifted the chair across so she could get a good look.

"Adam wanted to show me some voodoo shite, I was going to make tea instead but he insists this is a good one," Brent summarised pointing to the video which was paused on the screen.

"Any good?" Lucy replied.

Brent snorted, "it's a good CGI stunt if that's what you mean." Adam rolled his eyes at that.

"Wanna see the video Lucy?" Adam asked eagerly pushing the laptop towards her.

Lucy said nothing as she examined the video title on the webpage: 'Headless Horseman spotted in Ireland! Not Fake!'

"Adam the fact it has to add not fake in the title proves it is fake," Lucy dismissed.

"Hey! At least give the video a try," he implored.

Lucy yielding, clicked play on the screen. Brent leaned in to watch again while Adam studied both their faces excitedly. The video was only 50 seconds long. It was in the dark and Lucy guessed it was being recorded on a phone as currently all they were seeing were some dark green wellies trudging in the mud. It was a man walking his dog as it happily bounded right in front of him. The man sounded like he was struggling walking through the field as all they could hear was some heavy breathing. Suddenly the dog stopped and started growling, it eventually grew to a bark.

"Stop it Lassie! You'll wake the Fowlers!" the cameraman hissed at the dog but it ignored him and carried on barking. There was a bright flash of green which happened off camera. The camera then whirled around to the source and the video quality quickly fell. A green light of some kind was approaching rapidly the man's breath got fearful.

"Lassie!" he yelled scooping up the dog in front of him and what Lucy thought he had fell backwards. The man grunted in pain as the dog carried on barking. He adjusted his camera and where the dog stood there was green flames sparking on the floor. In the distance, a horse was neighing. The video ended.

Adam looked excitedly at Lucy. Lucy took time to ponder what she saw. "There was no actual headless horseman in that video Adam," she complained as if it has wasted her time.

"Not you as well, I suspected Brent would not be convinced but you said you believe in ghosts back when we met."

Brent sniggered, "I remember that! You swore you had a 6th sense or something."

Lucy's cheeks burned. "That was the alcohol talking!" she snapped. Lucy never drunk much and that one time on freshers' week is never going to be forgotten by anyone.

"Pass the laptop over," Adam interrupted not caring about the fresher's reminiscence. He fiddled for a little while by clicking play and pause to get the best freeze-frame. "Yes!" he said triumphantly thrusting his fist into the air. "Here." He whirled his laptop back to Brent and Lucy.

The image was blurry, and only half of a figure was caught on the camera. As the man was falling back a feminine figure showed herself. The peculiarity is where her face should be was a great beam of green light.

"The Headless Horsewoman more like," Lucy corrected, "but I see what you mean that is very... paranormal."

Adam smiled in exhilaration, "it was put up yesterday and going viral! There has been witness reports of it being sighted near Cork. This is some of the best evidence yet for the occult to exist!" Despite his smart appearance Adam was massively superstitious and believed in many irrational things.

Brent snorted louder this time getting out of his seat to the fridge. "It's frigging video editing. No sorry sod records their dog walks early in the morning. I bet you have gullible tattooed on your arse Adam," he jeered.

Adam eyed Brent becoming unreadable. "Please tell us almighty lord of the Celts how will we ever gain your wisdom?" Lucy started quietly laughing, they had started again.

Brent growled taking an aggressive chunk out of an apple which Lucy was sure he had stolen off Libby's shelf. "Alright let me tell you what always happens in these videos. When put online, time and time again do we fail to get a proper shot of anything it claims is real. They all make the disclaimer they are not fake which means they are fake. They all fail to be recorded in any decent quality making me think they are easier to fake. I mean c'mon, that video looked like he used a potato to record his dog nearly being run over."

Adam gasped in mock shock, "that's racist Brent, the Irish do have phones you know."

"What? No! I was not referencing the potato famine it's a common internet expression! To record with a potato shows the quality of the video must be like 44p." Brent became very defensive as would anyone in this day and age if accused of being racist.

Lucy zoned out of their regular playful bickering to see a head swoop over her shoulder to peer at the computer screen. Lucy recognised the feminine face to be Libby her neighbour and probably closest friend in the flat. Libby was a light-hearted girl wearing her bright yellow dressing gown. This time she had a purple towel around her head clearly drying her hair after a shower.

Libby has been known to be a very relaxed character often walking around the kitchen in nothing but an over-sized T-shirt when she thinks it is quiet, which Brent incessantly complains about. Lucy had to turn away from her blushed face as she felt her personal space was invaded.

"What's a Dull-han?" she asked prompting Adam to stop winding up Brent and turn to her.

"Dullahan," Adam corrected, "an Irish grim reaper of sorts. Think of it as some kind of headless horseman," he summarised enjoying the interest only to be quickly disappointed as she stood upright readjusting her bathroom towel.

"Cool." Libby had clearly lost interest.

"Put some clothes on woman!" Brent hissed, "my catholic upbringing can only deal with so much skin."

Adam appreciated that and started laughing weirdly unperturbed by her getup. Lucy secretly agreed with Brent, she should be more self-conscious.

Libby ignored that comment fixing her hazel eyes on the nearly eaten apple. "Is that my apple?" she accused.

Brent suddenly realised who he stole from. "It's just an apple, you can literally find them on trees."

Libby smiled mischievously, "yeah your right, apples do grow on trees. It's a shame pudding doesn't." She crossed over to the fridge opening it up and leaning down, Brent had to avert his eyes.

"Put some clothes on," he thundered, "if this is your behaviour now imagine what you would be like at the club later! You've gotta get more awareness Lib!"

Libby got out a piece of chocolate cake taking it to the table. "It's fine!" she said in a rather annoying sing song fashion. "I feel comfortable here amongst you guys, I walk around naked at my home all the time!" Lucy wondered if she was just born self-confident or didn't have any brothers. "Besides," she continued spooning some cake into her mouth, "you guys are all like family here."

Adam let out a low whistle while Brent made an indignant coughing noise. "Did she just family-zone an entire room?" Lucy said under her breath to Adam.

"I think she did," he answered bemused.

"Say Lucy," Libby said through chunks of chocolate cake, "how come you haven't been replying to my messages you are usually so prompt with messaging."

"Ah…" Lucy managed fumbling in her pocket to fetch her phone. She placed it on display on the table hoping the evidence would speak more than words.

"Woah fuck! How did that happen?" Brent asked suddenly very sympathetic.

Lucy paused for a moment. Could she tell them a ghost made her scared out of her wits so bad that she forgot she had her phone in her hand? That this thing, groped her and made her fear for her life?

"I dropped it," she answered in monotone.

Adam smirked, "you were never a great story-teller, predrinks taught me that."

"Yeah whatever, just message on Facebook now if you want me or better yet talk to me. I'll go get it fixed when I can," Lucy addressed the room but was notably irked by Adam's remark.

"Talking? Sounds like effort," Brent huffed he was now starting to get work on the greasy hob, cooking what looked like eggs. The kitchen's work surface which bordered the whole room besides the door way had more grease on it than a fast food restaurant's deep fat fryer.

"So you did not get my message?" Libby continued finishing her cake and licking her lips.

"If it was after 10:30am definitely not."

"Shame, well I'll ask you now. Wanna come out tonight with us?" Libby fixed Lucy with a hopeful stare.

Brent sighed with his back turned to them focusing on the hob. "Stop pestering her Lib, she didn't want to go the last 20 times you have asked her. She made it clear it's not her thing."

It was true Lucy only went out clubbing with the group once at the start of the term. She had no memory of it and the shame welled up in her when she thought of it. She was never a fan of alcohol she had a bigger reason than most not to touch the stuff. But that night… Was not a proud exception. She did not mind a causal few drinks but the all-out stuff? No thank you.

"You should know the answer Lib," Lucy said almost apologetically.

"No I don't, somethings bothering you Lucy," Libby replied hotly.

Lucy looked at her in surprise. "How did you-"

"Oh please Lucy you are not hard to read. For the time I have got to know you, our private chats? I have told you about me. I have not heard you once talk about yourself or your own problems."

"Libby, she hasn't exactly asked you to do that. You just swooped her up and made her your best friend within three days," Adam interrupted.

"You make it sound like I am her doll," Lucy growled.

"Sorry Lucy I didn't mean it like that," he apologised.

"And I am not angry she has not told me her stuff either," Libby interjected returning focus to her, "she is a good listener, I just hope I can return the favours in the ways I can, by cheering her up being around friends!" Libby gave a cheer at the end to try and diffuse the atmosphere.

Lucy softened at the gesture. "Look I dunno, last time did not go so well. You guys don't want a dead weight. Even worse, you don't want someone to ruin the fun. I don't intend to get drunk."

"Oh c'mon Lucy what is so bad about getting a little drunk?" Brent joined in now looking hopeful.

"A lot of things!" Lucy snapped, bolting out of her seat. Lucy's mouth suddenly felt very dry. She felt embarrassed from her outburst. It was childish. She muttered an apology and picked up her bag and left the room.

As she opened her door to her room she could hear Adam admonishing Brent, "well done jackass!"

Lucy moved inside putting her head in her arms. She was all tense; her fuse was trigger happy. She didn't need to snap at Brent or any of them. They were doing what they thought was best. To them, alcohol was escapism, uplifting and temporary happiness. They didn't realise Lucy's experiences with it were less than favourable.

Suddenly a voice popped into her head, "you're closing yourself off again." Lucy groaned and leapt nimbly onto her bed. The room was always in the light she never switched the light off. It was cluttered with clothes and dirty dishes. She lazily kicked off her duvet off to the bottom of the bed to make it more comfortable. She could sleep right now. Or could she not? Was it a chance of another nightmare?

She could hear the bickering from next door. The others would probably be arguing at who upset her. Was this what she had become? The one they had to tiptoe around. The weird recluse? She admitted her actions could seem like it. She had no desire to be that person but her circumstances…

Lucy grabbed hold of the duvet as she tightened her grip in frustration. Her problem was unconventional and it was ruining her university life. No! Don't let it beat you. This is what it wants! Lucy thought.

Lucy did not recognise this train of thought it was almost coming from another person. *You can't let it control who you are! Believe in yourself more!*

Belief. There is that stupid word again. Why am I finding it so significant though? Lucy pondered but not before she got out of bed. She had lost all interest in sleeping.

Lucy creaked the door of the kitchen open as the other three had resolved to eat in silence. Things looked sour when she was gone. Libby looked up sadly looking ready to apologise but Lucy beat her to it.

"I have given it some thought, and I have taken you up on your offer Libby."

Libby's face lit up like November 5th as she rushed over to Lucy giving her a hug. Lucy was taken by surprise unsure with how to deal with the amount of skin touching her own. In recompense, she gave Libby a light tap on the back.

"Glad to have you on board," Adam said, Brent nodding in agreement.

"Just promise me one thing Adam," Lucy said as Libby let go of her. Adam looked at her smiling Lucy knew his charismatic personality was the one probably organising the pre-drinks.

"Your desire Ma'am," he said melodramatically.

"Do not peer pressure me into drinking more when I have said enough," Lucy warned fixing Adam with her best glare.

He became unreadable but then stood up giving a flowery bow, "your wish is my command!" liar, Lucy thought.

Brent snorted through his egg sandwich muttering, "you are so gay."

*　　　*　　　*

The pre-drinks went well. Lucy was unable to ignore her feeling of mass fatigue and the rest of her day through communal laughter in the common room. There were some surprised faces and she had to introduce herself to this group Adam assembled, but they proved easy to talk to and welcoming enough. There were eight in the group it seemed the four from their flat and four from below. No one else from their flat wished to join in. Lucy was dressed in some skinny jeans and a black sleeveless top, for her this was too flamboyant but after Libby's constant harassment at her fashion sense she yielded and allowed her to choose the clothes.

The whole process of getting ready was such a rush. She had barely anytime to eat let alone shower. Adam had accelerated his plans for the evening. Lucy therefore had no time to unpack her bag or get on Facebook and let people know her phone was bust. She hoped it'll be fine, Andrea can wait for at least a day. Phillis as well, she'd want to know what's up but she knew Lucy was grown up enough not to cause concern by not messaging a day. It is at times like these that she realised how dependent people were on their phones, as everyone checked every so often during the pre-drinks. Not having her phone was… refreshing.

Lucy had limited herself to three beers that evening keeping a low profile in order to miss penalties from the drinking games. Brent who had as much subtly as a nuclear bomb got plenty of penalties, some were just rookie errors, she wondered if he did them on purpose.

The clock chimed 10pm and they were ready to brace the cold. The British club goer as one of the Spanish girls from the flat below laughed at how, no matter the weather, they would go without coats. This proved to be true as they all left only warmed with the alcohol in their bellies and their breath as cold wisps in front of them. All the girls besides Lucy had high-heels which created some moaning as they climbed the road up to the club.

The club was a first-year favourite in Aberstahl. It was often joked that ambulances wait outside to pick up the first years not taxis. The club was called 'Frenzy' having never been inside it yet, Lucy had nothing but cynicism. She did not enjoy crowds. She wondered why she agreed to come out again but there was no turning back now, she was committed and enjoyed the company.

The club was popular and thus a queue had already formed outside the entrance. That meant they had to queue in the cold. Lucy who had drunk the least, was really feeling the cold. She really should have brought a coat.

"Ah man this sucks! You said if we left now we would not have to queue!" Andrew cursed directing his comments to Adam who was at the back of the queue. Andrew was the tallest of the group and a friend of Tom's from rugby. He very similarly liked to throw his weight around Lucy noted how much he wrestled power from Adam during the pre-drinks.

Adam who was next to Mike the other guy in flat 2a gave Andrew a withering look. "Do you want a refund for these queue jumps Andrew?"

"No, no I just hope we get in quick." Andrew seemed wary of taking things further as he had other things on his mind, he kept glancing at Libby who was next to Lucy. Lucy would have to keep an eye on him.

"Stay with me Lu, you don't have a phone so it's best you don't run off," Libby said unperturbed by the cold weather in her black dress.

"You're going to beeline straight to the dancefloor! I am not sticking to you like glue!" Lucy protested. Lucy hated dancing, she was more awkward at it than the stereotypical uncle at weddings.

"Oh c'mon Lu you don't go in the club to spend £5 standing still." Libby slung her arm around Lucy as to ensure she could not escape. Her eyes were glassy and Lucy could smell the alcohol on her breath.

"Who would have guessed that everyone bought a queue jump? Kind of defeats the purpose of them don't you think?" Mike projected to anyone in the group who was listening.

The queue was finally trickling forward and with Lucy and Libby at the front did they keep going forward.

Alexa, the girl from Spain, was suffering the most from the cold as her teeth chattered uncontrollably. This looked to be a sobering experience. Brent eyed her with bemusement. "You European's are like the bloody English!" here he goes again Lucy mused in her head.

Alexa eyed him testily, "you are European too. My friends back home were right the weather here is shit."

"No sweetheart I am Scottish, not European and certainly not English."

"I get it you're not English, so what?" Alexa retorted, Lucy was keeping her ears tuned in ready to save Brent from his drunken self.

Brent laughed hysterically, "so what? This weather is tropical for me. You shitesticks better grow some backbone or get some Scottish blood running through your veins." He was struggling to keep still swaying in the cold air as he pointed a finger groggily at everyone.

"Brent knock it off, keep your Scottish tales up your kilt where it belongs," Lucy snapped back at Brent which took him by surprise.

Alexa laughed at that and so did the rest of 2a. Adam kept quiet and Libby smiled but said nothing. All too soon they arrived at the front entrance with two burly bouncers checking their tickets.

Adam wisely stuck close to Brent whispering for him to be on his best behaviour. Brent scowled foully and paced off into the crowd not waiting for any of them.

As Lucy got in Adam approached her. "You should not have said that Lucy," he said.

"He was being an arse Adam," she responded waiting on the rest.

"True, but you know the reference to the kilt is not necessary. Not all of them wear kilts. He looks like a bit of a tool now in front of the other flat."

"I wasn't trying to alienate him in front of the rest Adam. He is not your younger brother. Leave him be. He'll calm down and I'll say sorry when he simmers down." Lucy saw Libby come through and she quickly took hands with Lucy.

"Adam we are going ahead! Usual place!" she shouted back as she dragged Lucy through some more doors.

"Thought I'd might save you from Mr adult back there," Libby giggled with Lucy as she took Lucy into a dark, bright, flashing room.

The sound was deafening as people shoved past. Lights bedazzled the room as the music perforated Lucy's eardrums. The room was almost impossible to make out except a bar light in a dark purple lined one side of the gigantic space that was the dance floor. Frenzy indeed. Lucy attempted to walk to the bar but was stopped by Libby who kept a tight grip on Lucy.

"Do you think Andrea would mind?" Libby shouted in Lucy's ear pointing to the held hands.

Lucy ran the scenarios in her head and came up with the most comforting answer she could think of. "I don't plan to tell her!" she yelled back.

Libby smiled at that dragging Lucy to hell which was the dance floor. For whatever reason since arriving at university Lucy felt safe around Libby. She was straightforward sometimes clueless on her situation but overall an earnest person. Her haste to tell Lucy personal stuff early on charmed Lucy; no one had been so open with her before. It was a pity Lucy never felt comfortable reciprocating.

Libby being herself dragged Lucy to the centre of the dance floor, she started to let rip. Lucy watched her go and attempted to mimic her in an embarrassing fashion. She hoped no one could see how red she was in this darkness. It had barely been two minutes into the first song and she felt a hand sweep across her behind. Lucy froze up in shock. She whirled around to check who it was but no one was looking at her. She returned to her dancing and barely a minute again a hand swept more adventurously across her rear.

Lucy gritted her teeth in rage. Libby had not realised what was happening and starting dancing with a guy who snuck in with them. Lucy eyed him with suspicion but he was keeping his hands to himself. The songs changed and Lucy attempted to change position on the dance floor. A hand seized her bum and squeezed.

That's it! Lucy's lightening reflexes kicked in and her hand snatched the hand grabbing her bum. She whirled around putting the arm into a wrist lock and applied pressure without remorse. The guy yelled in pain as she released him staring him dead in the eyes.

"You bitch!" he shrieked many people on the dance floor didn't realise what was happening but some close by watched intently.

"Hand's off dickhead. The last man who touched me got a broken nose and a trip to A and E!" she snarled. He looked at her in horror but Lucy did not wait for him to leave. She left herself shoving people aside without apologising leaving that grotesque mess.

She stormed out of the room clenching and unclenching her fists. Her rage was bestial. Men! While not all were bad she found those special few to be the scum of the earth. They did not deserve what they had.

She had moved without realising it to the smoking area outside. It was cold, but refreshing. Half of the people were not even smoking but contributed to plumes of gas with their cloudy breath. Lucy just needed somewhere to think.

She felt woozy, her lack of sleep evident to her as she embraced the cold air once again. The alcohol effect had worn off. The smoking area was just a small fenced off clearing at the back of the club building. It was dingy, but light and people were able to talk at normal volume albeit with drunken conversation topics.

She rested herself against an uncomfortable brick wall lamenting this to be one of her worst days at university so far. A boy groaned next to her slumped on the ground he was groggily smoking a cigarette. Lucy recognised this boy.

"Brent?" she identified bending her knees to be at face height with him.

"Fuck off Lu, don't want to talk to you." Brent was glass eyed and stared at nothing in particular. He did not trouble to look her in the face however.

"Look Brent," Lucy began, "I'm sorry for what I said earlier I have just been… short fused with everyone. I want to apologise for what I said back there."

Brent's expression softened, "ah, damn. You know it's really hard to stay mad at you. You know?"

Lucy smiled, "I'm afraid I get mad at myself a lot so, no, I don't know. You don't smoke either, where did you get that?" Lucy pointed to the cigarette which at this point Brent was practically chewing on. He shrugged and put up no resistance as Lucy raised him to his feet supporting him under the arm. She flinched when he put his hand on her shoulder but Lucy was prepared for it. He was in a bad way he needed some water. "Spit it out Brent, it's like your pacifier at this point." Brent complied grinning like a mischievous child.

Lucy kept hold of him as she frog-marched him back inside. The noise and flashing lights was not welcoming but Lucy powered through them to the bar. She rested him on the bar itself, "look sober!" she pleaded. Brent gave a mock salute and leaned against the bar surveying the dance floor. Lucy waited impatiently to get a bar member's attention. After what seemed 15 minutes one finally came over. Lucy asked for two pints of water while Brent tapped her on the shoulder.

"Adam is really going to town with Mike! Look!" Lucy decided to humour him and followed his unstable finger. The tall frame of Adam was a periscope amongst the dancers. Mike who was shorter was not so easy to spot.

"Can't see him, here." Lucy handed the water over to Brent while sipping her own. She began to take long deep gulps only then realising how thirsty she was.

Brent grinned stupidly, "you look surprised Lucy! Your gaydar is really bad considering…" he trailed off making incoherent words.

"Drink up Brent, after you have had that you and I are going home," she stated.

Brent raised the water to his lips but then started convulsing. He dropped his water and doubled over. A sickening wet sound sploshed next to her. Lucy felt warm specks stain her jeans.

"Hey man! What the hell?" a man standing next to the other side of Brent was angry. Lucy glanced but suddenly wished she hadn't. Sick plastered his shoes.

Lucy froze up. Her breath quickened and her pupils widened. Vomit. Oh no! Not now! She tore her eyes off the sight and tried to supress the memories. She could hear the gurgling, frothing noises from before. The black room. The convulsions on the bed. The pleas for help.

A bellowing shriek sounded from the middle of the dance floor. Lucy shot her eyes open trying to see where the cry had come from. Straight away as if like dominoes everyone stopped dancing and toppled fleeing from the middle of the floor. Lucy could hear one of the barmen on the radio behind her shouting, "Get security! Someone has a weapon on the dancefloor!"

People fled, the chaos ensued. Lucy's heart sank in fear. As the crowd cleared the centre of the room one figure stood looking at her. A kitchen knife was held in one hand. The matted shoulder length hair covered her face as it raised a hand to point at Lucy. It was dressed in a decaying nightgown and began lumbering awkwardly towards her.

Lucy screamed in unison with the rest. Her nightmare had returned. Bouncers surrounded the assailant screaming at her to drop the weapon. Lucy was trembling she could not find her feet. Run! She thought. You need to run!

Lucy snapped out of it as she grabbed Brent by the collar. He two had come to his senses looking in absolute horror at the zombie woman in the middle of the club.

"WE NEED TO RUN NOW!" Lucy screeched grabbing him by the hand and began pelting away without a second glance. She could hear further screams from some of the bouncers as she ran as fast as she could. Brent was still not able to run quick looking sluggish and queasy. Lucy kicked open the nearest fire exit she could see and ran through it.

Reaching the outside, she could hear yells from inside. She could also hear the sirens approaching. "C'mon!" she gruffed in frustration as she dragged Brent with her. She moved up the pathway onto the main road. She must have taken a different exit to the rest as she could not recognise anyone as many people were still running. Lucy saw a taxi mounted on the kerb. She dragged Brent towards it.

She began furiously tapping on the window as there was more screaming and shouting. The taxi driver who had his headphones in and was reading the paper winded down the window.

"What is going on?" he asked nervously.

"Doesn't matter, can you get us home or not?"

The taxi driver eyed Brent. "He better not make a mess," he warned.

"I promise you I will beat the living shit out of him if he does!" she opened the door and flung him roughly inside. "Put your seatbelt on!" she shouted at him as she closed the door behind her. Lucy's heart plummeted to her toes as she saw the figure lumber up the path. Blood was trickling down its blade. "Oh no! Oh fuck no! Can you drive now?!" Lucy thundered at the driver.

"I don't like that attitude young girl!" he said testily

"I'll pay you an extra £5 if you start driving now!" she yelled back. The figure was now on the path only a few metres away.

The taxi driver took one look at the figure and leapt into action. He put his foot on the accelerator and with a considerable amount of wheel spin powered onto the road. Lucy watched as the figure halted watching the taxi as it left.

Lucy sat down breathing a sigh of relief. Panting in adrenaline, did it hurt anyone? Lucy could never forgive herself if it did. Lucy felt harrowed as she remembered the blood that stained the blade it was holding. That thought was not comforting.

"What the hell was that thing?!" the taxi driver asked notably panicked.

"How the hell should I know?! She had a knife! I didn't decide to stick around!" Lucy in truth knew what it was but had no explanation for it.

"Where are you headed?" the taxi driver managed calming down somewhat.

"Sky's Razor," Lucy managed strapping herself in and holding back tears.

Brent looked pale and said nothing as he peered out of the window. Was he ok? Would he remember all of this? Lucy hoped not. A vibrating sound came from Brent's pocket. He fumbled with it and took out his phone. He squinted at the screen then handed it over to Lucy. Lucy accepted it and saw it was Adam who was calling.

"Hello," she managed quietly weeping,

"Lucy? Oh thank god! We had no idea where you were! Libby was petrified. Where is Brent? Is he okay?"

"He is with me, he is very drunk and not in the mood for talking," she explained trying to sound calm over the phone, her voice betrayed her by breaking.

"Lucy, are you okay?" Adam asked quietly.

"Yeah I'm fine," Lucy lied. Wiping away tears from her eyes. "The rest are with you?"

"Yeah we are all accounted for, on our way back now. Lucy, did you see what it was?"

Lucy paused and prepared to tell another lie, "some pyscho dressed in some Halloween costume. Was best to leave though as they were armed."

Adam grunted in a somewhat disappointed fashion, "how did they manage to get a weapon inside the club? And the costume?"

"Adam." Lucy cut off, "see you when you are back, me and Brent took a taxi."

Not waiting for his answer she hung up and handed the phone back to Brent. Brent gave her one glassy glance then looked back out the window.

The rest of the journey was done in silence. Lucy's problems were mounting. She had to act. She should have done the homework straight away. As soon as she was home no matter the time she'd do it then. Whether she liked it or not she had to meet Arthur Squire. She had no other option left.

CHAPTER 4

It was ten to nine in the morning. Lucy was waiting patiently outside the office labelled 'Arthur Squire'. She had a headache, a blocked nose and eyes that felt like they had been rolled on sand paper. She was not sure how much sleep she managed considering she got to bed around 3am and woke up at 7am, it was just not enough.

As soon as she got back home she did not bother talking to the rest of the flat and buried herself in her room. Of course, they asked if she was ok, Lucy lied that she was fine. Brent had sobered up and attempted to tell the story to the rest but from Lucy over-heard, he either denied what he truly saw or misunderstood. Brent was not stupid, Lucy quickly discovered he puts on a persona to appease his immediate friends. Lucy felt Brent knew what happened in the club was related to her but he never said it to anyone else. She was grateful to him for that.

She had spent two hours before bed writing what she believed in coming up with eight sides of A4 paper. Her writing was diabolical but she didn't care, she needed to see Arthur. She had to have faith in Caitlin's advice as she had nothing else to have faith in.

Lucy did manage to log in to Twitter and Facebook and saw a barrage of messages from Andrea. Lucy did send some hasty replies assuring she has not died. She also gave a status update on both platforms to let everyone know about her bust phone. Plus, she let netball know of her situation and gave a short message to Phillis hoping she was ok. No one replied. It was at 2am after all.

Lucy massaged her face as she leaned against the wall. She felt the bags under her eyes stretch with each palm that stroked across it. Her hands went through her black hair which felt greasy and unclean. She decided to put her hair back with the hair band she had kept in her bag. That way her bad hair day would not be so noticeable to everyone else.

It was at this time of perpetual lethargy and inattentiveness Lucy was suffering from, made her wish she had at least a coffee before this meeting. Breakfast was stale cereal and that was rushed in favour of getting the earliest bus. Lucy groaned putting her hand in her pocket to check her phone then realised she didn't have one. Residing herself, she put her hands in her jacket pockets and closed her eyes. The closed lids felt soothing against her irritated eyes, she wondered if this was a hangover or just massive sleep deprivation. It was not like she wanted to come in at 9am.

When she checked online for Arthur's contact hours they were the most awkward times. 9am-10am on a Tuesday or 9am-10am on a Wednesday. These times were not student friendly and Lucy had a suspicion Arthur was well aware of that fact.

People passed in the corridor but paid her little mind. They were mainly staff at the university and perhaps the occasional student. The building was coming to life as she meditated against the uncomfortable wall.

"Did you hear? Frenzy was attacked last night!"

Two men were chatting down the corridor both mingling outside a water dispenser. Lucy opened an eye to see who they were. They looked like PHD students one of them sporting the staff tag.

The second man waiting for his turn replied, "yeah it made the regional news." Lucy heavily cringed at that.

"It didn't say much but to think it happened in this boring place." The first man had finished filling up his water bottle and moved to the side to allow his colleague access to the fountain, he continued, "do you think it was one of the students?"

The second man shrugged, "could be, worrying thing is he or she got away. They have no leads it's like the attacker just vanished. I'm just glad no one died."

"First the arson attack on Aberstahl Manor and now this? Are things actually getting exciting?" the first man took a sip from his full bottle looking perhaps perversely excited about what he mentioned. Lucy had not heard about an arson attack, at least she wasn't the only troublemaker around.

The second man, watching his bottle fill added, "I reckon that was students as well. Bunch of junkies would use that place to take their fix, probably left a cigarette somewhere. Although this is just me guessing." When he finished his bottle they both started walking away. Lucy felt detached from the wider world because her phone was broken, so she was in the dark about recent happenings let alone the Frenzy attack. She breathed a sigh of relief, at least no one died.

In her unfocused gazing, she saw a man swiftly approaching the office. In one hand, he had a mug which was steaming and another a rolled-up newspaper. It was Arthur Squire. He was walking at a brisk pace and Lucy seeing him approach got a better chance to look at him than since the lecture.

His clothes were of the same theme as last time, they were old-fashioned. He was wearing a buttoned up white shirt with a light brown waist coat over the top. He had no tie this time so had a loose upturned collar. He wore matching coloured trousers which looked sizeable on him as they were fastened with a black belt. In his mouth was a tooth pick which he seemed to be chewing on. As he approached and made eye contact his face was not shy to hide his annoyance.

He walked up to Lucy moving his newspaper under his arm and took the toothpick out of his mouth; he then fumbled in his pocket for what she presumed were his keys to the door.

"You are not here for me, right?" he sounded hopeful.

"My name is Lucy and I am here to see you," Lucy said flatly turning to face him.

There was a clink in the lock as Arthur successfully opened his office door. Pushing the door ajar he turned back to her his face looking thoroughly displeased. "You are a first year, right? I'll let you off since you probably have not got the memo yet." He flung his newspaper onto his chair in his office and took a sip from his coffee as he sized Lucy up. "The reason I have contact hours is not because I want to talk to students about their first world problems, but rather, have some me time. In other words, young miss the reason I chose my contact hours at 9am is so I would not get harassed by entitled millennials. I do not see the point of contact hours, but I have to have them call it department bullshit."

Lucy seethed with hot anger. She knew he was a prick and she was now going to have to practically beg this man for help, with four hours sleep. "I need your help Mr Squire," she managed slowly and cautiously maintaining eye contact.

Mr Squire burst out laughing, "I am not your sodding teacher, if that was an attempt to butter me up you have me all wrong young miss." He then proceeded to walk inside his office and Lucy slow on the uptake reacted too late.

As he almost finished closing the door she blocked it with her foot. The pain of her foot getting crushed made her yelp. Arthur was startled, "what the hell do you think you're doing?!" he blurted almost losing his composure. "If you need help put your foot in the door of someone who would give a shit!"

He wrestled with the door for a short while as Lucy prised it further ajar with her hands. She was surprised at how strong she was in this instance.

"Listen up Arthur! I am not here to be turned away at the fucking doorway. Believe you me I would never have come to you if I thought there was another way, but there isn't. I need your help! What kind of professor turns away a student in need?" she thundered not afraid of making a scene.

Arthur who seemed much more fearful of a potential scene lowered his voice, "that professor would be me! Now leave!"

Lucy bellowed, "Caitlin sent me!" calming herself down she said again, "Caitlin sent me." Lucy stopped resisting against the door but to her surprise Arthur no longer forced it shut. His face had changed to one of surprise.

He swung open the door and sized her up. He put his hand up to the bridge of his nose massaging it gently. He gave an exasperated sigh, "let me get this clear. Caitlin Harkin told you, to come to me? The head of department Caitlin?"

Lucy nodded adding, "she is also my personal tutor and when she hears about this!"

"She won't," Arthur replied curtly.

Lucy frustrated at this man's arrogance asked, "what makes you so sure?"

"Because I have decided to help you. Now get in quick." He stood aside and allowed her entry. As soon as she passed the threshold Arthur slammed his office door shut. "Take a seat," he offered pointing to one of two sofa seats next to a coffee table.

Arthur's office was immaculate. Clean, tidy, organised and Lucy hazarded a guess that it was larger than Caitlin's. Books were on every shelf and his desk which took up a whole side of the room next to the window was shining off sunlight. A computer left powered off was to the side as well as many potted plants. Lucy noticed what looked like an old-fashioned chest was tucked underneath. On closer inspection, she felt like she had travelled back 50 years. Ornamental objects scattered the room, a painting, a cloak stand and a tall bell clock. Was he something of a collector? Lucy wondered.

Lucy sat on the chair and felt herself almost become absorbed into it. As she sat Arthur placed his steaming mug in front of her. Lucy blinked in surprise.

"Here, it's yours, you need it more than me," he said neutrally. She stared at it closely, there was milk inside but she cocked her head to see anything amiss. Arthur who sat opposite her snarled, "I have not poisoned it! If you are thinking this out of character for me, you misunderstand my purposes of giving it to you."

Lucy raised her head to focus on Arthur to find he was affixing her with a judgmental stare. She could tell he was reading her, she only hoped that she was not an open book. He swept his long fringe of his eyes revealing more of his face to her. They were grey, they looked old. Too old. Everything else about him was youthful except those eyes. When she stared at them she thought she was staring into bottomless pits of mist.

"Drink it. I will need you to be more alert." It sounded more like an order than an invitation.

Lucy complied secretly happy she had a chance to get herself out of this feeling of fatigue if only temporarily. As she raised it to her mouth and took a sip she found it at the right temperature but winced at the flavour. "It's bitter," she announced.

"Tells you wonders about me," Arthur snorted. He crossed his legs not troubling to hide his annoyance at a student in his office. The office was eerily silent as Arthur troubled to say nothing more as he watched her drink.

Lucy decided to take initiative, "why is it significant only when Caitlin sends me do you feel inclined to help?"

Arthur's eyes narrowed, "why ask me a question which is not significant to why you are here? Don't waste my time and let's get to the point."

Lucy growled through her coffee. He was going to be difficult, this guy loves his power trips. Was her pride really worth swallowing through this meeting?

Lucy sighed and fumbled in her bag to procure her homework. She placed it on the shiny coffee table and slid it across to Arthur. "My homework," she said flatly.

Arthur took it off the table to examine it. "You won't get any first prize for being the first boring student to complete their assignment the day after it was set," Arthur goaded. He was smiling, but not maliciously and the smile did not seem related to what he just said. It was a smile of an excited child.

Lucy clicked her tongue in frustration, "in future I'll hand it in last if it saves his grace from burdensome marking."

"Sarcasm huh?" Arthur leaned in to peer over the lump of paper he was holding, "there may be some redemption for you yet."

Lucy could not figure out this guy. She expected him to lash out at her disrespectful comment one she said with butterflies in her stomach. It didn't even phase him, in fact, weirdly, she seemed to have gained some points from him.

Arthur spent a few minutes looking over her written account of what she believes in. It was not an account of a God she believed in. It was not the belief in star signs either. It was ghosts. What Lucy believed in was ghosts. One in particular would not leave her alone, the embodiment of her fears.

After not reading all of it Arthur dropped the work on the coffee table and moved his fringe back again. He then fixed her with a curious look. "What made you think completing this homework would be vital to this meeting? Did Caitlin suggest you do it?"

"She suggested it," Lucy admitted which made Arthur scowl.

"That woman! She blunders around sabotaging my work. Okay, let's leave that aside. Why do you think I set this homework?"

Lucy shrugged, "you wanted something interesting to read in comparison to what was supposed to be set?"

"I asked you to think, not give cheap-ass answers," Arthur retorted.

Lucy took another swig at the bitter coffee while she pondered. "It's related to my problem." She said finally, not looking at Arthur but at the ceiling thinking aloud. "My problem is unusual, it is paranormal. Your homework is asking what paranormal things we believe in…" Suddenly something clicked in Lucy's head like a switch which lit a room. "This homework was to find me!"

Arthur's face showed mixed feelings. "You were close, but no. I did not know or care of your existence Lily until this very hour."

"Lucy," Lucy corrected.

"Point proven," Arthur said raising his hands innocently. "You are correct in your assumption that this homework was seeking the paranormal as you put it. You are also correct if what I suspect is true that your problem is very much related to it. But you are not special. This homework was more of a survey intending to find more than just one person in your position."

"Then you know what is wrong with me?" Lucy blurted out excitedly.

"Perhaps, but I will need more data. And it will not be for free."

Lucy halted at those words. What? Did he want money? She was a student clearly not made of money.

Arthur detected the halt in her enthusiasm with a patronising grunt, "did you think I was as charitable as the NHS? They are not my employer and my employer certainly does not ask me to fix student problems. I teach not pamper."

Lucy hunched up for a moment gripping her jogger bottoms tightly, "name your price," she said wearily.

"I don't need money if that is your concern. I would like to study you."

Lucy looked up in horror at Arthur. Which made his face go into genuine confusion, "I am in the psychology department all I'll want to study is your mind, that is it," he assured.

"What sort of study?" She asked.

"I cannot give you full disclosure otherwise it will corrupt potential data. What I can tell you is it will involve recorded interviews and participant observation. It is not covert in the sense you know you are being studied. But the information is sensitive. As in I cannot tell anyone what I am studying not unless they pass stage 2."

"Stage 2?" Lucy asked.

"I know you have what I suspect and I can diagnose you. In other words, I can tell you what is wrong with you."

Lucy became increasingly nervous was she mentally ill? How could she be? Others saw that thing as well.

"You are not mentally ill," Arthur continued as if reading her mind, "or at least Caitlin would not send you my way. No what you have, can be seen as a blessing or a curse."

"This all sounds really cryptic," Lucy interjected.

"It has to be. I'm not doing this for fun."

Lucy took herself back to the Monday morning lecture and felt a lot of the comments he made were just purely for fun. So she took that comment with a pinch of salt. Arthur got up and rummaged in his desk draw he soon withdrew a paper. He then took it back to the coffee table and handed it to Lucy. She scanned her eyes over it, it was a consent form.

"This the consent form for the study?"

"And two plus two equals four," Arthur patronised, "normally I don't see the point of doing forms but if it prevents you from suing me I take it as a necessary evil."

Lucy scowled and looked at the form in more detail. She begrudgingly signed the form finding nothing out of the ordinary on it. "So what now?" she asked impatiently.

"Now, we get to work Leeanne."

"Lucy," Lucy corrected again.

Arthur gave an exasperated sigh, "what is your surname?"

"Why would that help deliberate amnesia?" Lucy accused.

Arthur's lips curled slightly, "call me old-fashioned but I remember surnames better."

Lucy took a glance at him, the room, him then the room again. She didn't need telling he was old-fashioned.

"My surname is Baxter," she admitted.

"Right Baxter, you are now going to go through a 20-minute interview with me. It is to be recorded because I love the sound of my own voice and for me to annotate your responses. The answers are in free-form you can say whatever you wish, even swear, I don't care."

Lucy nodded believing he does love his own voice far too much. "This is going to help me with my problem, right?"

Arthur glanced up at her as he positioned a recorder on the table. "This whole interview is about your problem. So, if you plan to not answer questions no matter how difficult they are you can leave and I won't help you. They are going to be vital for me to understand what exactly you have."

Lucy can already tell this interview was not going to be in her comfort zone. Then again last night was not exactly comforting either. She'll have to roll with it if there is a chance it won't happen again. Wait a second, Arthur said diagnose, did he ever suggest cure? Lucy realised.

"Alright let's get started." Arthur pressed play on his recorder. "I am here interviewing a Miss Lucy Baxter." So he does remember her name Lucy thought. "A hungover student of roughly 18 years of age. She has approached me fearing she has a condition that only I can solve. Subject came here under the direction of the devil herself Mrs Harkin. I will now proceed to ask questions to ascertain whether she is plain cuckoo or might have something worthy of my time."

Lucy gritted her teeth. Bear with it Lucy. Keep going, it is just in his nature to antagonise everyone he meets.

"First question, I am now showing the subject her written homework piece. Is this your handwriting?"

Lucy blinked stupidly taken aback by the seemingly mundane question. "Yes? It's mine."

"Did you write this under pressure? Or have you always had comments from peers saying they cannot read it?" Arthur pressed waving a random page of scrawl in front of him.

"Teachers at high school often complained but I always wrote like that it's fast and efficient," Lucy defended feeling the impending criticism.

"Clearly they feel like me and are witnessing a birth of a whole new character set," Arthur commented looking at the piece again.

"Look, you can read it, can't you? I don't see the relevance of my hand-"

"Second question," Arthur cut-off not interested in her excuses. "You have made a written account of how you believe in ghosts. You are not the first person I have encountered to believe in ghosts, so why do you believe them? What is your reason for believing in them?"

Lucy pondered what seemed to be a more legitimate question. Arthur was patient watching her very intently as she decided on a response. "I know this sounds stupid, but I have seen… ghosts."

"Seeing is believing, right?" Arthur added, Lucy thought he would laugh at her but he accepted the fact she has seen them. Does he believe in ghosts as well? "You saw what you think is a ghost? Or an actual ghost? Can you verify that what you have seen is actually a ghost?"

A tricky question. Lucy felt nervous, she had always assumed what she saw was some apparition haunting her. It had to be a ghost it was something her mind used as logic to explain the otherwise unexplainable. Lucy fidgeted as she tried to come up with a suitable answer. "I haven't exactly asked it," she mumbled.

Arthur raised an eyebrow, "so it cannot communicate? Have you tried communicating with it?"

"I have told it to fuck off several times. It doesn't get the clear message."

Arthur smiled somewhat. "So you have seen it more than once? This ghost is harassing you? Have you not tried getting a restraining order?

"Can you be serious with me?!" Lucy thundered, "I am telling you it's a goddamn ghost."

"Yet you provide no proof," Arthur responded coolly, "you want me to take you seriously provide me with a serious reason why you think it is a ghost!"

"Because it looks like my mum!!!" Lucy yelled slamming the table in anger making the recorder shake. Small droplets of water welled in her eyes but she quickly rubbed them away. She was sick of crying. She was sick of all of it.

Arthur's face softened a little and he asked with a lot less accusation in his tone, "is she...?"

"She died, almost over nine years ago," Lucy settled.

Arthur took a notepad out of his waist coat pocket and jotted something down. He looked back up at her. "This is clearly a touchy subject. I should return to it but first let's move onto my other questions. Also, I'm sorry for your loss."

"Don't pity me," Lucy growled. "I don't care if you look down on me for being a naïve student lost in an adult world. But don't you dare! For one second! Pity me!"

Arthur blinked in surprise this time, "understood," he said neutrally. "Third question, where do you find this ghost?"

Lucy calmed down, slowing her breathing. She took off her jacket to get a bit more comfortable. "I guess it is always around me. Unless it goes elsewhere when I don't see it. It is not haunting one place, it's haunting me."

Arthur scribbled more on his notepad looking thoughtful. "So this ghost it reappears and disappears?"

"Yes, it appears like behind me or wherever I am not looking."

Arthur nodded again as Lucy sees the cogs work in his head. "Got any ideas where it goes?" Arthur asked.

Lucy looked at him incredulously. "I was hoping you would be able to tell me that."

Arthur gave a disappointed sigh, "yes, but I was wondering if you had any idea yourself?"

"I have no clue."

"Fine, we will move on to my fourth question. If this ghost only appears at certain timed intervals. It could well be because of external stimuli triggering its appearance. What I ask of you is, recollect; is there any patterns on its existence. For example, does it only come at night? Or does it only come when you are alone etc?" Arthur was starting to show his prowess in an interview. His cool collected demeanour made him appear extremely rational. He was breaking down her experiences in ways Lucy never really thought to do before.

Lucy felt these questions were now getting to the heart of the problem. She recognised it had some link to her but only appeared when… "It appears only in darkness," Lucy answered expanding on it she continued, "it only comes where there is little or no light."

Arthur nodded looking pleased with the answer she gave. "Is that the only trigger? I mean to say does it always appear whenever you are in the dark?"

Lucy pondered this question for what seemed like half a minute. "No, not always, but I am always on edge as a result in the dark."

"Are you afraid of the dark Baxter?" Arthur pressed.

Lucy afraid of being ridiculed lied, "no," her interviewer looked sceptical at her answer but did not press further. Lucy realised the metaphorical mic was still on her wracked brain for other reasons this ghost has appeared. "It did appear last night when I saw vomit."

Arthur looked perplexed, "vomit? This creature comes when you see vomit? What? Does it eat everyone's sloppy seconds?"

Lucy agreed that vomit on its own was unlikely to be the reason for its appearance. She had a phobia of vomit having a small panic attack whenever she saw it. Hang on, Lucy realised she was scared of both vomit and the dark. "It comes whenever I am afraid. That is its trigger."

Arthur smiled slightly, "good, you are starting to piece things together."

"Does this thing sense fear?" Lucy asked with some trepidation.

"Perhaps, I cannot say for certain. I do feel however that we have a three-step process here. You see something that potentially scares you or you have a strict aversion from it. Your emotional response is one of fear. That build up in fear results in the appearance of this entity which scares you even further. Does this sound about right?"

Lucy nodded. Finally, someone gets it! Arthur is getting it better than herself and she has lived with this problem for a while.

"Let's move on to our fifth question. Simply put, what does it look like?"

"I don't exactly like to make eye contact."

"So, it looks like a human?"

"Yes."

"Is it transparent like a ghost?"

"No, it looks very real."

"What is it wearing?"

"Why does that matter?"

"Answer the question Baxter."

Lucy shifted about her chair not making eye contact with her interviewer. "It… It… does not wear the same clothes each time," Lucy admitted.

Arthur began furiously scribbling away on his notepad not troubling to look up he snorted, "at least it knows wearing the same pair of clothes for more than two days is unhygienic."

"I'm trying to be serious here!" Lucy snapped.

"So am I," Arthur retorted, "any important features on this being?"

"You mean, like what stands out?"

"What is consistently always there? What does not change each time you see it?" Arthur pressed harshly clearly getting impatient.

Lucy closed her eyes visualising the creature in her head, her heart beat racing as a result. Opening her eyes thankfully seeing it was light she answered, "it always has a knife in its right hand. A kitchen knife."

"It has a bloody weapon!?" Arthur said shocked.

"Yes. Yet it has never hit me with it."

"There is so many things I want to ask about that but we'll keep on track," Arthur said massaging his temple. "Anything else?"

"It always has grey, ghoulish skin. It is always bare foot and has long black matted hair which covers its face."

"All of the face?"

"Just the eyes. It spews bile from its mouth on occasion making disgusting retching sounds and smells of…"

"Smells of?"

"Smells of a corpse," Lucy admitted.

Arthur raised an eyebrow but did not comment any further. He finished jotting down his notes and fixed her with a piercing glare. "6th question, only two more after this one," he promised, "tell me, what is its behaviour when you encounter it?"

"It is always drawn to me. If I flee it pursues me, it generally ignores other people unless those people get in its way."

Arthur mouthed silently what Lucy guessed was a swear word before he leans in. "How many people have seen this thing other than you?" his voice was deadly calm but Lucy could tell an outburst was imminent.

"I can't control when it appears!" Lucy protested.

"How many?" Arthur growled.

"Did you hear about the club attack last night?"

Arthur's face sank into abject horror. "That was? Was it….?"

Lucy grimaced and nodded slightly.

"Jesus fucking Christ!" Arthur bellowed getting out of his chair. He started pacing up and down his room furiously muttering to himself. "Are there any other times?!" he shouted back at Lucy while pacing.

"A few, but only one or two people saw it before that occasion I swear!"

"Anyone who sees it other than you have just made this horrendously more difficult!" Arthur snarled.

"Oh, I'm sorry for increasing your workload!" Lucy yelled back finding her backbone.

Arthur stopped in his tracks looking at her. His face slowly regressed into a calmer expression. "You're right," he said sitting back down, "my outburst was only thinking of myself. Forgive me." He bowed his head like he was a Japanese samurai begging for forgiveness.

Lucy was completely taken aback by this behaviour that she decided to move past this eccentricity, "can we just get back to the interview please?"

Arthur collected himself and returned to his interview face. "So this thing is dangerous it will attack, knife in hand, anything that stands in its way of you?"

"Yes."

"What happens when it gets to you? Has that happened?"

"Yes." Lucy became notably uncomfortable, "it.. er… kinda… gropes me."

Arthur looked unperturbed at that statement, "and it does not use the knife?"

"Correct."

"Interesting."

"Is it?"

"Very. But we'll move on. Question seven is more personal and about you Baxter."

Lucy steeled herself for the coming barrage of questions.

"I suppose question seven is more an amalgamation of questions. First you said your mother died? How did she die?"

"Car accident."

"And the father?"

"Ran away before I was eight."

"Where are you living when not at university?"

"With my registered guardians, Phillis and Joseph Sloane."

Arthur turned over on his pad to write some more. "May I ask why guardians?"

Lucy shrugged, "don't know any family."

"At all?"

"None," Lucy said with finality in her tone.

"When did this creature first appear then? I'm presuming after your mother's death?"

"Pass," Lucy said holding up her hand.

Arthur looked shocked, "pass?! This is crucial information!"

"Look Arthur, I appreciate your ability to help me piece things together in my head, but I think that can be done without going into my life history."

"You do not get to decide what is important or what is worth knowing! Baxter if you want my help you need to tell me what I ought to know!"

"As far as I can tell, you have no entitlement to know about me. All you are entitled to do is solve my problem. That's it." Lucy folded her arms to suggest her attitude was immovable.

Arthur ground his teeth in frustration fixing her with a steely glare. His eyes were scanning her whole body. Perhaps trying to read her. Perhaps to find a weakness. He found none.

"Eighth question." Arthur resigned to move on went to his final question. "Do you dream?"

"Huh?"

"Do you dream?" Arthur repeated.

"This is your final question?"

"A simple yes or no will do and I can end this interview." Arthur closed his notepad and put it on the table folding his arms and leaned back into his chair.

"I... everyone dreams, don't they?" Lucy said a little unsure of herself.

"Then why are you struggling to remember a single dream you have had?" Arthur asked as he hit home. "It is common to forget dreams. But for you to not even recall the faintest memory of a dream, that is rare."

"Do nightmares count?"

"No."

"Then I don't recall a single dream," Lucy said begrudgingly.

Arthur clasped his hands together, "time. Thank you, Miss Baxter, the interview is now over." He switched off the recorder then turn the look back at her. "Go home get some sleep, you look horrific."

Lucy felt wounded by the last statement. "What happens next?" she asked hopefully.

"You sleep," Arthur dismissed.

"What? You know I can't sleep very well because of this problem, right?"

"Then sleep with the light on, it's what you do anyway right?" Arthur asked smugly. Lucy glared at the man who knew too much.

"I have a timetabled day," Lucy muttered.

"Skip them, I'll explain to Mrs Harkin why." Arthur got a fresh page and his pad and started writing again. "I need you fresh," he explained handing a torn piece of paper from the pad.

Lucy looked at it. It was an address and a time. "What are we doing there?" Lucy asked,

Arthur pulled a huge grin. One of a boy who realised he had brought the biggest water gun to the water fight. "We are going to be ghost busting."

CHAPTER 5

Beep beep. Beep beep.

Lucy stirred from her hibernation groaning like a mother bear. Her eyelids were heavy, it was too painful to open them but still the alarm continued.

Beep beep. Beep beep.

Lucy outstretched an arm to press the button for snooze. Without looking Lucy was touching all the wrong things. She felt herself knock something to the floor making a loud clunking sound.

Beep beep. Beep beep.

"Alright fine, you win."

Lucy took her face off the pillow and groggily aimed her hand to the power button on her alarm clock. She saw the time was 4:17pm. She had gotten an extra four hours' sleep. It was something. She rolled ungracefully from her covers and onto her feet expertly missing all the clutter scattered on her bedroom floor.

Lucy switched off her lamp and at the exact same time powered on her main room light. Her eyes did not need adjusting to this new light. Lucy stretched and yawned as if all was well, she felt already a lot more rested. A lot calmer.

Lucy proceeded get some clothes from her open wardrobe. One thing that impressed her about her uni room was how much room for storage there was. Her wardrobe took the remaining wall space at the bottom of her bed and was sizable to boot. Rummaging in it she realised her choices were limited. There were a few choices of underwear left indicating she needed to do laundry. She conceded on wearing the black lace underwear set Andrea had bought her for her 18th among other things.

Lucy secretly hated the design but never told Andrea this. Andrea thought it was something more adult. Lucy disliked the colour and for someone who mainly wore bright clothes was conscious they could be seen from underneath. They were still better than doing the laundry however.

Slipping them on, Lucy found her last pair of clean blue jeans with holes where the knee caps were. Again, her last choice. Lucy found a band shirt that crumpled at the bottom of the wardrobe which would do. It was a dark blue so hopefully conceal her choice in bra. With a glance out of the window she expected herself to be wearing a jumper at least. Condensation was forming on the windowpanes.

Lucy was meeting Arthur at 8pm. She had time to kill but was nervous with anticipation. She didn't want to sleep any longer for risk of losing her sleeping pattern and felt she needed to eat something hearty beforehand. Still the postcode he gave her was weird.

Opening up her laptop on her desk she searched the post code again on google. It came up on a warehouse right next to Aberstahl Lake. A 40 minute walk or 15 minute bus journey.

The lake was big but polluted, it was right of the bottom of the basin as Aberstahl; was surrounded by hills. It was used for a time by a brewery and cannery factories but the waste from such industry in 18th and 19th centuries stopped any fishing from really being possible. The lake is arguably making a recovery.

So, why there? Lucy looked through any information Google had about this warehouse. It is non-commissioned and abandoned; the council has plans to demolish it but have yet to do it. So why here? It was unavailable to public access and has been fenced off. Lucy looked around the area to see what else was significant. Besides a ramp for boats and other used warehouses it was a boring, grey industrial estate.

Lucy could only guess but whatever they were going to do, Arthur wanted it out of sight of anyone else. That made sense, and Lucy preferred this way, but still, what were they going to do? It did dawn on her several times she was going to an isolated location with a man she had only met twice. She was considerably nervous as a result, deep down Lucy's judgement of Arthur would suggest she had nothing to fear, but alas, her judgement can be wrong.

Lucy decided to help ease her conscience she would look him up along with the Lake she just viewed. Typing his name in the search engine, the first result was an Aberstahl staff listing. Clicking on it she saw a list of names of staff associated with the Psychology department. Clicking on Arthur she saw a profile lacking a photo but with plenty of text to compensate. His title was associate professor. Lucy continued scrolling and found out he had joined the university in 2014, two years ago. He had published many papers associated with journals in Sociology, Psychology and even History. He was well referenced too; the man certainly had some accolade in the academic world. Some of the paper names took Lucy's notice one was 'Challenging the normative conceptions of Human Belief.' He did seem obsessed with the concept. However, the most surprising thing Lucy saw was when she scrolled to the bottom of the page. He had a PHD awarded at 22. What?! Lucy did a double take, she recognised he was young for an academic but to get a PHD at 22 is insane. Furthermore, it seemed to be a Sociology PHD rather than Psychology yet, he is now a Psychology professor. Lucy was baffled but her fear of him had somewhat been reduced. Whatever it could be, she perhaps wrongly thought such a young achieving academic would have devious intentions in regards to tonight. This did not stop her from feeling she best bring precautions.

While pondering that further Lucy decided splash her face and brush her teeth. Her hair was a bit crazy after lying on a pillow but she showered before bed so was not too bothered.

Lucy after drying her face, made it to the kitchen for a browse of what food she had left.

Already in there was Brent. He looked up from his sandwich chewing in an exhausted sort of way. He had bags under his eyes, and he was sweating. Lucy realised what happened the last time she saw him and faltered. It was supremely awkward. He met her eyes as he probably was wondering what to say.

"Afternoon," Lucy mumbled breaking the silence. She broke eye contact and went straight for her cupboard labelled in her name with a sticky note. Brent grunted. Lucy sighed quietly to herself. It was relief, his grunt was characteristic, normal. He carried on chewing pulling up his hood over his buzz cut head.

Lucy rumbled through her cupboard finding pasta and some tinned tomatoes.

"The police came to our door while you were gone."

Lucy froze mid squat, not troubling to turn and face Brent. She carried on pretending to not care and asked casually, "what did they want?"

Brent carried on chewing before answering. Wolfing down his sandwich before replying. "Was asking about last night," he began, Lucy moving to the hob to pour pasta in one of her pans. "They were asking if we went to the club Frenzy. Been askin if I saw anything about the girl who attacked the staff."

"What did you say?" Lucy said cautiously.

"Said that I was the only one in and could not speak for the rest. You know it's my free day." He paused again as Lucy poured water in her pan and got ready the tin opener.

"And?" Lucy pressed trying to not sound fearful.

"And, I said I saw someone dressed up in some Halloween costume holding a knife. They didn't run and were clearly fucked up in the head."

"Were the police happy with that?"

Brent shrugged, "dunno." He finished his sandwich looking up at Lucy as she stirred her boiling pasta gently. "Would you have said the same thing?"

Lucy glanced over her shoulder at Brent who fixed her with suspicious eyes. The kind of eyes who already doubted what Lucy was going to say next. "I would have said roughly the same thing. Did they say anything else?"

Lucy tried to move the topic gently away but Brent seemed keen to continue, "they said for me to strongly encourage anyone else I knew who saw what happened to come forward."

Lucy tested the pasta with a fork as she decided to say nothing.

Brent clicked his tongue in annoyance and asked again, "well? Are you going to go talk to them?"

Lucy turned to face Brent to give him a full sizing up. He looked concerned but also irritated. His arms were crossed and he had turned his chair so the backrest was against the table. "I have nothing else to add Brent," she said finally.

"Bullshit," he muttered but Lucy pretended she didn't hear.

After a short while Lucy's food was ready. She placed the steaming plate of tomato pasta on the table ignoring the stains which pockmarked the surface. Brent was browsing on his phone and looked up at her once she had started to eat.

"Lucy if you are in danger-"

"Can you give it a rest Brent?" Lucy exasperated letting go of her fork which clattered against the plate.

"Lucy, she followed you. She ignored everyone else and followed you. How else am I meant to interpret that?"

"You're just guessing," Lucy said with a mouthful of pasta. It was hard to meet his gaze. He was concerned for her, but she knew, the less involved he was the better off he'd be.

"Fine, I'll tell the police myself."

At that Lucy looked up at him. He was a stubborn one. Lucy always knew that. "Do you trust me Brent?"

Brent's heated face did not falter, "no," he managed bluntly.

Lucy smiled, "guess we both have trust issues then." Brent faltered at that instead.

"Why are you so calm?" he insisted looking at her as if she was insane.

Lucy wondered that herself but she had to subdue Brent. He seemed convicted, she had to throw off his suspicions, "because you are making something out of nothing. You are the one which is scared. It was a prank which was meant to make us like this. You were drunk Brent, I was drunk. It ruined the fucking night. And now you are making it ruin our friendship."

Brent looked worried after that last sentence. "Look Lucy, I'm just worried about you. I thought I was… Am doing right by you."

Lucy chuckled a little, "I'm touched!" she said it half mockingly, half meaningfully. "I'll talk to the police," Lucy lied, "if it makes you feel better, it'll get that bitch which made us very nearly shit ourselves."

Brent laughed, "nearly? I was lucky that I was wearing brown chinos."

Lucy laughed back and soon the conversation lost all tension. It became what she wanted it to be. What she always wanted it to be, free from conflict, free from suspicion. It was just a pity she had to lie in order to have that.

*   *   *

Lucy stood outside a steel fence clearly stating 'Private Property, No Entry' on one of the signs cable tied to the rungs of the two metre-tall fencing. She glanced at the map she had printed out at the street name.

'Fishers Road' she looked at the street sign 'Fishers Road' Lucy groaned. This was indeed the place. It was dark now, the overcast sky made no room for the stars or the moon as Lucy felt incredibly unnerved. She stayed in the lamppost light like some moth refusing to leave its glare.

Lucy really wished she had her phone. She could have called Andrea, browsed the internet, anything. So long as it distracted her from the dark.

The warehouse was uninviting. Even in this lack of light she could tell is was brown with rust. The translucent plastic panes which covered its roof were murky some littered with bird poop. No one had cared to be to this warehouse for a long time. It was large enough, by Lucy's estimates to store eight fishing boats. Its front entrance loomed in front of her, the wooden doors fairing no better than its metal body. Behind it was Aberstahl Lake. Lucy thought it would sound like a seafront with the sound of water crashing on the beach. But no, nothing. The only sounds were the bustling traffic behind her leading back into Aberstahl central which she missed already.

She checked her watch. It was 8pm. Lucy would not want to keep Arthur waiting. If he was even in there at all. She made a hurried break for it, crossing the road to a street lamp across the road. So long as she was basked in light was she safe.

Lucy looked at the fence wondering how to get in. She hoisted her rucksack further up her back as it sagged when she ran. Lucy was not sure of what to bring. She felt the random things jangle in her bag. One thing she was happy she brought was a torch. She ruffled it out and switched it on using the beam to look for gaps.

Was she meant to wait for him? Or was he already inside? Christ! Lucy simply did not know. She already felt a bit foolish dressed in a black jumper and rucksack, if she had a mask she would definitely look like a burglar to other people. She had brought all sorts of equipment, a rope, bandages, a drink, a knife…. Lucy felt nervous having it there but if she was to deal with this thing. She wanted to be able to defend herself, the ghost had a knife as well; it was only fair, right?

She gasped when she eventually saw a gap. It was not massive, but someone had clearly cut the gate open to sneak in. Was this Arthur? Lucy didn't care. She ran to the gap five fences down flinging her back over the fence and virtually crawled through the gap. Picking up her bag she nervously flung her torch light all around her. She was waiting for that inevitable ambush, of when that thing appeared before her again.

Thankfully there was no sign. She approached the warehouse cautiously, she wondered whether she should knock on the front door but thought better of it.

Instead she circled the dilapidated building for another way in. Sure enough she found one, a side entrance, possibly a fire exit, stood wide open. She shone her torch inside but could not get a clear view. Braving it, she stepped inside.

Suddenly there was a great clang! Lucy felt her eyes get pierced by some bright light. She raised her arms to shield them as her eyes desperately tried to adjust.

"You came! Guess that makes you either gullible or desperate."

Lucy knew that voice, that tone, it was most certainly, "Arthur!" Lucy snarled. As she blinked feverishly trying to take in her surroundings. The source of the light was two flood lights on stands, something you would see on a road works site. They shone brightly illuminating the entire inside of the warehouse. The warehouse itself was bare. Nothing inside besides the walls, concrete floor, those two lamps, a stool, several bags, Lucy and Arthur.

He stood their grinning somewhat mischievously as he stepped in front of the lamps which were placed in two corners of the building facing towards the lake. His clothing had not changed still wearing a brown waistcoat and trousers. He was fiddling with another toothpick in his mouth, which he neatly pocketed.

He glanced up and down at her before commenting, "did you manage to get any good TVs on the way down?"

Clearly remarking on her choice of clothing Lucy almost bared her teeth like some wild dog. "None of them were airing Ghost Busters unfortunately," she growled.

Arthur laughed. "That's a shame, at least you might get a theatrical adaptation tonight, if you are lucky."

Lucy didn't think that would be a sign of luck. "What is this place?" she nodded to the set-up with the lamps and the bags by the stool. "Is this what you would call your private dungeon?" Lucy heavily implied with her tone exactly what type of dungeon it would be' but it fell on deaf ears as Arthur dimmed the lights on his lamps. "Is this place yours?" Lucy asked again.

Arthur glanced up after dimming the second light, "oh no, this is private property. We are most definitely trespassing. Not that anyone has cared beforehand."

"So you have been here before?"

"Yes, it is quite convenient you see. Away from prying eyes, and in a large enclosed space. It is just perfect, also free, that is a big plus." Arthur had an excited tone about him. He was a lot more active, a lot livelier than when she met him this morning. Was he a bad morning person just as much as she was? Lucy pondered.

Lucy subconsciously dropped her bag by the edge of the door she had just came through. The noise attracted the attention of Arthur who stared at the bag suspiciously. "What's in that?" he asked shrewdly.

Lucy glanced at the bag realising what was in it, "just some stuff," she answered ambiguously.

Arthur's eyes narrowed, "is that your attempt of a ghost defence kit?" he asked almost sneering.

Lucy almost gave it away as her ears became red and she averted his stare. Arthur noticed and starting laughing. Yep, he may be more active but he was still an arsehole Lucy thought as she balled her fists besides her.

"What's in there? Salt? You going to throw salt at your foe? Like it is some kind of devil spawn? Sorry for rubbing salt in the wound but salt only works well on slugs," Arthur said through barely controlled laughter.

"Enough already!" Lucy shot back, "you like being a twat I get it. But what I brought in my bag is nothing to concern yourself with!" She made a mental note to return Libby's salt when she got home. "Besides what's in your bags?" she accused.

Arthur stopped laughing narrowing his eyes again. All he managed was, "touché."

"So you do have something in there to defeat it?! Why laugh at me like that when all I wanted to do is come prepared?"

Arthur shook his head like Lucy was a five-old asking if Santa was real. It was obviously patronising. "Okay, A. You can't prepare for something if you don't know what it is. B. We are not fighting this ghost. And C. It is funny because it is so predictable of you millennials, don't take it so personally."

"Millennials this, millennials that, you say it like you are an 80-year-old man, by the looks of you were only born in the 90s. If you want to mature so early, and believe you me, you will need a lot of practice. Go and start playing bingo!"

"Thanks for the compliment. Now close the door we have work to do."

Lucy growled but complied. It was hard to say no despite how much of a dick he was. He was the only way she could see dealing with her problem. She did not know why, he had yet to show any real evidence of knowing what he was doing, but his whole composure came with a relaxed arrogance. It was really annoying, but weirdly, Lucy felt she could rely on it.

"Now I want you to sit on that stool facing towards the lake. Leave your bag where it is."

Lucy again complied without comment sitting on the stool. She wanted to throw insults at him all day but that would be forgetting why she was here. She shifted on the stool nervously. This was too weird. The apprehension too fierce. The stool too uncomfortable.

Arthur walked to face her standing about three metres away. He gave a curt nod, "thank you for trusting in me Baxter. Many girls in your shoes would have definitely caused alarm by now." There was no hint of sarcasm in his words, it was genuine.

Lucy didn't pretend that it had not crossed her mind. She was going somewhere with a stranger out of reach of others and alone. Lucy looked at him again. His figure was not intimidating in the slightest Lucy reckoned he barely did any form of martial art, whereas she had. Even so it did not stop her from bringing the knife which she had slipped into her pocket before entering the building.

"Well I am kind out of options and desperate here," Lucy admitted.

Arthur simply nodded. "Okay, let me give you a rundown of what is going to happen. This is a controlled environment, one which I will attempt to bring your ghost out to meet us." Lucy glanced at him, she clearly looked worried as Arthur said, "I said controlled, no harm will come to you here. You have my word." Lucy was not yet sure how much that was worth. "Upon you giving me the details of the triggers of its appearance and behaviour I am confident we summon it and even make it docile."

"How?" Lucy asked.

Arthur pointed at the two industrial lamps, "I will power them off, we will be plunged into darkness."

Lucy shook her head, "we are not doing that."

"Baxter, the whole reason you are scared of the dark is because of that ghost. I have reason to believe your fear is what makes it appear. We need it to appear before we can go any further."

"Can we at least leave a torch on? Please?" Lucy implored shakily.

Arthur's expression softened a little, "I did not say this would be easy. I am here, you will not be alone for this one."

Lucy whimpered a little but nodded her agreement. "What happens when the lights go off?" Lucy said it with utter dread.

"Then we wait for it to appear."

"And when it does?"

Arthur pursed his lips looking notably awkward. "Then we observe it."

"Huh?!" Lucy leapt off her stool, "we observe it?! I thought we were going to kill it!"

Arthur's expression hardened against Lucy's outburst, "first of all, it's a ghost according to you. That means it is already dead."

"Then banish it or whatever the correct verb is," Lucy retorted.

Arthur became notably shiftier, he mumbled something prompting Lucy to glare at him further before he finally raised his voice. He let out a deep breath and said, "I don't know how to yet."

Lucy stood gobsmacked. "You don't know how to get rid of it?" she yelled incredulously, her voice echoed all over the empty warehouse for added effect. All traces of her fear almost gone.

Arthur kept his gaze with her not even flinching with her raised voice. "The key word is, yet, Baxter. I never once promised you I would get rid of it straight away. That is virtually impossible, each case is different I need to observe the creature before I decide what action to take."

"You said and I quote we would go 'ghost busting'!" Lucy jabbed a finger at Arthur in accusation. It was his turn to avert his eyes.

"That was me trying to say something cool," he admitted.

"You lying son of a bitch! Why did I even bother going through with this?! Fuck this! I am not being treated for a fool, I am leaving!" Lucy got up and tried to move away but Arthur shouted after her.

"Baxter, you are letting your emotions get the better of you! I can still get rid of it but it requires observing it first!" Lucy was ignoring him heading towards her bag.

"Lucy!" Lucy paused at the use of her first name as Arthur bellowed it in the warehouse. It echoed around the open space as she turned to glare at him. "I normally don't do this, but…" he trailed off looking uncertain. Lucy just carried on glaring. He gave out a large sigh, "fine, you said it looked like your mother correct?" Lucy still glaring at him nodded slightly. "Then, I already have an idea, but it is not a sure-fire way to remove it. If you want it gone tonight this is your best chance."

"Why did you not go through with this method before?" Lucy asked suspiciously.

"Because this method is sloppy. It leaves all the work pretty much up to you. I cannot really help you except cheer from the side-lines."

Lucy started walking slowly back to the stool. "What do I have to do?"

Arthur sighed again massaging his temple. "No patience," he muttered. "It's quite simple really you have to doubt what you see."

"Huh?"

"You have to disbelieve. You must believe in what you are seeing cannot be real. That it is just an illusion. That you were dreaming of it all along. You have to believe that it does not exist whole-heartedly there is no room for doubt. If any inkling of yourself still believes in this apparition this will not work."

Lucy mulled this over as she sat back on the stool. "Seems hard," she said finally.

"Exactly, so if we go with my way-"

"Will your way guarantee a way to get rid of it before the end of this night?" Lucy asked.

Arthur fixed Lucy with a long, hard stare. "There are no guarantees," he exasperated.

"Then we will do it my way," Lucy answered flatly.

Arthur looked set to argue but he backed down. He walked past her and towards the lights. "You are an impossible woman Lucy Baxter!" Arthur shouted from behind her. Lucy ignored him as she saw one lamp dim and its light vanish. She heard some footsteps as Arthur walked to the other lamp. "Oh, and another thing!" he shouted, "bingo can be played by all ages! It is not just for old people!" Lucy smirked. Even as the light started dimming she took in the comfort, that she finally was able to push one of his buttons.

But as the light disappeared from the room, Lucy's smirk vanished as quickly as the light, leaving only the dark to loom in.

*   *   *

A blanket of darkness drowned all of Lucy's senses. Her heartbeat started doing rollercoaster dives and her breathing started to become shallow and rapid. Lucy clutched her jeans like they were her lifelines as her eyes skirted the total black fruitlessly.

At any second it would come. Any second it would leap out and seize her. Could it come from behind? Lucy span her head around so fast her neck cricked but she did not care. Could it come from the left? The right? Up? Down? Where would it come from?!

Lucy felt like a sacrificial lamb on an altar waiting to be killed in order to become an offering to a malevolent being.

Forgetting all of their angry exchanges Lucy whimpered the only name she could "Arthur?"

"I'm here," he whispered softly.

Lucy felt a small rush of comfort. "Can you see it?"

There was a pause, "no, Baxter control your breathing. You won't do any good sucking up all that oxygen."

Lucy tried but she seemed unable to slow it down, her breathing was still increasing as objects started to form. She flinched as blurry images flew at her as her eyes tried to make sense of it all.

"Baxter I am going to touch your shoulder, relax, calm your breathing." Sure enough a hand rested gently on her shoulder. It stayed there making no other movements. "Calm your breathing Baxter, you need to focus. Don't you want this fear gone?"

Somehow those words soothed her. He was right, she needed to face this fear, not get consumed by it. Her breathing slowed and Lucy slowly was regaining control. The darkness terrified her but at least she was not alone in it. Her eyes adjusting, she could now see Arthur behind her his eyes scanning ahead.

"Can you see the other side of the warehouse?" he asked.

"No? Why?"

"Tell you later, let me know when you do."

Lucy wondered if he saw the thing, "is it her?"

"No."

And then there was silence. Nothing. Lucy and Arthur kept scanning the whole room for any sign of a monster leaping out. Nothing,

"Arthur?"

"Hm?"

"I can see the other side of the warehouse now."

He groaned at that. How long have they been here in the dark? Lucy who was still notably uncomfortable with the lack of light was not so scared now. They both waited, it almost became boring.

"Ah shit I was afraid of this," Arthur cursed. He moved away still in the dark towards the bags coming back with one in hand in moments. "Looks like we are going for plan B. Turn around on the stool and look at me."

After turning around Lucy asked, "what happens if it comes at me from behind?"

"Oh it most certainly will now. You can see the whole warehouse right?"

"I don't understand."

"Have you ever seen this ghost appear in front of you? Or where you were looking?" Lucy thought for a while.

"No I haven't."

"Case rested. Now, I think what has happened is the darkness trigger only works when you are alone in the dark. Since I am here, the plunging you into darkness plan A has failed."

Lucy eyed the bag trying to make it out in the dark. "Something about this plan B is fishy," she said.

With no warning, Arthur started giggling, "you impress me Baxter, what an excellent pun! Although…" his laughter trailed off and then he sighed in a defeated sort of way. Lucy saw him point a finger at her, "let this be burnt into your memory! That I had to lose my dinner over you!"

Lucy looked confused but he rummaged in the bag and withdrew a fish fillet still in a packet. Lucy almost scoffed, "are you having a snack now?!" she hissed.

"What? Raw fish? No thank you."

"Then why have you brought it?!" Lucy hissed again forgetting the darkness around her and the peril she could well be in.

"You remember when you told me about how you unleashed the ghost in the nightclub?"

"I didn't unleash it!" Lucy protested.

"Whatever, you know what your other phobia is?"

"I don't see how that's… wait… how out of date is that fish?"

"About a week, I reckon."

"Arthur no."

"This way is guaranteed to make me puke my lasagne. Its smell is almost enough."

"You're crazy!"

"Crazy yes, but a genius to boot."

"There has to be another way!"

"Sure there is!" Arthur said like she had won a prize. He moved the packaged fish towards her. Lucy repulsed leaned away from her stool. "The other way is you eat it. Truth be told I would prefer if you did."

"No fucking way."

"Exactly! And since I am not in the business of force feeding rotten fish to jumped up little shits. This is the only way."

"You are just doing this for joke aren't you! This is all fun and games to you!" Lucy accused.

Arthur's response was laced with sarcasm, "yes Baxter, nothing is more fun than consuming rotten, smelly fish which is raw. Did I ever tell you it's one of my guilty pleasures?"

"Then why?" Lucy pressed truly not understanding this man's eccentricities.

"You wanted to get rid of it for good, right? Believe me, this is not being done for fun."

Arthur started removing the packaging from the fish fillets and suddenly Lucy caught a pungent waft. She gagged as the smell threated to drown her. "Don't do it Arthur, do not do it!"

"Sorry Baxter, but we do have bigger fish to fry after this one." He chuckled to himself at the crudely chosen idiom, but with that Lucy winced as she heard soggy flesh part from bone. After a few seconds of hearing Arthur chew, she heard him starting to wretch. Soon enough like a fish flopping out of water there was sickening splat on the concrete floor.

Arthur started hurling. "Blaurrgh," was all he could manage as Lucy saw the vomit cascade out of his mouth and hit the floor in sickening plopping noises. It was wet, it was foul and again she felt the warm specs fly onto her legs.

Lucy froze up. Those warm flecks that hit her legs, it was just like then. That dark room. That bedroom. That convulsing body on the bed. The pleading eyes begging for help.

Lucy clutched her head, "NOO!" she shrieked. She won't bring it back. She won't!

Through Arthur's coughing and wheezing and Lucy's cries they heard footsteps. It was here.

One step, two step. It was bare feet. Slapping against cold concrete. It was slow, it was purposeful.

"Arthur?" Lucy practically wailed. All of a sudden Arthur was right beside her. His eyes widened in surprise at what he was seeing, as her back was still turned she could only hear the creeping footsteps. Arthur was pale, he dabbed at his face with a tissue clearly removing all evidence of his vomit.

"Wow that is one ugly ghost, although that is a nice choice of dress. A real juxtaposition," he remarked.

"What do we do?!" Lucy asked in fear.

"Okay, Baxter, on the count of three I will turn you around to face her. Remember what I said, you must not believe in her! You got that? She is not real. Keep repeating that in your head!"

"I don't know if I can!"

Now she could hear that retching. That sickening sound of bile stuck in the throat, Immovable, always there, always making that monster foam and spit,

"One."

Lucy was trembling not wanting to go through with this after all. Was she to face this thing again?!

"Two."

The bare feet were edging closer. The retching becoming the domineering sound in the entire warehouse. Its sounds bouncing off every surface.

"Three!"

Arthur whirled Lucy around to face her fear incarnate. It was close. Far too close. Eight more steps and it would have her.

Its face again was mostly covered by that black matted hair. It dangled in front of her like a curtain. This time it was wearing a one-piece dress which was white with faded images of flowers imprinted all over. In its right hand was that same kitchen knife. This time it was not bloodied, but stainless not a blemish on it. Its left arm was free but the bracelets covered the arm jangled like chains, tethering it to this earth.

Lucy's instincts kicked in as she averted her gaze.

"No! Baxter you must look at it! Give it eye contact tell it you do not believe in it!" Arthur yelled taking a step back but still within arm's reach, Lucy whimpered. "Baxter!" he shouted again.

Lucy finally found her courage and looked straight at the demon in front of her. Its grey sinewy skin repulsed her but she kept looking at it. *You are not real!* Lucy thought. *You are not real!*

Amazingly the creature stopped cocking its head to the side like it was a confused dog.

"Yes! Baxter keep at it!" Arthur encouraged.

Emboldened, Lucy tried harder. *You are fake! I do not believe in you! You do not exist!*

The creature gargled in response. Was Lucy hurting it? She kept going repeating the phrases in her head staring down her tormentor. It started gargling shrieks whipping its face to the ceiling.

This sudden movement forced her long curtain of hair to fly up to briefly reveal her face. That face. That nose, they were similar to Lucy's. "Mum?" she whispered.

The creature whipped back to face her. The hair returning to cover the face. It started shambling forward with much more vigour.

"Baxter! You are faltering, quick, regain your thoughts! Quick!"

Lucy tried to repeat the phrases in her head but then the creature was upon her. One hand clasped her throat which made her cry in pain. The force of the impact flung her off the stool and hard onto the concrete floor. "Arthur!!" she choked.

"Lucy listen to me! Repeat those phrases! You have to!"

"Arthur I am dying!" she choked again as the pressure on her throat got more severe. She cried in agony. "NOOO!" she wailed hitting the monster with her fist who now was on top of her. The knife still in its other arm.

"Ah fuck!" Arthur cursed. Leaping into action. He grabbed the stool, and swung it down onto Lucy's attacker. As he did, the creature retaliated slashing its knife across Arthur's forearm cutting the white shirt and finding the flesh beneath. Arthur yelled in pain as blood spurted from the wound he staggered back clutching at his arm. The stool had lost the force behind it and just clonked off the creature's head.

The clonk caused the hair the move apart and for the first-time Lucy made eye contact. Those eyes. The green ones of her mother's. Were unfocused. Glazed over. Dead.

"NOO!" Lucy cried for a final time using as much strength as she could muster to lift the being. Her grip on her throat was still vice like and Lucy felt her eyes start to bulge. Lucy had to. She had to. She grabbed her knife which in the struggle was hanging out of the pocket. Lucy felt it cut her flesh as she gripped the blade and pulled it free of her pocket. Spinning in around, Lucy plunged it hard and fast right into the side of the monster's neck. Lucy expected it to be incorporeal. For her blade to swoosh through it like smoke. But no, it connected and Lucy felt it lodge firmly in the ghost's flesh.

It howled in agony and loosened its grip. Lucy then used both of her legs to launch it off her. It flew off her and ungracefully landed onto its back two metres away. Lucy coughed and spluttered there was black dots in front of her eyes as she forced herself to her feet. Her spectral foe was doing the same, the knife still sticking in the inside of its neck. There was no blood oozing out.

Instantly a figure crossed in front of her. It was Arthur. "Go run Lucy! I'll distract it!" his arm was bleeding profusely and he had no weapon in hand.

"But…" she began.

"It is after you Lucy! Not me. Go!"

"But what can you do?!"

"Just fucking run Lucy!" he shouted as the creature came bearing down on them.

Lucy didn't need telling twice. She ran. She ran as far as she could. Out of the warehouse and into the cold night air. She could hear the howl of frustration come from the ghost as it lost sight of its prey.

She could hear Arthur yelling back at the creature, "look here fugly! She's gone and you have to get past me!"

It was a clear sky. The moonlight shone her way as she ran and ran, past more neighbouring warehouses. Her throat was dry and painful like she was swallowing gravel. The shouts from the warehouse became more distant. There was crashing sounds and more of those retching shrieks. Lucy felt her lungs burn as she scrambled across gravel not looking back.

Lucy's body screamed in agony. She went past the sixth warehouse. Keep going! The seventh warehouse, she stumbled, her hands grazing the gravel cutting skin, but kept momentum, if only for a few more metres. She could not keep going. She had to stop. Eight warehouses down she practically collapsed on all fours wheezing, spluttering and crying.

The noises from the warehouse from where she ran suddenly stopped. It became eerily quiet. All besides Lucy's pained breaths and sobs the whole world became quiet again. Lucy leaned against the warehouse doors massaging her neck as she felt numb around the whole area. This was the first time it had hurt her. It was just like back then. Lucy whimpered. She was at the end of her tether. She had failed. Whatever had happened it didn't work. She'd lost. Lucy cradled her knees and brought them into her chest. She buried her head between her legs wishing the world would just simply go away.

There were footsteps coming from where she just ran. Lucy raised her head listening intently. They hit the gravel in a pit pat fashion. No! Lucy had not recovered yet how has it found her so quickly? She could hear the wheezing, the footsteps which were definitely heading her way.

Lucy tried to get up but her body resisted her. Was this it? Killed by the ghost of her own dead mother?

She glanced at the shadow in the moonlight. It was just around the corner now. It carried a knife in its left hand. Lucy whimpered but had nothing she could do to stop it. It was over. She closed her eyes wanting it to be quick.

The footsteps halted, the wheezing continued. There was a thump on the gravel in front of her. Lucy opened her eyes and saw a knife lying in front of her. Her knife. Puzzled she looked up and saw Arthur. He was clutching his left forearm which was covered in blood. He had a deep gash on his cheek and he had torn up his waist coat to stem the bleeding on his arm. The rest of his white shirt was bloody and a cut was evident on his chest but shallower than his forearm. He was wheezing like a man who had not jogged in a long time.

He fixed her with a steely glare wheezing and bleeding, looking just as rough as she did. "That's why," he began wheezing with each breath, "we do it my way, you bloody stupid girl!"

CHAPTER 6

The situation was utterly awkward. Lucy through her pained gasps tried to ignore Arthur's presence. His eyes were daggers. They hurt when they looked at her. She still cradled her knees in some pseudo-foetal position feeling vulnerable. What made it worse is Arthur said nothing. He just glared, his fury palpable coughing and wheezing, leaning against the warehouse door. The silence continued as both tried to catch their breath through pained gasps. The air was cool, so soothing as Lucy felt hot and ill. The air was therapeutic, very needed as it attacked her blushed cheeks.

Drip, drip, the patter of liquid against the concrete slope made Lucy glance up. Arthur was bleeding badly. He held his arm gingerly as his other hand covered it sodden with his own blood.

"Stay here," he instructed noticing the blood flow was not ceasing. Lucy said nothing as she watched him walk away. He was heading back to the warehouse they both had just left. Fighting her demon neither of them could beat. Lucy felt very tired, it was weirdly comforting being in this position. She felt her eyelids droop as the world turned black.

"Stay awake!" someone barked. Lucy felt a rough kick on her side which made her jolt upright. It was Arthur again. Sometime must have passed since she had closed her eyes. He was back carrying the bags he left behind in the warehouse in his good arm. The other arm was still dripping. He looked pale.

"We should go to a hospital," Lucy said meekly.

"No hospitals," Arthur responded flatly. He moved to sit next to her unzipping one of the duffel bags. Lucy saw a green case, it was a first aid kit. His uninjured arm started rummaging in the box as he grunted. He picked up a packet of needles and a roll of thread.

Lucy realised he was planning to stitch his wound on his arm. "Can I help at all?" she asked quietly.

Arthur gave her a stern side glance, "have you ever stitched a gaping, bleeding wound before?" Lucy slightly shook her head. "Then don't. I'd rather do it myself."

"Are you going to do it without painkillers?" Lucy said becoming more alive.

Arthur looked ready to explode. "I don't need your unsolicited advice. Kindly stop talking. If you can't do that just piss off and hail us a taxi." Lucy was too exhausted and actually considerate of Arthur's predicament to bite back now. He winced in pain as he laid his arm across his leg. He had placed bandages there to soak up the blood which is still oozing out. He looked very pale and clammed, sweat bowling down his face. He held the needle in his teeth as he threaded it through with his good hand.

Lucy could not watch anymore standing up and giving him a wide birth. Lucy left Arthur alone by the warehouse to tend to his wounds.

Lucy realised again, that she had no phone. Will there be any taxis nearby? She decided to not ask Arthur for his phone as she could hear groans of intense pain coming near the warehouses.

Lucy decided to go back through the fence and head onto the road. She needed to be visible. The only gap was next to the warehouse where she had just fled but oddly Lucy did not feel afraid of it anymore. She still kept a wary eye on it as she slipped back through the gap and onto the pavement. She could no longer hear Arthur, probably for the best. What now? As she embraced the orange tinge of the lamppost lit street, Lucy was at a loss.

Get a taxi? To where? And why a taxi? And not an ambulance? How is she going to get either down here? Which direction should she run to? They were on the fringe of Aberstahl in a place where no sane person would venture around in at night. Well, besides herself and Arthur, neither of which Lucy realised could she label as perfectly sane.

Lucy reached up to cup her chin to think but instead felt intense pain. Gingerly tapping her fingers on the underside of her cheeks she realised the pain was consistent all around her neck. It must have been when she was being strangled. Still, where to? Suddenly something caught Lucy's attention, a phone booth!

She made a hurried jog towards it, its glass was filthy but see through. One window was smashed in and glass littered the pavement around it. Glancing at the glass as she pulled the door open Lucy noticed a purple bruise engulfing her neck. It looked very bad, Lucy had to ignore it for now.

She picked up the handset and raised it to her ear, she heard a static hum which confirmed to her it was still functional. Wait, did she know a taxi number? Lucy again had to think hard, none were coming to mind.

"Shit!" she muttered feeling already cramped in this booth. She had never used this before. She doubted anyone around her age would. Lucy identified a slot to put coins in. A sticker which was almost scratched off read '20p a minute'. Lucy rummaged in her pockets and got out her wallet. Only two 20ps that'll be enough. Something drew her attention in the booth another sticker which had seen better days. Part of it was ripped but she could make out half a number with the letters 'xi'.

That was it! Lucy could not believe her luck. It was half a number but Lucy suspected if she put in the area number first it should be fine. She started smashing the buttons on the phone and held the receiver close to her ear. She could hear the dialling noise meaning it had connected. Lucy sighed in relief, at least something was going alright.

"Beep, Beep."

"Hello?" Lucy spoke down the phone. But the double beep continued incessantly. "Is this a wrong number?" Lucy wondered out loud. She again spotted the coin slot, "oh right! Stupid!" Lucy muttered to herself slotting the 20p in. It made a satisfying clunking sound and the beeping stopped.

"Hello Atkinson Taxis," a man spoke down the phone in an overly jolly fashion.

"Hi, um hello?" Lucy was a bit taken aback by the friendly voice.

"Hello madam! How can I help you?"

"I er, would like to, um, order a taxi please?"

"Certainly ma'am! Where from and where to?"

"Umm warehouse 87?" Lucy instantly regretting saying that.

"Eeeeer where is this warehouse 87?" the phone receptionist sounded unsure.

"By Aberstahl Lake?"

"Oh there! What on earth were you doing down there? You lost?" Lucy thought this receptionist was perhaps a little too chatty.

"Fishing," Lucy answered, "we got carried away and missed our bus."

He must have bought that lie as he proceeded onto the next question, "how many ma'am?"

"Just two."

"And where are you two heading?"

Again, Lucy paused at this. The phone started making a beeping sound so Lucy put in another 20 pence. Where should they go? Lucy wanted to go home but she had no idea where Arthur lived. She checked her watch, it was close to 10pm.

"Ma'am?" the receptionist pressed to see if she was still alive.

"Yes, hello I am still here. Can it be Aberstahl University campus please?" That'll have to do for now. She could get a late bus home and Arthur probably meant to go back to campus anyway.

"Right you are! The taxi will be ten minutes. Can we have a number to contact and name?"

"It's Lucy, Lucy Baxter and er, my phone is out of charge, so it won't help, don't worry though we are not going anywhere!" she assured.

"Very well ma'am thanks for calling."

Lucy put the receiver back on the hook. She had got it sorted, thank God. Deciding it was enough time to give Arthur a bit of space. Lucy walked back to where she had left him. On the way back Lucy picked up her bag still left in warehouse 87 and slung it back over her shoulders. She noticed the blood stains on the floor of the warehouse and the broken stool and a pool of vomit towards the back of room. Not wishing to stay any longer she placed the knife she had picked up from Arthur in her bag and left as quickly as she had arrived.

Approaching the place where she and Arthur had collapsed from their ordeal she saw Arthur squatting against the warehouse door. His eyes were closed and his face was tilted towards the sky, he looked like he was meditating. His breathing had calmed down, they were deep but placid breaths. His arm was resting gently to one side and Lucy could see a bandage around it. He had managed to stitch it back up which Lucy secretly thought was quite impressive.

"You all patched up?" she asked.

Not opening his eyes, he mused, "it is as you can see."

"Still, if you do not mind me saying, it is really impressive that you did it without painkillers." Lucy did not hide the obvious awe in her tone.

Arthur with his eyes still closed made an uncomfortable expression. "Yeah, well… No matter how many times I do it, it still hurts like a bitch."

"Then why no painkillers?"

Arthur's expression returned to a neutral tone, "It's the pain, I don't dull it, I like to remind myself I am alive, pain is what reminds us all that we are alive." Lucy felt like she had just received a lesson on a very sinister subject so she attempted to change it.

"Have you chilled out now?"

Arthur finally opened his eyes meeting his grey ones with her green, "for now," he said coolly. He grunted and then got to his feet gently testing his patched-up arm. Lucy could see him wincing. "You ordered a taxi?" he inquired.

"Yep, should be here in ten minutes."

"You told them to come here?" Arthur said shocked.

"Well where else would they go?" Lucy defended.

"You mug. It'll be suspicious to them! Two people covered in bruises and cuts out here in the dark where no one else is. What are they going to think?" he hissed.

Lucy folded her arms. "I told them we went fishing."

"Fishing?!" Arthur blurted loudly but then he paused making a childish grin, "oh that bloody irony." He smirked as he picked up his bags in his good arm. "It is not untrue I may have another fish in here." Arthur was slowly turning back to the excitable and humorous one she met in the warehouse.

"Don't tell me you have another fish in that bag?" Lucy groaned as Arthur started walking.

"Yep, in case the first one didn't do its job of displacing my dinner," he said.

Lucy walking next to him exasperated and put a hand to her forehead, "and I suppose that is our evidence of us going fishing? A fish which is in a packet with a use by date on it?"

Arthur gave her a reproachful glare, "we can blame it on the lake pollution," he said as if that'll explain it. "Besides you chose the excuse that we were fishing. It'll be up to you to convince them we really were. With your purple neck and my bandaged arm and one fish between us I'll be just as interested in the story as the taxi driver."

He made an evil grin which Lucy instantly resented. Why was it up to her to come up with the excuses? By now they had both made it onto the pavement by the road. Arthur had found it difficult to get through the gap in the fence with his mangled arm, Lucy decided to not help him as she waited for the taxi. By the time he had caught up Lucy could see some headlights coming down the road.

"Which company did you book with?" Arthur asked.

"They called themselves Atkinson's taxis?"

Arthur groaned, "great! They are nosy fucks, just so you know. I cannot stand their receptionist."

The cab pulled up to where the pair was standing. A window pulled down with a man's voice asking, "Lucy Baxter?"

"That's us!" Lucy responded keenly opening the back door. She paused and then swung it open for Arthur to go first. He moved in without saying thank you which made her scowl. She then went in closing the cab door behind her.

The cab interior was certainly a lot warmer than outside, it was only until she was inside did she realise how cold she was.

"To Aberstahl Uni, was it?" his voice was muffled by the glass panel which separated him from Arthur and Lucy yet there was a speaker for the back so they could hear him clearly. The taxi driver was a middle-aged man who wore a flap-cap. He was beefy and with a grizzled beard.

Lucy noticed he kept glancing at the pair of them through his rear-view mirror, she could tell he was already very suspicious. "Yes, that's right! Any idea how much?" Lucy asked attempting a pleasant friendly tone.

"Whatever it is I'll just pay for it. Can we get going?" Arthur cut in rudely.

The taxi driver grunted and then began to pull away. Lucy attempted to get comfortable as the taxi drove off and back into civilised Aberstahl. Several minutes passed with no one saying anything. Arthur had made a point of staring out of his side window not making eye contact with anyone. Lucy kept fidgeting messing with her hands and knees putting her hands on different places.

It was the taxi driver who broke the silence, "so, what were you two up to back by them warehouses?"

Lucy was taken aback by the directness of the question. That all she managed was a, "huh?"

"Folks in the office told me you pair were fishing?" he continued as he made a left turn.

"Oh, yeah! No they are right! That is what we were doing!" Lucy said awkwardly still trying to keep her tone upbeat.

Arthur gave her a glance before returning to look out the window, his expression immediately pissed her off as he looked smug.

The taxi driver also looked unconvinced. "If you pair were fishing why on earth does he have an arm bandaged up? What happened to him?"

Lucy looked pleadingly at Arthur but he continued to stare out of a window. When no help came Lucy quickly formulated her excuse.

"A fishing hook! Yeah, a fishing hook! He got one caught in his arm you know how sharp those things are?"

The taxi driver looked shocked, "is it still in there? Shouldn't he be in a hospital?" Lucy also wondered the same thing.

"Oh no! It's not that bad! You see, he is a bit of a beginner and made matters worse by deciding to rip it out. He is a bit of a slow individual you see."

Arthur made an annoyed cough but did not turn around to look at her this time. The taxi driver while not fully convinced turned his attention to her. "What about you then? That is some bruise you got around your neck."

Lucy knew straight away this would be harder to explain. She suspected the taxi driver thought they had a fight or something much worse had gone on.

"It's embarrassing to admit it but that was because of a fish."

"A fish?" the driver took his eyes of his driving to glance in his rear-view mirror to look right at her. Arthur again peered over at her quizzically.

"Y-yeah, you know they are actually very strong animals. Us fishermen... uh fish-man and woman need to mercy kill them once out of the water. They are often hard to hold you see. My student here." She pointed to Arthur whose eyes narrowed in a deadly sort of way, "was too much of a pussy to do it so when he handed me the first fish he caught it smacked me right in the throat with its tail! Honestly the other students are going to have a laugh with this story!"

The taxi driver chuckled, "if you don't mind I may tell the kids that story as well."

"It is yours to tell, I admit it is pretty hilarious but it was not at the time." Lucy beamed smugly at Arthur who turned to look back out of the window.

Lucy hoped the drive would be over soon. There were obvious flaws in her stories, but she hoped the taxi driver would not notice them.

"What about you sonny?" the taxi driver addressed Arthur who gave the taxi man a sideways glance, "you're awfully quiet, did you not enjoy this evening with your teacher?"

Arthur's nostrils flared at the word teacher but he said nothing. Looking back outside he managed dryly, "I guess you could say I was hooked."

Lucy snorted with laughter turning her face from view, giggling into her palms.

The taxi driver eyed the pair curiously as he made a turn off a roundabout past a sign directing them to Aberstahl University.

Lucy thought they were in the clear. Sure, her excuses were a little dodgy but they were believable enough she felt. It was now only a few minutes' drive away as she recognised the street they were driving down.

"There is one thing I don't get though. If you pair were fishing, then where are your fishing rods?"

The atmosphere in the taxi got eerily quiet as Lucy bit her lower lip. It was their toughest question yet.

"That is because… That is because we store them at the warehouses, they are big things you know? It's easier just to store them right by the lake. My friend's dad lets me as he is the owner of one of the warehouses." Lucy hoped that explanation would suffice, she was quite impressed she managed to make it up so quickly.

"Hmm," the taxi driver sounded as they passed the sign saying Aberstahl University. They had reached the campus. "And here is me thinking you stored both rods up his arse!" The taxi driver nodded towards Arthur which made Arthur look livid and Lucy snigger.

The driver was laughing as well, as Arthur snarled like a dog, "I guess we can forget about your tip mate."

The taxi man came to a halt next to the student's union wiping tears from his eyes, "still worth it," He muttered. "That'll be £13 then please."

Lucy who had cheered up got out of the cab still laughing as Arthur got out of his side. Lucy walked up the grass verge onto the SU's courtyard. She waited there as she saw Arthur handing over the money. Lucy realised something was up as there was angry whispering amongst the pair. Lucy could not make out what was being said but the taxi driver was jabbing a finger aggressively at Arthur.

Did Arthur come up with some witty retort? Lucy wondered, but in response Lucy saw Arthur withdraw something from his pocket. It was attached by a chain and was golden. It was a pocket watch. It did not surprise Lucy that Arthur had possession of a pocket watch judging by his dress sense but what good would it do having that now?

Arthur jangled it back and forth in front of the taxi man. Was he offering to sell this for the taxi ride? Lucy always recognised he was weird but not daft. Yet, somehow the argument had died down. The arguing stopped completely and Arthur came around the back of the taxi as it and the driver went down the road and out of sight.

"Why are you up there?" he asked looking up at her.

"I'm going to the bus stop so I can go home. What was that all about?" Lucy pointed to the watch which Arthur quickly pocketed.

"Never you mind," Arthur snapped, "I can't have you going home yet. I need you to come to my office. Now."

"Why? Can't this wait till tomorrow?"

"No," Arthur dismissed, "you still want my help? You come to my office right this second we have more to discuss."

*   *   *

Lucy was admittedly surprised that Arthur had all the keys to get to his office. He had the front entrance key, as well as the key for several hallway entrances. He explained he did not have all the keys but members of staff are sometimes expected to stay till very late doing work. Arthur also explained he was one of those who did it the most.

Lucy followed him down the silent corridors as he whistled swinging the keys around his outstretched finger. No one else was in the building even the cleaners have gone home. Lucy expected to see a security guard but maybe they were patrolling other areas of the campus.

They had reached Arthur's office door. He proficiently found the relevant key and opened the door. Going in first Arthur pushed the door wide enough so Lucy could follow in. It made a satisfying slamming sound that probably echoed around the dead building. Arthur flicked his lights on and moved to his desk. Lucy stood uncomfortably by the door unwilling to go into the room without knowing what came next. What was in store for her? They had failed this faux exorcism, and it seemed pretty clear Arthur was blaming her. His arm was a bandaged mess Lucy could only see this going one way. One thing was for certain on her part, she would not let him walk over her, not again.

Without turning to her Arthur spoke up, "let's put the elephant in the room to bed, shall we? We have both withheld information from each other." He then turned wincing with his bandaged arm keeping it close to his chest and using his good arm to lean on his desk. He fixed Lucy with a level stare. "I believe what went horribly wrong was a lack of trust, between you and I and that cannot be allowed to continue."

Lucy narrowed her eyes but said nothing still standing by the door.

"If we are to overcome your apparition we need to trust each other."

Lucy finally spoke up, "you seriously expected me to trust you? What? After the five hours I have been around you."

Arthur did not react but said, "I admit I did expect you to have more faith in me. I was wrong. Such is my folly to blindly assume you would. You have not told me everything, have you?"

Lucy could not continue to meet Arthur's cool gaze. He was right. She had still kept secrets from him. "Everyone has secrets they like to keep."

"Indeed, but I am not asking for you to tell me every embarrassing memory. I am asking you to tell me everything you know about your undead mother."

Lucy flinched at Arthur's wording. It was cruel and unemotional having little sensitivity. "Get fucked," is all she managed.

Arthur raised his eyebrows. He looked like a parent who for the first time had their child swear at them. His facial expression suddenly changed to that of exasperation. "Fine," he muttered, "I'll come clean first." He walked to his chest underneath the window sill withdrawing a key from his pocket. Lucy could not see what was in the chest but it did catch her interest. Without thinking she walked around craning her neck to try and get a better look. He opened it with ease squatting down to rummage inside. Unfortunately, he found what he wanted very quickly. Barely three seconds had passed and he was shutting the chest and locking it.

He turned to face Lucy with an old brown book in his hand. It had no illustrations and looked aged beyond recognition. He brandished it like it was a poster showing it to Lucy.

"A book? What's this book got to do with anything?"

Arthur's eyes sparkled with excitement he looked more invigorated than at any other point this evening. "This book was written by a man who history has never recognised. A Russian by the name of Vladimir Pehov he lived some 300 years ago, I would give you the book but it is written in Russian."

Lucy did not recognise the name but was also getting impatient, "so?" she responded folding her arms.

"Let me finish," Arthur scolded before continuing, "the book title if roughly translated to English is called 'The Mind as an Architect'." He put the book down on the desk. "You Lucy, are what he calls an architect."

"I do not follow at all," Lucy said shaking her head in confusion, "I'm a what?"

"An architect," Arthur said cuttingly. He then began to start pacing from his desk to the other side of the room and back again. "Your condition, your affliction, is not a mental illness or a psychological trauma, although it does not stop you from having them in tandem. You carry an extremely rare ability. The ability to create with your mind." Arthur proclaimed this last part like it was the end of a play, the audience however was not applauding.

Lucy folded her arms, "are you having me on?"

"What? No! Listen damn it. I appreciate this is a hard thing to believe." He then paused half-smiling, "oh that irony," he muttered before continuing, "you are an architect. You have the ability to create things with your imagination and belief alone."

Lucy still looked sceptical.

Arthur looked more annoyed, "think back," he said with a touch of irritation. "Remember when I said your condition can be seen as a gift or a curse?" Lucy nodded. "Do you remember my first lecture from Wentworth? How I asked people to question what belief truly is or could be?" Lucy paused but nodded again. "My homework," he continued emboldened by Lucy's nodding, "was to find and identify possible architects like you Lucy. Architects work off belief unlike the normal person, an architect's belief in something can manifest outside of their mind and turn into a physical or corporeal form. You can create just by thinking and believing in something's existence." Arthur paused before adding dramatically, "be careful what you believe in Lucy because it will more than likely become true."

Lucy looked dumbfounded this information was going way over her head. Architects? Belief? What is this nonsense? "Let's say I humour you on this," Lucy said cautiously, "if I can create with my mind, why have I not noticed this myself? And why has no one else?"

Arthur nodded thoughtfully. "Excellent questions Lucy." Lucy could now see the professor coming out of him. "The first question is always depending on the person. As I have mentioned you are not unique in the sense there are other architects no matter how rare. Your case I suspect is following the trend I see with most people in this country. You are taught from an early age to rationalise everything you sense with the knowledge you have been given i.e. science. You have probably gone through your whole life dismissing the peculiar, the abnormal, as fantasy. Science is taught like it has an answer to everything, it knows it does not but that is not the point. The power of an architect is no different. You have it since birth. Any evidence that you have it without knowledge of it creates your wilful dismissal of it. Tell me Lucy with your haunting how many times did you consider yourself mentally ill before realising it was something much more unexplainable?"

Lucy faltered. How many times did she kid herself? How many times did she convince herself she was just dreaming? Just hallucinating. Lucy looked nervously at Arthur as realisation came sinking in. "Are you saying that ghost thing is of my own creation? That I made that thing?"

Arthur nodded hesitantly, "that is what I am saying yes. It is what people in my line of work would call a 'figment'."

A tear fell down Lucy's cheek without warning. She did not even feel it, only saw it drop onto the carpet. "So, that thing I faced is a thing I made?! That it looks like my mum because it came from me?! That thing is not actually my mum. It's just a fake of her?" she looked at Arthur lost as more tears came flooding. She was in shock.

Arthur looked panicked, "you are overthinking it! Ah shit, hang on!" he opened the draw in his desk getting a pack of tissues he dashed over handing them over to her. "Um I have more to say. Do you want to sit?"

"Get away from me!!" she screeched knocking the tissues out of Arthur's hand. Lucy tried to collect herself putting her forearm to her face. Composing herself through mid-sobs she glared at Arthur who looked stony as he gave her space. "This is just a sick joke by you isn't it? You tell me I am a freak, I'm different! You tell me that the thing that is out to hurt me is just a fucking figment of my imagination. You are telling me that ghost is not my mum. That she is not haunting me?! That I am so pathetic that I am just haunting myself?!"

Arthur softened his tone, "it won't make it any easier by thinking I am a bastard. I told you I am coming clean." Lucy continued sobbing looking away from Arthur. "You wonder now? Why I did not say what you had? For one you would have never believed me. Two, you would hurt from the truth. Three, it is a kept secret from as high as the government that architects exist."

Lucy whirled around grabbing Arthur's shirt in a fistful and aggressively pulling him towards her. He did not react and allowed himself to be dragged. Lucy put her distraught face dangerously close to Arthur's collected one. "You are one massive twat you know that?! Tell me! That this is a joke. That this ent the truth! That you are some crackpot delusional prick who delights in telling his student's they are freaks who conjure up monsters to scare themselves in the dark. Tell me!" she shook with rage barely maintaining a grip on him.

Lucy was pretty certain she had just spat on Arthur through her anger. He did not look angry he still looked calm, like he was attempting to tame a beast. "You are forgetting something Lucy. If this was all a joke of mine why did Caitlin point you to me? Do you seriously think a head of department would be in on a joke like this?"

Those words rung true with Lucy. She let go of Arthur and stepped away from him. Caitlin, her personal tutor. Did she know about this as well? Did she believe in this architect nonsense as well? Why would she?

Arthur brushed down his shirt and took one of the tissues off the floor to wipe his face clean of spittle. He gave her a withering look. "You are an architect

Lucy. Face it. I do not know what you were expecting but that thing that attacked both of us is not the animated soul of your deceased mum. You just rationalised it to be. It's a figment, nothing more nothing less, in a sense there is no such thing as ghosts the undead souls of the once living. Just creatures created in the mind's tool box, they are real. They can be dangerous, they will act how you would expect them, as the architect expects. You are not a freak. An architect is just a human with high creativity that is so concentrated their own beliefs can become a very close reality. You are no different than any other person to walk this earth. You are not a freak, you are either cursed or gifted depending on which you prefer."

Lucy collapsed onto her knees. She felt so very tired. Her sobbing had stopped and now she rested, defeated. "Can I be cured?" she asked feebly.

Arthur squatted down close to her to be at her level. "No, it is not a disease. It is a part of you. However, you can learn to cope with and supress it. As for that there is no better teacher to help you deal with it. That is why Caitlin sent you to me."

Lucy raised her head to meet his. Her cheeks red and her eyes were bloodshot. "Are you an architect as well?" she asked quietly.

Arthur gave a cautious smile, it was the first-time Lucy saw him make that face. "Bingo!" he said energetically, "to top it off I study architects and figments as part of my research into them. I have dealt with many people like you coming to terms with what they have." He held out his good hand to offer Lucy a way up.

Lucy eyed the hand hesitantly but stomaching her pride grabbed hold of it and allowed herself to be pulled up. When she got back to her feet Lucy instantly felt pangs of regret for her outburst but she repressed herself from giving a vocal apology to Arthur. Lucy blew out a breath to calm herself and asked Arthur, "right. How do we stop it?"

Arthur nodded, looking relieved, "got there in the end, huh?" he pointed to the two chairs where they had sat to the interview earlier in the day. They both sat in the same chairs where they sat at this morning.

Lucy leaned back and let the seat almost swallow her up. She was not sure whether to still believe Arthur but she could not deny it made connecting all the mystery surrounding her ghost a lot easier. Why it would target her, why others could see it, why it was unnatural in appearance. It was a representation, of something she feared made manifest out of her own mind. Her mind still was racing with other questions.

"I think I'll start by saying this whole evenings attempt was not fruitless. Despite you attempting to rush things and me, to my fault, letting you do so, I managed to identify the entity for what it was. If I can identify the class of the figment and proceed from there I can go about figuring how to remove it."

"There are classes of figments?"

Arthur waved his hand dismissively, "for the sake of my own analysis, yes. Although obviously, they probably will not identify in the same way."

"Wait, these things are sentient?"

"If an architect believes them to be, then they will be," Arthur answered, "but let's not get side-tracked I could spend all night explaining what I know. We neither have the time or leisure to do so."

Lucy merely nodded in response keeping her questions under lock and key for now. She would have a better opportunity further down the line. The two continued as if her emotional outburst never happened.

"Your class of figment from my observations seems to be a shadow class." Arthur paused to see if Lucy had any questions, when she did not present any he continued, "the shadow class is perhaps one of the less serious figments. They are called shadows because they often stalk their architect, forever attached like a shadow." Lucy shuddered at his description it did explain the ghost's fascination with her.

"So, does it come out of my shadow or something like that?" Lucy asked hesitantly.

Arthur chuckled lightly, "nothing that fancy. Remember when I asked you to stare away from the end of the warehouse?" Lucy nodded, "well that is because a figment always appears outside the Architect's peripheral senses. Call it a quirk of the human mind. If you see the thing materialise in front of you the mind subconsciously doubts its existence. Doubt of its existence by the architect makes it impossible for the figment to appear. Hence why they somehow always appear wherever you are not looking. This also applies to their disappearance, shadow figments typically appear for very short amounts of time."

"Sounds like a cheap horror film rule," Lucy remarked.

Arthur chuckled again, "quite so. Note that this only the architect's senses, if normal people are around they will see it materialise out of nowhere. There is another reason why I have named them shadows."

"And that is?"

"They are just like your own shadow, a part of you. I like to see the shadow in a poetic sense that it is the parts of us we want rid of, but whenever the sun shines out it reminds us that it is still there."

Lucy shifted uncomfortably in the chair. "Why not just become a poet?" she tried to joke masking the connection she felt with Arthur's words.

Arthur snorted derisively, "it's mainly because I have ambition." Arthur shifted forward in his chair lowering his voice but still caring for Lucy to hear him, "your apparition Lucy, the monster that haunts your every step, is your shadow. You've discarded and repressed feelings that you have yet to come to terms with. Its characteristics, its behaviour and appearance are all clues as to what you have been trying to run from. Yet it pursues you in the form of your deceased mother that is why I know it is yours."

Lucy felt the intensity of his grey eyed gaze drilling hard into her skull. "Are you saying that this thing? Is just my intense emotions? Do we need reminding I'm quite an emotional person?"

"Let's stop using the humour to hide from uncomfortable truths, shall we? It's all for your own good. You need to come to terms with what you face. It's an entity of your own trauma. It torments you every time you feel fear, it reminds you it still exists deep down in your memory. Remember the triggers? This figment only appears when you are vulnerable when your mind gets triggered about your past. Something to do with the dark and the sound of sick?"

Lucy shuddered and felt a rush of panic. "Stop! Do you want it to come back?!" She saw a brief flashback of that dark bedroom all those years ago.

Arthur looked unperturbed. "Eventually yes, as to remove it we need to confront it. But rest assured it won't appear here. This is a safe space. There is light and you are not alone. Besides even shadows struggle to appear many times a day."

Lucy still not entirely convinced glanced over her shoulder then back to a bandaged Arthur. "Are all architects this fragile?" she managed sheepishly.

"No. Then again not all architects are the same. They have not lived your life nor feel like you do. We may have the same label or ability but it doesn't mean we experience the world in the same way. Anyone would be fragile in your circumstances this is not easy information to process."

"Then tell me this, this thing is part of me right?" Arthur nodded, "it is an embodiment of my negative emotions, memories, etc. right?" Arthur nodded again. "Then why does it look like… look like… my uh… mum?"

Arthur leaned back staring to the ceiling at this puzzling question. "I can partly answer that," he began still looking to the ceiling. "Every figment has its creator architect that is undisputable, figments would not exist if architects did not. There is a relationship of creator and created even if the creator does not realise it. The human mind cannot make something entirely new, if they have I would give them a million pounds. All stories, art pieces and other things made by humans have had inspiration from other sources be it their own memories or someone else's work. I call this the inspiration rule. A figment has been crafted subconsciously in the architect's brain. It takes the imagery the architect encounters to make a physical being." Seeing Lucy's confused face Arthur changed his direction, "I'll give you an example. Say for one moment I believe in Frankenstein's monster. I see an image of it off the internet and that is my inspiration. I like you, get overly stressed with a plethora of things keeping things bottled up inside. My mind needs release. So say it happens in my dreams I see this monster and get scared." Lucy retreated down the chair as she saw too many parallels from this example. "Very soon I start seeing a version of Frankenstein's monster chasing me all around the place. The end."

"So, the bottom line is?" Lucy impatiently quizzed.

"That a figment will probably take on a form that the architect has already seen. Usually relevant to why it exists but not always. Understand that your memory is not perfect it won't look exactly like your mum but your mind takes inspiration from how you remember her."

Lucy thought about this for some time. She had always wondered why it was not a perfect image of her mother, with the ghoulish green skin and that long matted hair. She had always thought it was her decaying body, but her mother had been cremated…

"You must realise you must also answer now."

Lucy looked up as Arthur looked serious, "answer what?"

"I have come clean now it is your turn."

"I… uh don't know what to say." It was right that Lucy was unsure of what Arthur wanted off her now. Her mind was doing constant gymnastics coming to terms with his revelation.

"Let's start with how your mother died. She did not die in a car accident, did she?"

Lucy froze and felt her heart plummet as the all-knowing Arthur had sussed where she had lied. "How did you…"

"Figure it out? Please. It's your mother's appearance, I believe it has something to do with her death. You know how she died, and so does your subconscious. Does a knife wielding woman with a frilly dress look like a car accident victim?"

Lucy averted her gaze and said nothing.

"Lucy, we need to be open with each other here. Now is not the time to be ruled by your emotions."

"Why?"

"What?"

"Why must I tell you this? All it does is bring misery to me and you find out something I have never told to a soul at this university."

Arthur started to look irritated as Lucy dug her heels in. "Did you not just hear me this past half an hour? Did you not realise that you were nearly killed by that thing?!" he pointed to her heavily bruised neck. He groaned in frustration, "look! The method I gave you tonight was the easy ticket. It does not have a high success rate but it was by far the easiest. To get rid of your shadow you need to either disbelieve what you see or come to terms with it and welcome your shadow back into yourself. Since option one has blown out of the fucking window we are going with option two."

"I still don't see how my mother's death has anything to do with that!" Lucy replied hotly.

"Because you idiot girl! It is clear as fucking day your negative emotions, your troubled past, your trauma made manifest is all about your mother's death!!" Arthur dropped that bomb harder than the United States did on Hiroshima. Lucy almost reeled in shock. Steadying herself on the arm rests. Arthur calmed his tone slightly before saying, "that's why you are being punished by yourself, by your own figment. A memory of long ago that you have desperately willed yourself to forget and remove is coming back with a vengeance." Lucy sat there wide-eyed as Arthur could as well have just slapped her. "To heal this mental wound, I cannot do it without knowing the story. I need to be let in Lucy. Otherwise I am plucking guesses out of thin air as I am utterly bewildered as to why your mother's death still haunts you to this day. I will not be able to help you unless you tell me what happened. Tell me what happened and we can plan to remove this thing for good." Arthur held out his hand as if to the seal the deal with a handshake.

Lucy looked at the hand in front of her blankly. If she shook it, she'd have to tell him everything. If she shook it he would know everything. This man, this Arthur who she had met only within this week was asking off her what she saw as the impossible. This could no longer continue. Instead of shaking it she moved to get up instead. "Thank you for your time Arthur Squire, but I do not think I can continue this charade any longer." Her voice was cool and professional she sounded like a business woman terminating a contract.

Arthur's face was aghast, "you're leaving?" he said it like he could not comprehend it.

"Yes, it's getting late and I need some rest the last bus is going to be gone in ten minutes."

"Wait! You cannot just leave! We haven't finished yet." Arthur stood up now in shock himself.

"I can and I am."

Lucy moved to pick up her ruck sack and other belongings as she moved to the door.

"Is the death of your mother so precious to you that you won't share it with the only person able to help you!?" Arthur thundered as Lucy opened the door.

She glanced over at Arthur, at his bulging eyes his angry, emotional outburst of being denied. She secretly liked him being on the receiving end. "I'm sorry Arthur but I simply do not *believe* in you to help me. My past is my past and you have no right to know it." With that she started walking down the corridor not troubling to give a backwards glance. She could hear Arthur's incredulous splutters of indignation he clearly had not predicted this outcome.

"You are making a terrible mistake! Lucy! You'll be back!" she could hear Arthur yelling, "they all come back in the end! You are no different!"

His cries fell distant as Lucy kept walking. All she did was just keep walking away. That's what she had done all her life, just walk away.

CHAPTER 7

"How about this one Lucy?"

"Mm?"

"C'mon look!"

Lucy reluctantly tore her gaze from the rows of phone cases in front of her to look at another one of Libby's suggestions. She held in her hands like a model on television a phone case in plastic packaging. It was one dotted with a dog-like pattern having protruding ears and what Lucy assumed was a nose for where the home button on a phone would be. Lucy could not hold back pulling a face.

"Libby," Lucy began wondering how to best word it, "when I asked you to come out with me into town to help me search for a phone case, I meant a case which would actually protect my phone not have a case which makes me look like I am in year eight."

Libby looked dejected flinging the case back into the rows roughly, her eyes then suddenly lit up, "are you a cat person instead?"

"Libby!" Lucy protested, "I said I wanted a protective case."

"Fine, but you know they are largely pointless if you never drop your phone. They never fit in your hand bag or pocket and they look ugly."

Lucy gave Libby a knowing look, "all true, except I actually dropped my phone and while we wait on a £200 repair job I would like to find a £5 case. You get me?"

Libby smirked and then rolled her eyes moving to where Lucy was looking at the stall. It was Friday afternoon, it would so have it that both Libby and Lucy finish their week by 12 on a Friday. Libby despite being a chemistry student had Friday afternoons completely off.

It was three days since Lucy stormed off from Arthur. She had not seen him since. She was dreading the lecture she had with him next week fully expecting him to single her out, despite their less than amicable separation Lucy has had no episodes since then. The bruise around her neck had faded and it required some imaginative stories to explain its presence to anyone who asked. Lucy knew she was by no means 'cured' and it was difficult not to rationalise her circumstances in any other way than what Arthur told her. He did still infuriate her and she had no plans on going back.

"Everything ok their ma'am?"

Lucy woke up from her thoughts to see a young boy nervously hanging around the market stall. He had blanked Lucy and asked Libby who was closer. Lucy gave him a scanning glance estimating he was no older than 15. He was taller than Libby by a head height and even slightly taller than Lucy. Around his waist was a money bag giving the clear signal he was the stall attendant.

Libby gave a small glance to Lucy with a knowing smirk before turning to face him. Lucy was helpless to watch as Libby played the game.

"Hiii there! My names Libby and I am looking for a phone case for my friend over there." She gestured to Lucy who just stood arms crossed, the lad quickly glanced at her but obviously was more interested in Libby so focused his attention back on her.

He nodded enthusiastically, "yes, I could not help but overhear..." he began as Lucy tried her best to not roll her eyes. "I have to agree with you though Libby? Is it? A case is to help make your phone more appealing. You would not need a heavy-duty case if you were not prone to dropping them." He gave a sideways glance to Lucy which made her almost scoff in indignation. Was she being judged by a 15-year-old they have just met?! She was the customer here! Lucy thundered in her mind.

Lucy decided to butt in, "I am the one paying here, not Libby. I would like a protective case please." Lucy was surprised at herself at how neutral she kept her tone despite her internal annoyance.

Libby exasperated unintentionally a puff of air which misted onto the boy's face, he looked notably flustered at that. "I er, well." Composing himself further he said, "why not a compromise? A phone case which does both!"

"Ooh good idea!" Libby encouraged although Lucy was pretty sure she already had thought of it and was intentionally annoying Lucy earlier.

The boy goes around the stall picking a selection of cases and bringing them back. "How are these?" he asks handing them to Libby. Lucy cleared her throat and raised an eye brow, "oh! And here are some you can look at!" He said quickly passing the rest of them in his hands to her.

"These are £10 not 5," Lucy interjected.

"Ah well, the price of a compromise I guess?" the lad responded.

"What about this one Lu?" Libby interrupted handing a thick set case. It looked promising. Lucy looked it over, it was rubber and purple a colour she could live with. On the back was a huge red heart.

"Screams not me," Lucy answered throwing it back to Libby who dropped it by accident.

"Can we not throw them around please? My Da won't be happy," the store attendant chastised.

"You no longer need to wonder why she broke her phone huh?" Libby sniggered to the young boy. Lucy decided not to say anything, saying a ghost of her dead mum made her drop it was not the best comeback.

They spent the next five minutes looking through the cases till Lucy found one she kind of liked. "Typical," Libby muttered looking over Lucy's case, "can you not just get cute stuff Lu?" Lucy glanced at her dark skull in a hood case.

"It's Grey-skull! Off He-Man the cartoon!" Lucy said in such a way to defend her choice.

Libby huffed clearly not knowing the show. She placed her case labelled, 'Party girl' in the attendant's hand. He looked at the two fairly contrasting cases in bemusement.

"That'll be £20 please," he said opening his satchel.

Lucy moved her hand to her jeans pocket to fetch her wallet when Libby spoke up, "can you make it £15?" she pleaded giving the attendant one of her cute smiles.

The attendant blushed at that considering her offer. "Libby!" Lucy hissed.

Libby giggled, "I was only teasing, here is my ten." She handed him her share of the money which Lucy quickly followed suit.

The attendant still flushed red gave the cases away in a flustered manner. Was this the first time he had been flirted with? Lucy wondered as he merely nodded shyly.

"Well then we better get going my phone is probably fixed now." Lucy began to walk away. Libby nodded and waved goodbye to the attendant.

Managing the courage, the attendant shouted after them which attracted stares. "My name is Ryan! I hope you come again Libby!"

Libby looked back and said, "see you around Ryan!"

As soon as they rounded the corner back onto Aberstahl town square Libby sighed in relief. "I needed that," she said like she just had her addiction sated.

"Have a boy fawn over you?" Lucy asked nonchalantly.

"I can tell when you are judging me Lu," Libby replied glancing at Lucy who was a few inches taller than her. "If you didn't grow a conscience we could have saved ourselves £2.50 each."

"He's a 15-year-old boy Lib, he is bound to think with his penis."

Libby snorted, "that is not exclusive to the 15 year olds at least they are innocent."

"Who's rejected you now?" Lucy asked bluntly.

"Wha! Lu! If that was called jumping to conclusions you have just reached China!"

"Was it at the club?" Lucy pestered.

Libby grumbled, "he said he already had a girlfriend. You don't get it Lu, being single sucks. I know you would never be able to cope."

Lucy brushed that jibe aside as they got out of the square and past the bank. "So, you thought you would go to 15 year olds? I'm not sure the law would allow that."

Libby gave Lucy a reproachful glance. "Stop playing dumb, I had no plans of courting him."

"Just boost your confidence?"

"Precisely."

"You need to get a dating app. They are great for that kind of thing."

"Here we go again."

"I don't need it. You clearly do," Lucy argued more for just teasing her friend.

Lucy remembered the last time she had this conversation with Libby. It surprised Lucy how quickly Libby admitted her vulnerabilities to her. Lucy has not opened up to Libby at all or anyone at uni for that matter. Libby though, who Lucy found herself getting on with the most in the flat quickly bonded with her. Within a week they had deep chats about Libby's life, Lucy didn't mind that. Before uni Lucy never had anyone besides Andrea confide to her, she found it comforting to know other people had problems, albeit the problems being 'normal' in comparison.

Libby wanted a uni debut. A fresh start. She was shy at school but now wanted to experience uni as an outgoing person. Lucy thought she sometimes tried too hard to do this. Although it has had some success and she definitely got attention from the opposite sex yet either it was nerves or she was just picky; Libby didn't always reciprocate.

"I know Andrea would kill you if you got a dating app, now that I think about it," Libby said bringing Lucy back from her thoughts. They had reached the phone shop.

"Let's do this and head back yeah?" Lucy said as she opened the door. As the glass parted past her Lucy saw a ghastly green figure leering at her. It had long hair and a knife in hand.

Panicking Lucy shot around to look back on the high street. Libby was there looking at her curiously. "What's up Lu? You see a ghost?" Libby started giggling off Lucy's behaviour as Lucy's eyes darted around and beads of sweat started trickling.

Giving off a long sigh Lucy convinced herself she saw nothing. Beckoning Libby to come in she thought to herself that she really wished people would stop saying the word ghost around her.

*   *   *

"We're back!" Libby announced as Lucy opened the door back to their student accommodation. Only one person responded. Libby beelined to the kitchen to investigate who was there as Lucy closed the door behind her.

Following Libby in Lucy saw Adam on his laptop surfing the internet. "Hey guys!" he said in an upbeat way munching on a crumpet and still in his dressing gown.

"You are still not dressed?" Libby asked incredulously.

"Nope, no reason to get dressed," he said through chewed crumpet.

"Well get dressed anyway. You stink," Libby scolded moving to the kettle. "Tea anyone?"

Lucy raised her hand to that and sat at the mucky table. Thank god, we have in house cleaners Lucy thought to herself.

"Geez you're demanding. Boys don't like that in girls you know?" Characteristic of Adam, he knew which buttons to press.

Libby looked prepared to smack him with the kettle in her hand but before she could utter a retort the kitchen door opened.

"I'm so sorry Adam but I still can't figure out the hot water on your shower the nozzle won't turn... huh?" Standing in the doorway was Mike. The guy from the flat below. He was only covered with a towel.

Adam let out a strangled groan as both Lucy and Libby grinned. "Oh um, tell you what Adam, I'll just have a cold shower. Never mind!" he raced out of the room.

Adam's usually calm collected face was flushed with embarrassment.

"OOH guess who scored first in the flat!" Libby yelled in laughter, "wait till I tell Brent this!"

Adam whirled his head around, his face as red as his hair, "please do not tell Brent this!" he almost begged, "he is the worst person to tell, he'll never let it go!"

"Tell me something Adam," Lucy said keen to join in on the ridicule. Adam glanced begrudgingly at her. "Please tell me your nozzle was a lot more responsive to him than your shower is"

Libby snorted with laughter doubling over.

Adam pulled an irritated face, "oh haha! Good one!"

Libby who barely contained her giggles said, "I think so too!"

"I am so blessed with such lovely flat mates," Adam proclaimed getting up to go to the sink to wash his plate.

"Is Mike joining the family?" Libby inquired.

"Shut up!" Adam grumbled hiding his face from view. "Stupid moron should have just texted me," he muttered.

Lucy took her tea off Libby as she calmed down her laughter. It was these moments that made university so enjoyable she thought to herself.

Knock knock. Someone was at the door.

"That Mike again?" Libby wondered sitting down opposite Lucy.

"I swear to god if it is him!" Adam thundered.

"No, you guys, it came from the flat door. I'll find out who it is." Lucy left her tea at the table to find out who was knocking. As she passed Adam's door she could hear yelps of surprise which could only be Mike, Lucy tried her best not to chuckle.

Reaching the door, the knocking came again. Lucy yelled, "I'm here just a second!"

Lucy turned the lock and opened the door. Standing before her was a man comfortably taller than her, taller than the 15-year-old they met today, very tall. He was an imposing presence, dressed in a long woollen coat parted at the chest where a shirt and tie was visible. He was old, the handlebar moustache was superbly grey and the eye brows were just as bushy. He wore a grey fedora which gave him an eccentric appearance. His eyes were beady too small for his imposing look. The man glanced down at Lucy who was at a loss for words.

He rummaged in his coat pocket holding out a badge. A police badge. "I am DCI Percival Truman, I wonder if you could spare a moment of your time to answer a couple of my questions?"

Lucy gulped. Brent's words of warning drifting back into memory. "In what regard are these questions um inspector?" Lucy almost squeaked.

"The incident on Monday at the popular club known as Frenzy no doubt you've heard?"

Lucy merely nodded. Oh shit! Did he know? Did he know about her involvement? Impossible! But… wait… do the police know about figments? About architects? Surely not? But… How was she to know? Arthur never mentioned this. Shit Lucy! Stop thinking about him, he is not relevant anymore.

"Er what do you want to know?" Lucy squeaked again, feeling like the world's smallest human.

The inspector relaxed in posture, "calm down, no one here is in trouble, not unless it was you who caused the incident?!" the man boomed eyeing her intensely.

"Ummm I er well… that is to say… I."

The inspector chuckled, "not to fret, I was merely joking."

"Oh!" was all Lucy could manage as her heart stopped doing gymnastics around her chest. He didn't seem to know, but Lucy was not stupid to lower her guard.

"I'll be brief, I know you students have a lot to do with your studies. Were you present at Frenzy Monday night?"

Lucy paused. Should she lie? No! That be awful! Wait why should she lie? She hasn't done anything wrong! Right?! Why is there a guilty feeling then? "Yes, I was, our flat was." Lucy answered less squeakily than before.

"Then can I have your name?"

"Lucy, Lucy Baxter."

Truman raised his eyebrows at that. Oh no! He definitely recognised the name. Lucy realised she had still had hold of the door handle gripping it intensely.

"Do you know the flat below?"

"Why do you ask?"

"They mentioned you by name in their answers."

"Oh, they did? That's weird."

Truman got out his note pad and pen and started scribbling down details. "Why would you say that is weird?"

Lucy licked her rapidly drying lips. "I er, I am just surprised I left an impression on any of them. I only met them once."

"According to a Miss Alexa Castellon, you were right by the assailant when they assaulted three members of the door staff, inflicting deep lacerations with a kitchen knife." Lucy could only gulp as the inspector continued, "in Miss

Castellon's words it looked like it was following you. Could you care to comment on that?"

Oh fuck, shit, fucking shitty fuck Lucy cursed to oblivion, thankfully only in her head. Lucy tried to keep her face devoid of any response. That girl had really put her in it. The pause must have been suspicious as DCI Truman repeated, "Miss Baxter, care to comment?"

"Oh um ah yes. I would dispute the fact it was following me. I didn't see the person for very long I heard screams and shouts and judged it best to scram. I grabbed Brent and ran away."

"Brent? Brent Cox?" Truman asked.

"Yes, he lives in this flat with me, if you want I can go and get him?" Lucy completely didn't question how he knew that name as well.

"No need," Truman answered flicking through his notepad, "some officers collected Brent's testimony a while ago, it would be pointless for him to repeat himself." Damn! Lucy thought to herself. "Hm, his testimony seems to match yours, except he mentions that it followed the pair of you. Do you disagree with him as well?"

This has to be the hardest thing at university to date, Lucy thought, being cross-examined by a DCI! "I do, and I have told him that," Lucy said with feigned confidence.

"Then what could you tell me that has you so convinced this person was not after you?" Lucy hesitated. She needed to be smart here. One slip up and she'll be put under further scrutiny. Was it worth lying to this DCI? Then again, would he understand? "Miss Baxter, do you have reason to believe anyone would wish to cause you severe harm?"

"What! No!" Lucy didn't need to lie on that one.

"Have you received any threats over the past two weeks?"

"None, honestly officer, I have only been at university for three weeks, I would have hoped in that time no one would want to kill me that soon."

"Miss Baxter, I must advise against lying to me. The police are here to help if needs be." Truman's eyes were too intense but Lucy had to meet them.

"I am telling the truth officer." By God I had better not regret this Lucy thought to herself. "If someone wanted to harm me personally, why would they target me in a night club? Wouldn't they target me with less people in the way? She or he just went to the same exit as me and Brent by coincidence. That's all it was." Lucy felt like she had struck bingo with that remark.

"That point has merit," Truman conceded, "but that is on the assumption we are dealing with a rational individual. In my line of work, I rarely am." Truman adjusted his hat looking disappointed. "I am therefore correct in assuming you have no idea as to the nature or identity of the assailant of Monday night?"

"None," Lucy lied hoping it'll never come to being hooked onto a lie detector.

"Lucy! You have been at the door for a while! Everything alright?" Libby opened the kitchen door and walked up the corridor. "Oh! Um friend of yours?" Libby asked awkwardly taken aback by the imposing inspector.

Truman glanced at Libby and then softened, "it's clear I am taking too much of your time. Thank you for your time Miss Baxter. Please note, I may require a further session down at the station if anything else indicating you crops up. Understood?"

Lucy nodded meekly.

"Very well, have a pleasant day." Truman tipped his hat and prepared to walk off. As he did he reached into his coat and withdrew a golden medallion of some kind. Only till he placed his hand on the button on top did it flick open revealing it to be a pocket watch on a chain. Lucy stared at it, it was vaguely familiar, where has she seen something like that recently?

Curiosity killed the cat. "Umm that watch?" Lucy called after Truman who glanced up at her. "Where did you get that watch?" Truman quickly put it back in his coat eyeing her suspiciously. Lucy hurriedly tried to find an excuse, "I er think it looks quite cool, do you know where I can get one?" Lucy lied.

Truman sized her up, his character changed. Something definitely was off. "Do you dream Lucy Baxter?"

Lucy froze at the question. Arthur had asked that. Why was he asking that? Taken off guard Lucy blurted, "well yeah, doesn't everyone?" It was a lie. Another damn lie.

Truman huffed smiling to himself, "apologies for asking a daft question. Do not know what came over me. Have a pleasant day."

With that, Truman walked upstairs no doubt to interview the next flat in the building. Lucy was left stunned as she wondered to herself. What would his reaction have been if she had told the truth?

*   *   *

"The police visited me today."

"What?! No way! Let me guess it's about Monday, isn't it?"

"Yep, a DCI as well, they are treating this very seriously."

"No wonder! Nothing like this happens in Aberstahl then all of a sudden a terrorist with a knife!"

Lucy paused before responding. It had been awhile since she had texted Andrea and she was going in full drama mode.

Considering her response, she typed back, "Andrea do you think the police know what truly is going on?"

A few minutes pause then a paragraph came back, "that DCI guy you said he was asking all the flats, right? If the police have to widen their search doesn't that mean they have no idea? I mean think about it, an investigation is narrowing possibilities, if he only came to you then yeah I would say expect a follow up buuuuuuuuut…" the message ended there as Lucy waited for the follow up paragraph. "They must be clueless. We both know what happened but who is going to believe us? They ain't the ghost busters, they are the police. I wouldn't worry Lu we have dealt with it before we can deal with it again."

Lucy grimaced at that. She had not, perhaps wisely, mentioned Arthur and what happened with him to Andrea yet. She would eventually but felt it would only anger Andrea. "You know I find it hard to cope with this thing without you," Lucy typed back.

"I know, but I have to sort out my family issues first. After that is sorted I promise I'll be back."

"When are you coming back?" Lucy pressed, she felt lonely without her. Andrea was her crux, her source of positivity it had now been over a week since she had to dash home.

"You're missing university. It's great here. It be even better if you were here," Lucy typed that in but before sending it on her phone deleted it. She huffed as the reply didn't seem to be coming anytime soon. Groaning, Lucy turned her attention back to the book she was meant to be reading.

It was now 5pm and the library was notably quiet. Lucy got onto campus early with the intention of doing netball practice at 8pm. She had missed a few training slots but was conscious of her wish to be on the team. It may be out of the question now but team allocation is still two weeks away.

Lucy heard her phone vibrate loudly against the wooden desk. Her neighbour looked up from his own book to give her an annoyed glance. Lucy was meant to be in the silent area of the library. Mouthing an apology to him Lucy glanced at her repaired phone the message was curt and to the point. "Soon."

Lucy groaned in frustration and decided to get up from her desk. She had only been here half an hour and felt she earned a break. Leaving her book and bag where she was Lucy took her phone and walked in the direction of the coffee bar. Lucy was hoping they still had one of those double-glazed donuts left.

After walking through the door dividing the quiet section from the rest of the library noise trickled back to Lucy's ears. She decided to cut through to the lifts down by walking through some book isles, on her way she spotted someone familiar.

Wentworth. Sure enough it was the old and wizened lecturer that was before Arthur. He was peering at a few books looking confused. Wentworth must be around 70 but he had a mass of bushy white hair and glasses so magnified that made him look like a goldfish. He was slightly hunched muttering to himself. Lucy decided to say hi.

"Hello there Mr Wentworth."

Wentworth glanced at who'd spoken with a look of great surprise, "can I help you?" he asked. Lucy had confirmed it was him but he didn't seem to recognise her.

"I just wanted to say hi and hope that you are feeling better!" Lucy said trying to feel upbeat. "Arthur said you were unwell he said you had a stroke!" Lucy watched his reaction with rapt attention.

Wentworth looked displeased at what she said. "Arthur said that did he? That arrogant burke. It was a simple cold. A man my age cannot be expected to tolerate a cold in this weather!" he complained putting books back on the shelf.

"Ok good I thought he was lying," Lucy answered. "I'll leave you to it then Mr Wentworth enjoy the weekend!" as Lucy turned to leave Wentworth called out to her.

"Wait a moment! You are a first year, right?" Lucy turned back to face him nodding. "I haven't been able to get hold of Arthur since I have been back on campus, I was wondering if you could spare a moment of your time. You see, he hasn't told me what you covered in this week's lecture I was wondering if you could give me a summary?"

Lucy was very surprised at this request. She could believe Arthur at being uncooperative but not that Wentworth would rely on a first year to tell the material. "Um, I was about to get a coffee…" Lucy responded, it was a weak excuse but her curiosity partly wanted to see how Wentworth would react to what she had to tell him.

"I'll buy the coffee!" he chirped, "I could do with resting my poor legs, I promise it'll be half an hour, tops!" Wentworth began shuffling towards the lifts as he expected Lucy to follow him. Lucy stood there for a moment baffled by the invitation. You get a free coffee out of it! Maybe you could get the doughnut paid for as well. Lucy smirked to herself, you are such a gold digger she thought.

Remarkably Lucy got the doughnut paid for with no hassle Wentworth didn't even question the fact she put it on the tray. After settling the payment, the pair of them sat down at an empty table. The café was quiet as it often was on a late Friday.

"So, what happened on Monday's lecture?" Wentworth asked sipping his fruit tea.

Lucy began explaining in earnest all she could remember from Monday's experience. Arthur's focus on the word belief, the home work he set, the confrontation with Tom Stockton and the fact they went well into the next lecturer's hour. Wentworth remained devoid of reaction but Lucy could somehow tell he was not enjoying what he was hearing.

When Lucy finished Wentworth made a disappointed sigh, "and I have to a department with him," he muttered looking out at the rapidly darkening outside.

Lucy saw an opportunity, "why does the department keep him around? He clearly is more trouble than he is worth."

Wentworth went to look back at Lucy. "It is not professional to comment on a fellow member of staff's job tenure," he said, "although," he added quickly, "I have no idea."

"Harkin keeps him around right?"

Wentworth's eyes narrowed as he continued sipping his tea. "If you think she can keep him on a leash you are very much mistaken. No one controls Arthur Squire. He has the worst superiority complex I have come across in academia and that is saying something! He is young yet acts like he has been around since time began! If I was still a psychiatrist I would find him fascinating to study but no instead I have to work with him!" Wentworth had this bottled up for a good amount of time Lucy realised. Arthur must have done something to him to make him so mad. Lucy can easily imagine it.

Lucy however noticed something else in what Wentworth said "Sorry erm Mr Wentworth?" Wentworth glanced up at her from over his tea "You mentioned you were a psychiatrist? I was wondering if you could help me?" Lucy saw an opportunity. If her... condition was able to be explained by Wentworth she won't need to be sucked in by Arthur's fantastical nonsense. She had to be careful however, Wentworth could consider her to be virtually insane and take her to seek professional help. That is something Lucy didn't want, she knew she was sane although insane people would think the same thing...

"Ah yes, back in the glory days!" Wentworth chuckled he had spirited up perhaps realising gossiping about a member of staff to a student was treacherous waters to sail in. "I guess you could monopolise on that free advice since I asked a favour off you."

"Yes well," how to word it? Lucy wondered, "I think I have a problem like um mentally."

"You don't have a voice inside your head demanding you kill people? Because I get that as well," Wentworth joked Lucy just smiled lightly in response, yep, this is going to be hard to explain.

"I see things," Lucy blurted catching the attention of Wentworth who stopped chuckling. He put down his tea and looked at her in surprise. "Like illusions, things which I know are not real yet I see them." Lucy decided now would be a very good time to finish off her doughnut.

As she hurriedly stuffed her face in embarrassment for how silly that sounded Wentworth asked, "how do you know they are not real?"

Now that is a question Lucy did not anticipate he took her seriously this time. "Because I know they shouldn't be." Another lack lustre response.

"I must say it is very brave to announce you are seeing things to a man you have barely met. You must be desperate." Lucy went red-faced not able to look at him in the eye. He peered in at her through his magnified glasses. "You remind me of a patient years ago."

"I remind you of a patient?"

"Yes, perhaps one of my most memorable ones as I was unable to help her."

Lucy felt a pang of disappointment, "why couldn't you help her? Was it money?"

"Oh no nothing like that, I was private for sure but she had plenty of funds for our sessions. No, the sad thing is therapy never worked. It was utterly bizarre she was responding to treatment but it would be only temporary. She kept returning complaining the monster that comes from under her bed is still there. I thought it was childhood trauma manifested into a recognisable common child fear. But all investigations pointed to a loving household no tragedy, no negligent parents nothing of magnitude which a 38-year-old woman would still suffer from now." Wentworth was reciting the story lost in his memory lane as Lucy listened carefully. "After probably 20 plus sessions I was beginning to doubt my own methods, my own skill set but…"

"But?" Lucy asked leaning in herself.

"The final time I saw her she said she was cured!"

"Cured? You finally did it?"

"Oh no! I wish I had she made it very clear it wasn't me," Wentworth chuckled, "she came back to gloat at me for not listening to her. I remember she kept saying the thing was corporeal, that it could attack her physically when I doubted that assessment multiple times. She had bruises on her wrists where the monster supposedly would have grabbed her. I thought this was a multi-personality disorder as she had no recollection of doing to herself. Unfortunately, she had gone to see a third-party an identity she refused to disclose. They have performed what she called hypnosis on her, highly unethical if you ask me."

Lucy paused drinking in all that information. Was this patient an architect like her? Did she have to deal with a figment as well? Whatever it did prove, Wentworth had no idea of the concepts. "You don't believe in hypnosis?" Lucy asked tiptoeing around her real question.

"It's not a question of belief. The human mind can be manipulated that is without question. Hypnosis is just one of those methods, it's ethically wrong, you leave the patient so vulnerable to coercion it sets off all sorts of alarm bells. That being said I tried to see if I could be hypnotised after that."

"You did?! Why?"

"It infuriated me. The fact a patient so complex have been supposedly solved by a party trick. I went to see for myself if such a thing could happen to me."

"And?"

"Nothing. Waste of time. I was left convinced of my own methods and wanted to put the whole episode behind me. I knew I was not going to see her again, she had left town not long after being cured. I spent £150 just to have a golden pocket watch dangled in front of my face for half an hour. A con if I ever saw one."

A golden pocket watch? Lucy fearfully started to realise she was uncovering a much larger mystery. DCI Truman had one, she saw it earlier today! Was that coincidence? Who else did she see have one? She recognised it somewhere… Wait a second, the taxi driver and Arthur!

"This might sound a bit out of the blue but does Arthur believe in hypnosis?"

Wentworth marvelled at that question, "that is entirely out of the blue! Why? Did he mention it?"

"Yeah in the lecture," Lucy lied.

"Oh dear. Well I would have thought a man so pertinently cynical would focus on science rather than con-artists." I guess that answered Lucy's question, Wentworth doesn't know. Wentworth examined his wrist watch, "goodness gracious is that the time! I better hurry back before I miss my tea!" Wentworth finished his tea with haste hobbling to his feet. "It was nice catching up with you Lucy but I would go to a non-retired psychiatrist for help, get a referral from a GP."

"Before you go Mr Wentworth, can I ask you one more thing?" Lucy asked standing up herself. The room had got darker as looming rain clouds started trickling over the night sky. They must have spent a while talking. "How come I reminded you of that patient?"

Wentworth continued to fumble with his coat buttons as he replied, "because both of you said with such conviction that you knew what you saw wasn't real. Baffled me then, baffles me now. Have a pleasant evening Lucy." Wentworth nodded his head and shuffled away towards the exit of the library.

Lucy was left there standing watching him walk off. Was she getting closer to some truth? What was she missing? Lucy wracked her brain as she unconsciously sat down. Hypnosis? Why did she feel drawn to that subject, why? Ugh, another day, more questions.

Lucy got out of her chair her mind racing with the information. Come to think of it. Did Lucy ever introduce herself? He mentioned her name before she left and she was pretty certain she never said her name once. That must be it. Lucy glanced over at Wentworth as he finally reached the exit, there is a good teacher who remembers his student's names unlike someone else she knew. A good memory that.

*   *   *

"Alright that's enough girls! We've gotta vacate the hall in 5 minutes good work out everyone!" the coach blew her whistle ending the netball session. It was 5 to 10 and Lucy sat on the floor exhausted.

She really needed to make sure she comes to these sessions, they really help her de-stress.

"Lucy! The captain wants a sec! You got one?" one of the girls called out to her.

Lucy got to her feet as the others started moving to the changing rooms, chatting and joking. Lucy walked past them all to where the captain and vice-captain were talking. They both looked up from their sheet as Lucy approached.

"Nice moves today Lucy! You took one of our best players to town!" the vice-captain Trish praised.

"It's a wonder with those moves why she hasn't come to training more," the captain, Freya, agreed coolly.

Lucy knew from the resting bitch face of Freya that she was not all too pleased. She was a third year and got captaincy from Trisha last year. Trisha was a fourth year and by far more easy going decided to take a lesser role because of her studies. The two were an odd match Trish smiling in her headscarf to the pale Freya staring daggers into Lucy. "Erm sorry?" Lucy said not all too apologetically.

"If you wanna make the team as we are all sure you do, you can't just slack off our sessions!" Freya scolded.

"I didn't know I was paying nine grand to throw balls. Am I at the right uni?" Lucy asked sarcastically not enjoying Freya's tone, "look," Lucy added before Freya could get bitchier, "I said I am sorry and I do want to join the team. I just had other more pressing matters to deal with ok?"

Freya snorted, "could have let us know through a message."

"My phone broke."

"How very convenient."

"Alright that's enough guys!" Trish said clapping her hands to draw their attention.

"Freya she couldn't have helped it if her phone broke. Happens all the time with me!" Freya rolled her eyes but said nothing. "Lucy." Trish now rounded on her, "if you want to make the team you going to have to make every session from now on. We both really want you but it's not fair on others who want the place that turn up to every session. You get me?"

Lucy nodded to the far more diplomatically attuned Trish. Although Freya had yet to close the matter. "To make up for the missed sessions you can put the equipment away. Me and Trish have to go through the rest of the team selections tonight."

Trish gave Freya an exasperated look but Lucy spoke up before Trish could, "fine, I'll do it."

Freya gave a knowing smirk. "Thank you," she said without really meaning it.

"I hope I have given you ample time to choose correctly Trish," Lucy said deliberately leaving out Freya. Freya scowled as Lucy moved away to pack up the nets and balls.

As she robotically put the equipment away Lucy could hear the pitter patter of rain on the gyms ceiling. Lucy droned on for the next 15 minutes proving to the other girls she was capable despite being alone with Freya and Trish long gone.

Soon enough, after all the equipment was put away Lucy entered an empty changing room. She had yet to make friends at the club but she was pretty sure she had already made an enemy. No one was going to wait on her. Sighing, Lucy showered and changed in silence occasionally checking her phone for updates from Andrea.

It was 11pm by the time Lucy left the block and embraced the rain. It was cold and icy typical of the October month. Lucy cursed herself for not wearing a hooded jacket. She felt the shower she took moments before was now pointless as she sprinted towards the bus stop.

10 minutes of a brisk jog and Lucy saw a bus whirl away before she could reach the stop in time. "Shit!" she cursed realising the arsehole driver was not going to stop for her. When was the next bus? Lucy checked her phone for the time. She'll have to wait 20 minutes in the rain. Fuck!

Lucy sprinted to the bus shelter as no one was there. Everyone must have got on the last bus. How typical. She should have never had placated Freya should had told her to stick it Lucy thought.

As Lucy reached the relative confines of the bus stop Lucy heard footsteps behind her. They were slow, too slow for someone who would seek shelter in the rain. Each step was slow and purposeful. They were gradual and lumbering. Accompanying the footsteps was a gurgling. A sickening gurgle Lucy knew all too well.

CHAPTER 8

The world felt slow. Rain drops were almost floating down to the ground, Lucy experienced her body instinctively tense up.

Pat. Pat. Pat.

The foot falls were heavy as it sounded like a child jumping in puddles for fun. Lucy clenched her fists staving off the fear being pumped around her circulatory system.

Pat. Pat. Pat.

She carefully placed her bag on the dry floor of the bus stop. Lucy resisted from turning to confront her foe. She kept her eyes forward at the bus timetable not really reading the information.

Pat, "not another step closer!" Lucy yelled keeping her focus forward ignoring what was slowly approaching her. At first Lucy thought it was a miracle, there was a definite pause between the shuffling steps of the living corpse. Pat. Lucy winced, it disregarded her wishes and took another step. Lucy unconsciously ground her teeth as anger started to replace that familiar fear she had caged for so long.

"Did you not hear me?!" Lucy shrieked doing a 180 turn to stare down her tormentor.

The creature was soaking wet. The clothes now a raincoat and torn leggings that were blackened wet. Its hood was not up as rain trickled down the mangled, matted hair shielding its face from view. A few more steps and the sickly grey corpse would pass the bus stop threshold.

"Leave!!!" Lucy screamed. She took a step forward as she shrieked in fury. This was the last time. She would have no more. It dared to come out now, when she had finally recovered somewhat it comes again?! Lucy had no idea if anyone could hear her, but what was certain is there was no one around. No cars, no buses, no people.

It again froze at Lucy's cries cocking its head to the side like a confused dog. As soon as Lucy had stopped shouting it took another step.

"Haven't you had enough?! I came to uni, to try again. To free myself of you!" Lucy jabbed a finger at the monster it was close enough to seize her outstretched arm but it didn't, it remained placid, watching her. "Fuck off! I hate you with every fibre of my being!! I goddamn wish you would stay rotting in your grave!!"

Lucy, feeling emboldened, took a step of her own towards the creature. For the first ever time. She felt cornered, a trapped animal, her flight or fight response was kicking in. The creature did not flinch its arms remained limp, that accursed knife held loosely in its right arm. It took another step as Lucy started catching her breath from all her hysteric screams.

"I'm warning you. You get any closer and I'll kill you again. You hear?" Lucy growled softly her voice husked from the strain she put it under moments before.

This time her deceased mother made a new reaction. It raised its free hand to reach out towards her. Lucy started feeling intense fear as the hand opened and closed like a claw moving deftly to her face.

"No, stop," she whimpered, losing her courage. It was getting closer.

"No, no! Not again. I didn't do anything wrong mum! I swear." She felt like she was nine again.

It was mere inches from her hair. "NOO!" Lucy finding her courage shoved her dead mother away with her hands. It was aggressive, desperate but to Lucy's surprise, effective. The entity stumbled off balance with supreme clumsiness moving back several paces. Lucy was shocked. The creature looked vulnerable, weakened as it attempted to regain its balance.

Seeing weakness, Lucy went on the offensive. She let out a war cry and charged her foe. Rain started lashing her with icy coolness but the heat of Lucy's fury made her ignore it. She closed the distance to her mother raising a balled fist.

Smack! Her fist made a satisfying crack against the creature's jaw. It stumbled again like it was in pain. Smack! Lucy followed up with another punch into its bony chest. It let out a dry cry as Lucy could smell the death on its breath.

"Fuck you!!!" Lucy charged at it with all her might slamming into it with her shoulder. The force of the collision took the creature completely off its feet. It was flung on the concrete floor with a bone breaking crunch. The impact made the knife it loosely held clatter away into the darkness. Without thinking for the consequences Lucy mounted her mother before it could recover.

"Go back and die again!" Smack! Lucy started to pummel the defenceless ghost aiming repeatedly for its face.

"I do not want you. I enjoyed watching you die!!!" Smack!

"You deserve all of this! For what you did to me! You're a monster!!" Smack! Smack!

"I hate you!!!!" Smack! Smack! Smack!

Lucy paused her merciless beating. The rain poured onto her drenched body as she attempted to gather breath. She felt hot liquid on her face. It was not just rain, but tears. She was crying. Lucy raised one arm in an attempt to wipe them away. Lucy's mother stayed inert on the floor. It raised a hand slowly to its face as if to shield itself from more blows.

This move irrationally angered Lucy. "Oi! Why don't you fight back?!" she asked angrily. "Nothing stopped you before. You were all too ready to beat me, when I was unable to fight back. What about now?! What's so different?! Huh?!! Answer me!"

Smack! Lucy followed her demands by smacking her mother across the face again. "Fight back!" she demanded. Smack!

Smack! Smack! Smack!

Lucy's final blow was so vicious it whisked the long hair out of the way. Lucy's mother's face was left bare for Lucy to see. Lucy for the first time saw her mother's eyes. They were alive. Those bright green eyes Lucy shared with her mother and they were looking right at her. They looked sad the only emotive thing on an otherwise decaying face.

"M-m-mum?" Lucy asked instinctively.

The figure made no response to her question as it continued to allow rain splash all over it, the eyes did not blink. A drop of water formed at the corner of an eye. It started to trickle down a cheek before soon becoming diluted by the heavy rainfall. Her mother was crying,

"Why are you crying?" Lucy asked nervously, confused, muddled, unsure.

Her mother now had more tears streak down her cheeks as she bravely stared at her daughter crying over her. Lucy didn't get any answers.

Anger started to boil over her again, threatening to take control. "You don't get to cry! You are in the wrong! Not me! I get to cry! NOT YOU!!" Lucy unconsciously raised a fist past her shoulder preparing for another blow. "Say something!" she demanded again.

"I'm sorry."

Lucy froze all tears, all emotions. Did she just speak? Lucy did not see those lips move, but that was her voice. It was unmistakable. Lucy felt tears flood down her cheeks faster than the rain pouring around them.

"You're sorry?" Lucy asked through barely contained sobs. "Sorry is not good enough!!!" she clasped both hands together bringing them both down in full force of her fury.

"Are you quite done beating yourself up?" a hand came out of nowhere to clasp one of Lucy's wrists. It was rough and firm preventing her from exacting her vengeful blow.

Lucy shocked into reality flicked her soaked face to the source of the arm. It was a man dressed in a long brown overcoat holding in his free hand an umbrella which he brought Lucy under to shield her from the rain. Lucy recognised his face.

"Arthur," she whispered in confusion. Her face hardened, "let go," she ordered with a hint of threat in her voice.

"Not until you stop laying a hand on your shadow. You will stop this immediately you are hurting yourself."

Lucy gave a deranged laugh, "I need no twat of a professor to tell me what to do or what is best for me. Let go, or I'll fucking hurt you as well."

Arthur remained calm watching her placidly, Lucy attempted to wrestle with his grip but it was surprisingly strong. "Let go," Lucy demanded getting frustrated.

"No."

"I did not ask you to get involved. I told you I did not need your help! So, piss off!"

"You clearly do."

"I'm sick and tired of people deciding that for me! Stop looking at me like that! That pity! I hate it! I hate it! I hate it!" Lucy lost all composure and broke down into further sobs. They turned into wails as Arthur moved the umbrella to be entirely over her.

He bent his knees so he would look at Lucy at her level. "You're hurting Lucy. Hitting your shadow is almost literally hitting yourself, no matter how much frustration it exerts." Lucy said nothing as she used her ungripped hand to hide her sobbing face. "I'm going to let you go now." He gently released his grip as Lucy snapped it away and turned away to cover her face. Arthur did not place a hand on her but knelt there, waiting patiently. "Let's get you away from the rain," Arthur suggested lightly.

Lucy shook her head fervently, "she is still here," she managed.

"She's gone."

Lucy removed her hands to see all that there was beneath her was concrete floor. "Did you, did you see…"

"I saw a lot of it yes. I saw her. She is not an illusion."

Lucy started shivering as the hot emotions burnt out. "We need to get you warmed up. We need to get you inside."

"B-but the bus?" Lucy asked feebly as she felt a gentle hand pull up her numb body.

"I'll pay for a full taxi fare if you miss the last one. You can't go home like this."

Lucy submitted to Arthur allowing him to gently guide her away from the scene. "M-m-my bag," Lucy jittered. Arthur nodded and gave Lucy the umbrella dashing over to collect her bag still left in the empty bus stop. When he came back to guide her gently back towards a building entrance Lucy choked, "n-n-n-not your office."

Arthur let out a light chuckle, "got it. Probably too many painful memories," he mused. "There's a common room nearby which I know has an electric heater. We'll go there."

*   *   *

Lucy didn't ask how Arthur had a key to the English Literature common room. Lucy didn't ask how Arthur had come across her or why he decided to intervene. Lucy just felt numb, like she had just come out of a warzone. Any stimulus consequent was ignored, paltry to what she had just experienced.

Arthur flicked the light on in the sizeable common room rushing her inside. It was a large common room lined with plenty of bookcases suggesting what students would use this common room for. It was still not warm nor did it particularly feel cosy for her. Arthur guided her lightly to one of the sparse soft chairs guiding her to sit down. Lucy was amenable and accepted every direction from him without complaint. She must be in shock. She felt like a cushion was wrapped around her head, she felt drunk, ill.

Arthur took off his coat and placed it over her like a blanket. Lucy was internally surprised at this streak of compassion he was showing but externally she made no sign of acknowledgement. Humming to himself Arthur moved to the kitchen area at the end of the room rummaging in the cupboards. He flicked the kettle on as he got out two mugs and a bag of coffee. While he got them prepared, Arthur moved behind Lucy, grunting slightly he returned with an electric heater, plugging it in and switching it on. It'll be some time before it properly heats the room.

Some time had passed and Arthur returned with two steaming mugs of coffee. He sat not opposite her, but beside her in a chair next to her. Their chairs both faced a steaming up window which was dark but it was clear it was raining. Arthur took a sip out of his mug and handed one to Lucy. Lucy groggily took hers. She saw her mug had writing on, 'Life appears to me too short to be spent in nursing animosity or registering wrongs.' She recognised this quote, was it from Jane Eyre? Lucy glanced at Arthur who watched the window with some fascination, he must have selected this one on purpose. Lucy saw on his mug writing as well, 'Heathcliff x Cathy'. English students' mugs for sure.

"I see you are coming to. The coffee helping?" Arthur took a sideways glance at Lucy.

"Yes, erm, thanks," Lucy replied bashfully.

"It seems you have exhausted that fire. That's a relief I'm not sure I could be arsed with another argument."

"Were you following me?" Lucy quizzed.

Arthur hastily blurted, "no…. Well, I suppose that might be an appropriate verb."

"So, you were following me." Lucy was neither angry or happy, she stated the fact. She felt drained, too drained to find Arthur's stalking concerning.

Arthur continued sipping from his coffee, "I only started today. In my arrogance I expected you to come crawling back to me. Several days of nothing did I realise I was a fool. Luck would have it that I came across you in the rain, you seemed in a hurry. I had no intention of pursuing you after you got the bus. But, instead your shadow comes along and you become a cornered animal. I tried my best not to intervene but when I saw you virtually screaming at yourself it was then I realised this isn't just the shadow causing problems."

"Screaming at myself?"

"Your shadow is part of you Lucy. For better or worse, no matter what you truly project onto it, it is your mind's reflection. Not your mother." Lucy's cheeks flushed and she looked away. "Regardless of that I was hoping to find an opening to, how to put it? Apologise."

Lucy snapped her head back around faster than a bullet. "You?!Apologise?!"

Arthur raised a passive hand, "I haven't set the best impression, have I?" he grimaced placing his drink on a table to his left. "I realise I can be insensitive, I often forget that not everyone functions like I do. It was not professional of me. You enlisted my help and I failed you. You didn't fail me. I should have known better than attempt to bully an answer out of you. For that I am truly sorry."

Lucy scanned his face, he seemed genuine. No witty remark follow up, no snarl or condescending looks. He looked ashamed at himself. "I uh, don't know what to say."

"A 'you're forgiven' would help," Arthur answered smiling to himself slightly.

Lucy let out a light laugh, "okay, apology accepted." She smiled to herself, he does have some redeemable traits she concluded.

An awkward silence emerged between them. This was a first. The room started picking up in temperature now. Lucy moved her hands fully out from under Arthur's coat as she left it resting on her lap. It was Lucy who decided to break the silence.

"I suppose you want to know what that was all about?"

Arthur finally moved his face to look directly at her, he looked surprised. "I thought you had no wish to tell me or cooperate anymore?" It was not a taunt or a jeer but a question.

"I did, but I er, realise that I should apologise for how ungrateful and obstinate I have been. You tried to help me and all I have been doing is make it nearly impossible for you to actually help. For that, I am really sorry as well."

Arthur let out a triumphant whistle, "I wasn't going to say anything but I am so happy you realised that!" he said with relief.

He faltered when he saw Lucy's stony face. "Arthur? You are kind of ruining the moment here."

Arthur reverted his face back to being serious, "sorry, please continue."

"You clearly want to help me and I do not know how much more of this I can take. As you saw I lost myself back there, I think it'll only get worse now." Lucy let out a soul wrenching sigh. "I guess I'll tell you what happened all those years ago. What happened to my family when I was very young and why I see the ghost of the mother I killed all those years ago. Just promise me with what I tell you, you'll use it to help me get rid of her?"

Arthur nodded slowly, "I promise."

*   *   *

"My earliest memories were of a cottage house in the summer time. It was a village I lived in although I do not remember its name. My parents Kezia and Paul were raising me alone in this stone house. My first memory is swinging on the garden bench underneath a canopy of trees in the warmest sunshine. It was a peaceful place, quiet, I remember the car my dad had was a truck as the drive to the road was uneven. I used to giggle like a little girl when I was tossed around in the back seats as the car bumped over every pothole. My earliest memories of my mother were of her beautiful humming when she sat out on the garden bench admiring the garden, she would often allow me to rest on her lap when I would get tired after playing. It was soothing."

Lucy began her story sipping the rest of her coffee down, she started to focus on the best memories to steel herself for the later events. Arthur stared forward like her at the abyss beyond the window.

"I remember not many other people. The house was secluded with a massive garden, we weren't farmers but my dad was the one who loved the countryside. He often reared me as mum had the better paid job. I can't remember what it was but in the early days it was him who would play with me in the back garden, not my mum. I do think I was about six maybe seven not long after starting school did I start getting bored by myself. My dad started working from home. I remember him telling me to leave him alone in his study, which made me sad. My thoughts at the time, I remember them well."

"And they were?" Arthur asked after he sensed the pause.

Lucy glanced at him and she smiled guiltily, "I wanted people my age to play with. I had my chance not long after wishing that. One day I was lazing on one of our trees, I often climbed them, I saw kids in the fields. They were playing with each other, I was immediately jealous, they must have been kids from our village and I didn't recognise them from school."

"Was school far?" Arthur asked.

Lucy nodded, "you're getting it right? None of the friends at my school could play with me as they all lived in the city. It was a half an hour car journey as my parents took me to a good school rather than a local one. Back to the story, I did something I knew even then was naughty. I jumped over the fence and followed the kids." Lucy paused waiting for Arthur to ask more, but he didn't so she continued, "I ran after them excited, I ran through farmers' fields remember the feeling of elation of people my age. I followed them all the way into the nearby forest."

"And?"

"We played, I remember having a wonderful time one of them had a football, another had some water pistols they welcomed me straight away. Happy to have another join in."

"In the forest? What were their names? How many of them were there?"

"At the time I didn't question why, they called it their hideout and I found that so cool. I don't remember any of their names, my memory isn't the best but there were five of them, with me that made six. It wasn't before long I realised I was late for dinner time, time had flown by. I remember something odd then. I was the only one in a hurry to leave. They were all prepared to play for longer. I remember they looked sad when I said I had to go home, so I promised I would come back. Upon returning home it was dark I knew even back then I was in trouble. My mum came running up to me and embraced me she was crying. My dad looked worried too. It was the first night I heard them argue."

"Do you know why?"

Lucy scratched the back of her head, "I can only guess, but I think mum was angry at dad for not watching me. All I know for sure is things changed after that. My dad wouldn't let me outside when he was working. My mum would try organising for me to go to clubs after school. None of it helped, I wanted to see my friends I promised I would return. One time again I was lucky and managed to join them for more fun on a weekend. My parents were still in bed. I came back for lunch and a similar episode happened although this time my parents demanded explanations."

"What did you tell them?"

"It's hazy, but I for sure told them I had made friends who hang out in the forest. The look on their faces… It was not what I expected. As a 7-year-old I expected them to be happy for me instead they looked afraid and concerned. My mum attempted to sweet talk me away from the forest but I was a stubborn kid. It was my dad who offered the compromise."

"What did he offer?"

"He offered for me to go only if a parent accompanied me. So, I could still go and see my friends but an adult would be present. I resisted at first but caved in, I thought my parents would cramp my style." Lucy let out a short derisive laugh. "They did worse than that. The day my dad joined me to the hideout was one I would not soon forget. I did the secret password to come in but forgot to mention my dad was with me. I didn't think it was an issue." Lucy furrowed her eyebrows trying to remember. "The next bits are hazy again, sorry."

"Take your time," Arthur said.

"Several things almost happened at once. My friends disliked my dad, they attacked him. Threw stones at him so my dad got angry. But then he suddenly got scared for some reason. The next thing I knew is him picking me up and running from the forest. He was scared, but I have no idea why."

"Were your friends older than you? Did they play a nasty prank on your dad?"

"No, they were my age, but they didn't like adults but my dad was not one to scare easily my mum was an intimidating person and he stood up to her just fine. I just can't remember what got him so scared." Lucy scratched her head but sighed and moved on, "anyways my dad returned home and quickly took me to my room. He told me he would speak to mum and then to me, saying that I should never meet those friends again."

"And did he?"

A tear trickled down Lucy's cheek. "That's the last time I spoke or saw him," she sniffled. "I curled up in my bed as there was a heated exchange between my mum and dad. I remember my mum laughing cruelly and my dad yelling. It got worse, my mum stopped laughing and started yelling back. It all ended with a slamming of the door anyway, all I could hear was my mum sobbing not long after."

"Your dad left that very day?" Arthur asked incredulously.

"That's why I don't think I have all the facts, when I asked my mum where he was all she said that he was a coward and is no longer needed around. She looked upset about it though. My dad's departure is a mystery," Lucy conceded wiping the single tear from her cheek.

"Do you believe her?"

"I don't know what to believe Arthur," Lucy confessed, "whatever the case he clearly didn't love me enough to stick around," Lucy snorted, "anyway let's get back on track. With dad gone my mum was in a bind, she couldn't work as much and had to raise me. But for a while she found it ideal that I went to play with my friends. We would meet up and waste the weekends away. There was also school so for a time, things were ok. My mum started picking up a problem. An alcoholic problem. She was lonely and started drinking even when I turned eight I noticed she started behaving weirdly. She would often fall asleep at the table and at other times she would be crying in the bedroom. I would try and comfort her but I was scared of her."

"Have you ever been drunk Lucy?" Arthur asked absentmindedly.

"Once," Lucy admitted, "never again, my mum showed me how dangerous alcohol could be at an early age." Lucy gave an involuntary shiver.

"I thought as much," Arthur muttered, "please, continue."

"One night I had the audacity to take the bottle off her when she was sleeping. I was not a dumb kid. I knew this was the cause for her mood swings. I poured the contents down the sink, problem is my mum saw me do it. She stormed up to me and for the first time smacked me across the face." Lucy gently raised her hand to her cheek as if the blow still stung. "I ran to my room as she yelled after me. Things only went downhill from there. I used all my effort to avoid the house. I would use the opportunity where I could to play outside, even when it was raining. I would tell my friends all about what was happening and they started confessing similar stories. Weirdly, we all had similar problems and had no desires to return home."

"That whole group of friends, by chance, happened to have similar problems?" Arthur asked with a hint of cynicism in his voice.

Lucy raised an eyebrow. "I didn't really care. They were similar to me, they were all I had."

Arthur nodded conceding the point. "But isn't the fact all those kids having an unpleasant home suspicious to you?".

"Not at the time, I was just glad I could be around people that wouldn't hurt me." Lucy said honestly.

Arthur grunted his conceit and awaited her to continue.

"My mum got worse. She either got let off work or simply wouldn't go, she was in the house all the time. I would avoid her. And she avoided me, it was only when food was ready did I see her at all. We always ate in silence then. One day she asked me a question. 'Who are those friends you hang around with?' She would ask. I would give her vague answers. But one day I was followed."

"Followed?"

"My mum followed me without me realising it to where the hideout was in the nearby forest. I was careless. That woman was jealous of my happiness and sought to take it away from me. It was my 9th birthday and my mum hadn't gotten me anything but my friends had, we planned a party at the hideout away from all our parents. It would have been a great time if my mum had not gate crashed it. I remember seeing her face in rage as she stormed into our gathering."

"Was her reaction similar to your father's?"

Lucy shook her head, "worse. She had come with a weapon. A kitchen knife. She pointed at me with it demanding I go home with her. I remember refusing and all my friends trying to support me, until, until…" Lucy let out a small sob as she tried to contain her emotions Arthur watched her carefully with a neutral expression, "until she slashed one of them. That was the first time I saw blood, and it was of one of my friends. And it was all my fault." Lucy choked a little as tears nearly welled up again.

Arthur rummaged in his pocket and drew a napkin, Lucy took it gratefully dabbing at her eyes. "I'm ok," she muttered more to herself, "I'm ok," she repeated calming herself down.

"How serious was the wound?"

"I don't know, I had to leave that's all I knew. I had no choice. In order to stop her from hurting anyone else I came back without resistance. That was the last I saw of my friends as one rolled on the forest floor covered in blood. It was by then I knew my mum was insane." Lucy felt herself trembling recounting that horror was tough but the worst was yet to come. "I remember walking back watching the blood drip off that knife like it was melted butter. My mum told me never to approach them again. She said they were a bad influence on me. Her! The friends who were to celebrate my 9th birthday! Suddenly they were the bad influence?!" Lucy thundered. "You know what's rich?!"

Arthur looked at her but said nothing.

"She described them as one thing," Lucy paused for dramatic effect, "she called them demons! Her! I knew who the real demon was!" Lucy calmed herself down again. "Things never improved after that. I was kept prisoner in my own home, only let out for school. School was my only respite, I remember trying to tell the teacher my mum was sick but no one listened."

"Why do you think that is?" Arthur asked getting out of his chair to pace, "surely a teacher should investigate if a child pleads her case?"

Lucy lightly grimaced, "one time my mum was called in but she was a good actor. Out of the house she was the same beautiful cheery angel everyone adored in the village, when home she became ugly and demonic. My mum was careful. She had things figured out."

"This sounds like she was not insane. Or at least had a mental illness? Would you agree?" Arthur pressed.

"I don't know, my only guess from my memories is she became scared of me. She sought to cage me like an animal." Lucy took a deep breath to stay the emotions. "She started carrying that knife around everywhere, she was paranoid."

"Of a 9-year-old?"

Lucy shrugged, "maybe, I am not sure. I was nine." Lucy continued, "transgressions against her started becoming severe. I attempt to escape I get the knife brandished at me. One time, when she was drunk she cut my hair with that knife. It was long back then. I remember crying in the corner of the kitchen as she manhandled me taking chunks of hair out each time. I never felt so powerless. She hacked away at my long hair like it was a bush never even bothered to clean up the chunks of hair that littered the kitchen floor. I was left there crying holding my tattered, severed hair in my own hands." Lucy put her hand through her short hair as her bottom lip trembled.

Arthur lost his neutral expression and showed a face of horror. "You are being extremely brave you know? You don't need to tell me anymore."

"No!" Lucy interrupted, "I have come this far, please let me finish it." She gave Arthur a pleading look and he nodded regrettably sitting back down on his chair. "There are hardly any times now I can think of where she was sober, if was she wasn't crying or hitting me she was downing a bottle until she was passed out. Then one night I thought I had salvation. I was in my bed when I heard voices calling my name. I recognised them as my friends! I was to be saved! Or so I thought. When I made a dash for the back door to reunite with my friends I had not seen in over half a year someone was awake and preventing me from leaving."

"Your mum?"

"My mum, yeah. She snatched me before I could reach them. She held me by the neck and tossed me into our cellar. It was dark. And cold. I had never been in such a dark place in my life." Lucy's lip trembled again, tears began pouring down her face once more. "You know Arthur? You know why I am scared of the dark? It is because of that cellar. I was down there against my will powerless to stop what came next. I can remember the shouts of a fight. My mum screaming 'demons' as my friends attempted to rescue me. I saw none of the scuffle but I could hear shouting and screaming. All I knew was the victor. Not soon after the commotion had ceased the cellar door I had been shouting at opened and my mum stood there again with a bloodied kitchen knife. She gloated to me she had fended my demons off and closed the door onto me begging for her to let me out."

"How on earth were the police not involved?!" Arthur thundered he looked angry the story she was telling which got him heated up.

Lucy gave another hopeless shrug, "It's the past Arthur, we have the benefit of hindsight, simple answer is no one called them. Not me, not my friends, not my father, not my teachers and certainly not my mother. I had no access to a phone. At this point I had ceased going to school, my mum must have passed me off as ill. My dad never returned. The police had no idea! There was nothing I could have done, except weep on a cold cellar floor."

Arthur undid his top button as the room picked up in temperature. His grey old eyes looking wrenched with sadness. "Who else knows of this?" he asked quietly.

Lucy looked at him calmly, even the mighty Arthur could not help but show the same expression everyone had who she told this tale to. "My current guardians, Phillis and Joe, the police who eventually found me and my girlfriend Andrea and now you." Lucy looked at him calmly as Arthur wrestled with emotion. It was weird to see him express emotions, were they real? Lucy wondered, or an act? "The story is nearly over," Lucy reassured bitterly.

Arthur nodded as he collected himself back to a neutral tone waiting for her to continue.

Lucy blew out a breath and continued, "my mother did improve somewhat since that incident weirdly enough. She acted smug when she released me. She was still drinking but she started regaining some level of happiness. Which was weird, I guess she had achieved what she wanted, ruining my happiness. Although…"

"Although?" Arthur repeated as Lucy became lost in thought.

Lucy jolted back into her story telling, continued, "It didn't seem like that was her goal, on reflection. That was the last time she had raised a hand to me. Now thinking about it she was trying to make amends albeit poorly. Between my 9th and 10th years after that incident she allowed me to return to school and started to talk to me normally. Asked how my day was and started buying me stuff like new pencil cases and clothes. She never uttered the word sorry though."

"Guilt?" Arthur asked.

Lucy nodded, "I think so. Ever since scaring my friends out of my life for good she started coming back to her senses. But it was too little too late." Lucy grabbed onto Arthur's coat somewhat aggressively and squeezed as she knew what she had to tell next.

It was Arthur who prompted her to carry on. "You mentioned that you killed her?" he asked hesitantly sensing the conclusion was near.

Lucy took a deep breath "I might as well have. I condemned to her to death but that's just the same as murder."

"So, you didn't kill her?"

Lucy rounded on Arthur, "in my mind I did alright?"

Arthur raised an apologetic hand, "it's necessary for me to ask these questions, for me to better understand you. Please continue."

Lucy grumbled but decided not to pursue the matter. "It was barely two months after my 10th birthday. And when I returned home from school I could tell something was wrong. I often got a taxi as my mum was often too drunk to drive but this evening was a particularly nasty one. I remember walking in, intending to go straight to my room and avoid her as usual. But I noticed glass bottles all over the living room. More than usual, some even looked smashed. I remember just going to my room despite this oddity. An hour in and I had not heard or seen my mother. At this point she would have knocked on my door or tried at least to ask some sort of question, but nothing. I got curious and suspicious. Leaving my room, I did what I hadn't done in over two years go into my mother's room willingly." Lucy paused, she had to. What came next was the horror of it all. "I opened the already ajar door. And on the bed, was my mother passed out. Having drunk too much she lay on her back face up at the ceiling. And that is when that dreaded noise came. That retching, that accursed gurgling. That wet foam and bubbles seeping from her mouth. My mother was choking on her own vomit."

An eerie silence fell across the heated room. Arthur kept neutral but his eyes flitted all over her expression. Lucy had no idea what face she was pulling her face felt numb.

"At the age of 10 I sussed what was going on. 'She's dying!' I thought 'You must help her!' I thought. But my body and my soul did not make any haste. I just stood there watching. As the vomit seeps out of her mouth like magma from a volcano. I eventually did approach her as her body started convulsing. The lack of oxygen causing a panic in every muscle. I walked up to her and stood over her watching and felt nothing as I saw a spark slowly dim underneath me and then I thought, 'serves you right, you deserve to die.' Those thoughts plagued my mind at a tender age of 10. I watched my tormentor agonise and writhe with no feelings of remorse or interest to intervene. My mother was dying in front of me and all I felt was joy."

Lucy looked at Arthur tears blotting her vision. "I condemned my mother to death. I could have saved her but chose not to. A landline was on her bedside table. I could have picked it up and called an ambulance seek advice off the operator, but I chose not to. I had no wish to see my mother continue living. What does that make me? A murderer? A cold-hearted killer? Or the very demon my mum said I always was?"

Lucy broke down, after holding it in for so long. She had spent a week of crying but years damming it up and now that dam had completely collapsed and every raw emotion cascaded with it. "I LET MY MUM DIE!" she howled burying her face in her hands as she monsooned her tears non-stop. Lucy's every muscle shook as she convulsed herself in despair.

A gentle hand cupped the small of her back and even then it seemed unsure what to do. Lucy through her sobs saw Arthur had moved to sit on the edge of her armchair making eye contact. He creased into a gentle smile, "we won't continue until you are ready." Lucy who continued crying but yearned for human contact buried her face onto his shirt, wrapping her arms around him to prevent him from escaping. Arthur made no protest but he still had an awkward hand on her back unsure of what else to do.

They remained in this position for as long as Lucy's monsoon season lasted.

*   *   *

"I eventually did call an ambulance and the police when my mother stopped moving. I was smart enough to say that I found her dead rather than watch her die. I cried then but they were forced tears unlike now. I knew back then my life was going to change. I remember seeing the horror of the police women's faces at the state of me and the house. They quickly bustled me to hospital for a check-up and decided to arrange a guardian for me. I remember them unable to find a suitable family member or reasoned against my dad taking custody. It was decided with my unique case that they would place me under some foster parents I consented to that idea vocally opposed to living with my father. Luck would have it, that my social care and mental health nurse Phillis decided to take me under her wing. I am grateful to her for deciding to do so I cannot begin to describe how messy my life would have been if not for her."

"That's rare or even problematic for a social worker to take the child under their care directly," Arthur wondered aloud as he wiped down his shirt the best he can with the tear stains all over it.

"I often wondered the same thing," Lucy agreed, "whenever I ask, Phillis would cite that she and Joe always wanted a daughter and I was a special case. She always expected that to be a sufficient explanation to the point I just gave up asking."

"And the shadow?" Arthur pressed.

"That ghost of my mum? It never really appeared back then like it did now. I never saw it at high school but the image of her with vomit in her mouth often appeared in my nightmares. I would talk to Phillis about my nightmares as she often did, her counselling really helped me. It has only become worse recently. I would see it loom over me in when I would be half awake in bed. Always when the light was off to the point I insisted to sleep with the light on. I realised I was dealing with something paranormal when Andrea who stayed around mine turned the light off and saw it herself approach me, that was the second worst experience of my life." Lucy grimaced to herself, "only since I have been at uni has it appeared so frequently, why do you think that is?"

Arthur paused his attempts to dry his shirt to cup his chin thoughtfully. "The loss of the dependence I guess? I'm not sure, but if I were a betting man it would be that you always had Phillis to help counsel you, at uni you no longer get that. What Phillis probably did albeit inadvertently was help you bury your past and strengthen barriers. Now at uni you are alone, left to your own devices, if I was to draw parallels similar to what you experienced under your mother, was isolation. It is therefore little surprise to me that your past would come to haunt you, literally at this stage."

Lucy blinked stupidly as she took all that information in. "Huh, you are pretty good at this aren't you?"

Arthur grunted resuming to wipe his shirt, "I'm not sure I appreciate that sudden realisation."

"I never told Phillis or Joe that I saw my mum die, only that I found her dead. Only you and Andrea know."

Arthur nodded as he practically gave up on drying his shirt. Realising Lucy had done with her story, after a lengthy pause, he cleared his throat, "well anyway, thank you Lucy. What you have just said to me is under the utmost confidence. It's a burden I willingly share with you and you have done astronomically well to carry it with you all these years. I am somewhat comforted by your decision to trust me with this story but at the same time horrified you had to go through such an experience rarely shared by anyone else."

Lucy meekly nodded and remained mute.

"With that information, as promised, I have a strategy and perhaps an understanding of your shadow that I need to guide you through." Arthur got up and started pacing, "temember your shadow is a figment of your imagination but is still real, meaning it cannot be ignored and must be dealt with. A shadow is a terminology of my own making. I call these figments shadows as they are eternally linked to its architect. They are oft not always there but are part of you as much as anything else despite being external to your physical body. A shadow can be brought into being for numerous reasons, typically, and I'm sorry to say as it is in your case, this shadow is the embodiment of everything you have attempted to reject or keep buried throughout these years. It is a symbol of your raw emotion or trauma that you have not yet healed or come to terms with."

Lucy watched Arthur as he explained with gusto before asking, "how do I come to terms with it? I'm guessing this will get rid of it?"

"Yes, but remember this is a shadow, your shadow. It is not your mother. It takes on the appearance of your mother as clearly what you have not come to terms with is something related to her. I ask you again Lucy, for someone who said they killed their mother without remorse why did you cry back there?"

"I feel ashamed at being a murderer, that I killed someone."

Arthur stopped pacing to look at Lucy sadly. "Is that what you have been telling yourself all these years?"

Lucy felt liked she just been gut punched. That was how she still tried to rationalise it, her feelings of anguish for all these times gone. Licking her lips Lucy went about correcting herself, "actually, I feel guilty, I feel regret, I feel sorrow and that despite everything I wish I had saved my mother back then." Lucy looked down at her feet as her brain processed what it already knew.

"Well done," Arthur said approvingly, "the most haunting thing often is guilt and regret. I misjudged the shadow originally to be a warped childhood view of a parent rather than an embodiment of locked away emotions. Can you see why now I needed to know everything about you in order to tackle this properly?"

"I'm sorry," Lucy mumbled meekly.

"What? Oh you don't have to apologise! It's totally understandable to me now why you were reluctant to share your story with anyone." Arthur looked taken aback from Lucy's apology.

"So, what now?" Lucy asked expectantly, "I told you what you want to know, so what you are you going to do about it?"

Arthur let out a light chuckle, "I'm afraid I can't wave a magic wand and make it go away, but I think the hard part has been done. It'll still need to be you not me that'll make this shadow disappear. I can only tell you how to do that, the rest is up to you."

"Ok so what do I need to do?"

"Not now, come to the same warehouse tomorrow after 6pm and I'll tell you then."

"Why are we delaying? What happens if it comes out again tonight?"

"It won't come out. I'm sure of it."

"What makes you so sure?" Lucy's voice started to turn doubtful.

Arthur weathered her tone and smiled, "currently your shadow is the external locked away emotions you have attempted to ignore or even take a chance in believing in. If my hypothesis is accurate, which I have no doubts it is, half the battle is already done. What do you think those tears you sprayed all over me were? Just tears? Or those emotions finally seeping through after being locked away for so long?"

Lucy as usual attempted to find fault in what he said but this time she found nothing. Sighing conceitedly, she allowed Arthur to pick his coat off her lap as he rummaged in his pockets. He finally drew out a golden pocket watch which he took to examine at.

"Crap! That's the time?! We will need to book you a taxi as soon as possible."

Lucy's eyes narrowed at the pocket watch he was holding one that looked very similar to DCI Truman's watch.

"That pocket watch…" Lucy began by speaking out loud, Arthur hurriedly put it back in his pocket.

"Yes?" he asked neutrally.

Lucy paused, he was on guard about the matter. "No… its nothing, shall we get this taxi then?"

CHAPTER 9

Instead of foreboding which is what Lucy felt last time she was on Fishers Road, she felt excitement. The life story chat with Arthur was strangely therapeutic on par with her sessions with Phillis back home. Despite knowing it wasn't over Lucy did feel like a weight had been taken off her chest, she marvelled at how more relaxed she was in just a few short hours. Even her flatmates commentated on her shift in spirits. What was also weird was that Arthur, the insensitive bigot she once thought he was, helped her with this.

Therefore, her feelings of trepidation on the Tuesday where the first attempt to tackle her figment were no longer present. It was slightly before the arranged time of 6pm that Lucy found herself loitering under the same lamppost staring at warehouse 87. She had not bothered bringing a rucksack this time. No knife, or pots of salt, just herself and her phone. Andrea has been weirdly silent so that Lucy had not felt pressured to give her an update. She was still struggling with how best to tell her about Arthur and this whole progression of events. For now, it would seem, ignorance is bliss for her and Andrea.

It was notably colder than the Tuesday as Lucy watched her breath mist out in front of her. The reason why Lucy was waiting here was because unlike Tuesday, there was a car parked on the pavement by the warehouse. It was a flashy black jaguar making Lucy think it could be the owner or caretaker of the unused warehouses. She thought it could have been Arthur but then concluded he was not someone she could imagine driving a jaguar, besides, he was there last time and there was no car. Lucy was sure someone else was around giving cause for her to wait and survey for them. Being caught for trespass was on the low end of her bucket list.

"Still, it would have been nice if you had brought flowers." That's Arthur's voice Lucy realised. As the front doors of the warehouse creaked open. Lucy instinctively moved out of the lamppost light and crouched behind a nearby bin sensing it would be best not to be seen.

"You were too easy to find, you ought to be more careful," said a much gruffer voice ignoring Arthur's jibe. Lucy recognised the voice from somewhere. True enough a man walked out of the doors putting a fedora back on a whitehaired scalp. He turned around to look at the car parked on the road showing a brilliant white handle bar moustache. It was DCI Truman. Lucy gasped in surprise, they know each other?

"I'm not hiding anything, so what is the point in making myself hard to find? An old greyhound like you would sniff me out regardless." Arthur's tone was considerably more playful than the serious detective.

"I'm trusting you on this," Truman said jabbing a finger at Arthur who merely smirked.

"Would you go and retire already? I really don't need you dogging my steps, this place is far from London for a reason."

"I wouldn't have come out this far, if the incident in the club Frenzy didn't raise all the right flags for my involvement." Truman was now close to his car pressing a button on his key to unlock it.

"And I've already said I am handling it. Tell those bumbling bureaucrats at DACFE that I am on the case alright, next time just send a postcard."

Truman was now opening the door to his care as Arthur leaned against the doorway of the warehouse. "You know, if I told them that precisely, that would give them more cause for concern," Truman replied pointedly as Arthur rolled his eyes. Truman got into the car slamming the door closed behind him. Lucy heard a whirring of a window going down as she started struggling to hear what was being said. "Remember no loose ends, this has to be contained."

"How ominous!" Arthur quipped.

"I'm serious and so is the department. If you don't handle this appropriately we'll drag you to London and under our direct supervision, are we clear?"

Arthur's face became abruptly cold, but his tone went much icier, "you and your department should know better than to threaten me. Continue down this road and we both know who will suffer first." Lucy felt an involuntary shiver as she just saw a side to Arthur she didn't expect.

There was silence from the jaguar as the windows began electronically winding up. The engine started, and the car slowly started driving away. Arthur watched it go before walking back inside sliding the warehouse door shut behind him.

Lucy's mind was buzzing with what she just saw. There is more going on than she initially thought, and Truman seems to be in the loop. They must have been talking about her, there is no other reason she could think of. Lucy felt her feelings of trepidation crawl back in as she now began doubting Arthur once more. There were more things he was not telling her and yet she had come clean. What should she do now? The conversation between Truman and Arthur was suspicious enough with a higher organisation at play here. Yet she was so close to ending her own torment! Lucy quarrelled with herself for a short while before deciding she would proceed but be on guard. She was sure that Arthur had no wish to cause her harm but then again doubted his motives for helping.

Lucy hurried over the normal route and found a gap in the fence as before. Finding the same side entrance as last time she walked in to the lights already on and saw Arthur reading a newspaper on a new stool.

He looked up from the paper, "You're late," he stated.

Lucy walking in said, "sorry disaster with the pasta bake."

Arthur merely grunted not testing her alibi further. He got off the stool eyeing her all the while. "No bag this time?" he asked nonchalantly.

"I didn't think I would need it this time."

"No concealed knife?" Lucy felt like she was going through airport security.

"You can search me, but I promise no weapon of any kind." Arthur nodded satisfied with the response. "So, what's the plan for this time?" Lucy asked clapping her hands together showing an eagerness to get it over with.

Arthur rolled up his newspaper before chucking it by his bag next to the closest flood lamp. "Similar to before but no easy route. We are not going down the sloppy denial method that's for sure. It'll probably make the figment hostile again."

"Wait," Lucy interrupted, "you're saying that me attempting to disbelief it angered it?"

"Well, more so angered yourself, deep down you didn't want to forget, I mean now knowing what this is all about how could you? You getting angry is the same as your shadow getting angry, its actions however insane were representations of your feelings."

"And you failed to mention this before because...?"

"Because you pissed me off and I didn't know how deep and troubled you really were. That's why it pays to know these things." Arthur explained pointedly.

"Ah, well, sorry for that." Lucy said ashamedly glancing at Arthur's arm which looked like it was on the mend.

Arthur waved a dismissive hand, "we are not here to lament about the mistakes of Tuesday. We are here to get it done right and so we shall."

"Okay," Lucy said eagerly, "what is going to be different?"

"First, is drawing it out. The two triggers are vomit and isolation in the dark. Since I am not throwing up another time for you we are going for option two. I am not here to feed the rats." Arthur gestured to where the spot where his vomit used to be, now just a stain on the ground.

Lucy unclenched and clenched her fists nervously shaking her whole body out to prepare herself. "Okay, so that means you won't be in with me when it is happening?"

"Correct. During the materialisation phase I cannot be present. I will however return to observe once it appears. I'll know when. If it becomes violent I will intervene."

Lucy nodded hesitantly, "I don't think it will come to that this time."

Arthur showed surprise, "oh? Are you that certain?"

"Not certain, just know what has to be done this time."

Arthur smiled, "you have already changed since last night, you know that?"

Lucy looked at Arthur slightly grossed out by this soft touch approach. "Can we get this over with before you creep me out any further?"

Arthur's smiled turned to a frown upon hearing Lucy's response, "I'm the one getting lectured about being too nice now?" he muttered to himself, "I can never win."

Lucy plonked herself on the stool knowing the drill. Arthur proceeded to walk out of her view and to the flood lights to switch them off. "Remember," he shouted in a lecture like fashion "This is a controlled environment, we can pull the plug at any time. I have given you the advice and facilities to fix this, the rest is up to you. Remember, this figment of your mother is a part of you that wants to be let back in. We know violence is not the answer but perhaps…" he paused on the way to the last lamp "reconciliation is." With that the last light was extinguished and Lucy was enveloped in perpetual darkness.

Lucy never felt nervous up until she heard the door close and felt very much alone. Isolated. In the dark. Just like that cellar, all those years ago. Lucy shifted about on the uncomfortable stool as she felt her heart beat faster. Her eyes darted around trying desperately to pierce the darkness.

Lucy actually found herself closing her eyes and heard Arthur's voice in her head. "Remember, figments cannot materialise within your senses. They must materialise wherever you are not looking, this attributes to them becoming more believable to the architect."

Lucy waited on the stool patiently trying desperately to meditate herself, but her heart was not listening. The beats, they were rapid. Lucy clutched her chest in an effort to slow her overworking heart. Sure enough a sound echoed. A tap of bare feet on concrete floor. Her mother had materialised.

"Arthur," Lucy called out nervously.

"I'm here," whispered a response behind her.

"What?!" Lucy spurted momentarily distracted, "I didn't hear any door open."

"That's because I never left, now focus on your shadow not me."

Lucy hurried her attention back to her mother who was getting closer. She still had the mangled hair, the grey dead skin, the kitchen knife in hand but was now wearing her favourite cooking apron from all those years ago. The one she died in, all those years ago. Lucy grimaced to herself, at the irony presented to her. Her mind loved to betray her.

"M-mum?" Lucy stuttered nervously getting off her stool to stand.

The only response Lucy got was a strained gurgle, but it was something. A sign it could understand her.

"Mum, we need to talk. Can you just stay where you are please?" her figment ignored her wish and continued forward getting closer to Lucy with each step.

"Lucy!" Arthur hissed, "you cannot command your subconscious so what makes you think you can command your shadow? Try something else."

Lucy gulped nervously as her mother was now just as close as last time before lunging at her. It's a do or die a moment. It began to raise its free hand like a claw deftly opening and closing getting closer.

"Lucy!" Arthur nervously hissed.

But somehow Lucy remained calm as the hand was mere inches away. "You know, I never got a chance to thank you." Lucy was surprised at what she just blurted out and so was her shadow. It stopped. Frozen, like a statue. Lucy decided to roll with it, "not for the memories, they were terrible," she nervously laughed, "but thank you for being the mum I once knew, the one I adored, the one who would read me bedtime stories, kiss my cheek and told me what outfit I would look pretty in."

The figment remained still and even the arm flopped back down to its side. Was it listening? "Those memories are the ones I should treasure and sure what happened after were hurtful, miserable, tortuous." Lucy paused "But they weren't done by my mum."

Lucy continued unabated, "you weren't you. I know that, you know that. Whatever changed, whatever I did wrong, I know my mum wasn't there to witness that. I mean not all of your effort was wasted, look how I turned out now." Lucy pointed to herself doing a pirouette to show herself off to her own shadow. "It's not all that bad." Lucy suppressed a sniff.

"Figment or not, shadow or not. I was secretly happy you are here to witness me. Who I have become, I am not going to let the past define me. Nor do I think should you." Lucy pointed directly at her yearlong tormentor which flinched as Lucy took a step forward. "I regret that you are not here. Not fully. I regret what happened between us. I don't think I was to blame but I regret that I lost years of my childhood, I also regret making you and dad argue. I regret-" Lucy stifled another sniffle and took another step forward. This time it was her shadow who took a step back.

"I regret not saving you." Lucy finally managed, "I hate myself. I have carried this guilt around for years. That despite all you put me through I couldn't accept one crucial thing." Lucy took two more steps as her figment fearfully backed away. Lucy noticed there was no knife in its hands anymore. "That you're my mum. That I love you and always have. That if I could go back in time and save you, I would!" Lucy took so many more steps that her shadow was pressed against a wall with nowhere to retreat.

"Despite everything, I forgive you." Lucy then launched herself at her mother which instinctively pulled its arms to shield its face. Instead of hitting her mother, she embraced her. Lucy seized her own shadow and forced it into a hug. Lucy buried herself in her mother's chest her voice notably muffled as she now failed to hold back her tears. "I love you mum! I forgive you!" she started yelling through uncontrolled sobs, Lucy weirdly felt her mother warming up. She moved her face away from her chest and saw white skin. White perfectly healthy skin of a healthy young woman. The hair still hid her face. "My only wish now," Lucy said through her final cries, "is that can you forgive me?!!" And with that done. Lucy cried once more. She has cried too many times this week, but at least this time she could do what every child should be able to do. Cry in their mothers' arms.

Lucy continued to cry but paused when something short of a miracle happened. She was hugged back. Lucy stopped crying in shock as she felt the embrace of a loving mother hold her gently. Lucy felt warm breath on her neck as she stood rooted to the spot. And yet she heard something, something she didn't think possible. "I never blamed you, it is me who should ask forgiveness. You deserved so much more. You owe me no apology. I love you, my darling princess."

Lucy gripped onto her tighter, "mum," she practically wailed, "I missed you!" Lucy felt a gentle nuzzling on her neck.

"It's time to let go."

"I don't wanna!" Lucy replied gripping tighter devolving back to her seven-year-old self.

"It is the only way you'll be at peace."

Those words rung true with Lucy as she finally let go sniffing all the while as she finally saw a human face smile back at her. Lucy couldn't help but smile back. Lucy almost forgot! She had a witness to all this!

"How about it Arthur! Can a mere shadow be this standing in front of you?!" Lucy said triumphantly rotating round to look at an open-mouthed Arthur Squire. He was literally gobsmacked.

"See mum?! This guy always thought he was right and we proved him wrong!" she chuckled whirring back to face her mother. Alas, she was not there. "Huh? Mum where did you go?" Lucy started looking left and right but she was nowhere to be seen. Her mother had gone.

"She's gone. As soon as you took your eyes off her she disappeared." Arthur exhaled faintly.

Lucy paused for a short while. It was short, it was sudden, it was sad but, "yeah, it was time to let go." Lucy smiled to herself. She had got her wish. Coming back to her gloating self, Lucy fired Arthur's way, "you heard her speak didn't you?"

Lucy rounded back on a pale Arthur who this time looked like he had seen a ghost. "I heard something…" he muttered averting direct eye contact.

"Haha! I knew it, it was my mum all along!" she fist bumped the air.

Arthur raised a hand to stay Lucy's triumph, "let's not get carried away here, she was a figment that is indisputable. Whether she was a shadow though…" Arthur got lost in thought.

"It still wasn't really my mum is what you are saying?"

"Are you prepared to accept that fact? That was a likeness. Nothing more." He looked at Lucy with sad eyes, as if he had seen this tale many a time. Perhaps that was why he was so keen to burst the bubble.

Lucy smiled to herself gently, calming down. "I know. My mum has never called me a darling princess before," Lucy laughed awkwardly. It wasn't perfect, it wasn't really her, yet Lucy felt her sins cleansed. Her mother's forgiveness and touch even if fake are something she'll treasure forever.

Arthur pulled a sympathetic smile. "So long as you are aware." He nodded, "still I have seen many figments and met many architects but, what I saw there was a first." Lucy began walking back to the stool her back turned to Arthur. Arthur continued talking, following her. "Such a near flawless imitation, it wasn't quite a familiar class but nor was it a shadow class either. I feel like I just a saw a whole new type of figment! You have held up your end of the bargain, that experience will greatly bolster my understanding into shadow class figments. They are surprisingly rare and yet I saw its form gradually heal in front of me as a mental wound finally healed! Ah what poetic symbolism!" Arthur was now unable to contain what clearly was an intellectual orgasm.

Lucy moved to the nearest flood lamp to turn it on, her back still turned towards Arthur. "We did it!" she said triumphantly sharing Arthur's euphoria switching on the light to remove the dark she once was so afraid of.

Arthur exhaled, regaining composure he said, "yes we did, passed with flying colours which makes this next bit all the more difficult." Lucy heard a jangle of what she suspected was his pocket watch. "Come on Lucy, turn around and give me a handshake for a job well done!"

"No," Lucy said still not turning.

"What?" Arthur nervously laughed, "no handshake? I thought we made up?" He sounded like a hurt teenage girl.

"Drop the act, Arthur. I know what comes next."

Lucy felt a pause in Arthur's composure, "oh? What is that then? If you think I'm going to tell anyone else you're mistaken." He was holding his ground.

It was Lucy's turn to do a big exhalation. "To quote a DCI Truman, this situation must be contained."

Lucy felt the atmosphere change, "there was no disaster with the pasta bake was there?" Arthur said coolly.

"It was weird. You know all this time I wondered why, figments and architects weren't all that well known. I mean mine was pretty explosive, caused a whole night club evacuation. Then I remembered you said the government was aware about figments and architects." Lucy turned around but decided to keep her eyes closed. "So that got me wondering, how do they deal with these things? I mean I can tell first hand they are harmful, but then I got a delightful story from Wentworth." Lucy paused but Arthur said nothing, so she continued, "he told me a patient who suffered from the same symptoms as I was cured, by this thing called hypnosis. He didn't believe in it. But regardless she was never a problem anymore and disappeared. Then there was this weird thing of seeing pocket watches everywhere. I thought yours fitted in with your fashion sense, but it looked weird on Truman. Why is it you both have golden watches? Seems weird doesn't it? But somehow the only other person who knows what's going on has a pocket watch as well? So, then I piece it all together, and I guess you plan to hypnotise me. To contain me, to manipulate my memories so I will no longer remember about figments and architects. Well Arthur, do I get a first for that synopsis?" Lucy had her eyes closed the whole time for the fear of being tricked into a hypnotic state, but she must look ridiculous.

"You are one clever little shit, aren't you?" Arthur spat with venom. "There is no prize for being Sherlock fucking Holmes here."

Lucy sighed with relief, "so I was right."

"Right or not it doesn't change what needs to be done."

"Why? Why does it need to be done? Because Truman, the government told you to?"

Lucy could feel waves of Arthur's frustration flash over her. "Stop the questioning and stop the resistance. This is for your own good," he managed through gritted teeth.

"I'll decide what's best for me thanks."

"You bloody stupid girl! I cannot allow you to walk away with this information in your head, it's too dangerous, you are now a self-aware architect. This needs to be done!"

"So what does that make you? You're self-aware. You're an architect and yet you get to keep your memory? I don't think I have ever came across a study which requires me being brainwashed at the end of it!"

"Don't you dare question my motives, my ethics," Arthur shouted in indignation, "I'm different! They need my mind untampered with to study figments without me they would be helpless."

"So it is the government's call?" Lucy deduced.

"It doesn't matter, but Lucy don't make this any more difficult than it needs to be." Arthur was now imploring, from the change in his tone he sounded increasingly desperate.

"How could I possibly consent to having my memory removed?! A memory which includes perhaps the happiest and most relieving moment of my life?! You take that away and nothing will change!"

"I know what I am doing, don't make me come over there and do it by force!!" Arthur thundered.

"No! I refuse! I will not let you take this moment from me! I will not! You will have to do it by force if you think it's best!!" Lucy dug her heels in, bracing herself physically and mentally for Arthur's next move.

Arthur growled with uncontrollable rage, "fuck! Shit! Fucking shitty fuck! Curse that bastard Wentworth and his poxy stories and curse that fucking greyhound shoving his beak where it don't belong! Fuck em both! This is both their fault! Damn them! Goddamn them!" Lucy heard a yell of frustration and a heavy shattering sound as it sounded like Arthur chucked his watch to the floor. Taking a few seconds to catch his breath after that outburst Arthur said, "you can open your eyes now, you won."

"I don't trust you."

"You have made that pretty clear," Arthur snarled, "look, it's broken, useless. I can't hypnotise someone who is guarded against it. It is not some immense power if you know what is coming I cannot hypnotise you. Congratulations Lucy Baxter you have impressed everyone by solving the final puzzle! Hooray!!!" Lucy cautiously opened her eyes to Arthur's mocked clapping and to see a shattered watch on the concrete floor. "You don't get it do you?!! I don't enjoy this part of my life, I do not seek pleasure in manipulating people's minds. I have done this to so many people I have lost count! As the alternative is the government silences them, either be it a bullet or something else." Lucy gulped as she hoped she just misheard. "Once DACFE find out what has transpired here they will do everything within their means to shut you up. Killing is part of their routine."

"W-what?"

"You heard me. A bullet. You know those pieces of metal which can make your skull look like the inside of a tin of chopped tomatoes?!" Arthur was pacing non-stop constantly putting his hands through his hair."

"There must be some mistake," Lucy blurted fearfully, somehow beginning to regret her stance moments before."

"Oh, there was a mistake alright. I failed to hypnotise you because two wizened pricks have failed to retire back to the earth's soil!" Arthur practically yelled the last part.

"But I am a British citizen they can't just kill me?! I'm a student, I have not done anything wrong!" Lucy suddenly felt way out of her depth with this new feeling of her life being in danger.

Arthur scoffed and looked at Lucy in disdain. "Please, MI6 sends British citizens to Guantanamo bay without so much as a backward glance. Killing a self-aware architect is the weekend treat for them."

Lucy felt beads of sweat trickle down her face. She had not anticipated this. Not at all. "Maybe if I just kept quiet..." Lucy suggested feebly.

Arthur massaged his temple looking notably frustrated. "It's not the fact that you will talk it's the fact you could. Besides I cannot overstate how much of a threat they see self-aware architects as. You have a tremendous power that if left to your own devices you can cause devastation. Look at what happened at Frenzy! Imagine if you started believing in dragons. It's every Welsh persons' wet dream and you conjuring one up will be hard to contain! That's why I had to hypnotise you Lucy, to save you from that fate!"

Lucy spiralled to find a rebuttal, "I know dragons don't exist," she spluttered desperately.

Arthur cocked his head patronisingly. "Do you? I mean I've met one. You now know you can make these things reality because your brain is a factory of make-believe. You decide one day you want to make a dragon. You imagine him, give him cute little eyes and a nice spiky tail to impale people with. You think of it in enough detail and boom Aberstahl has a dragon setting the social sciences building on fire. The fact you know you can make things with your mind is enough to create the unnatural. The raw potential is terrifying no matter if you have no intention of conjuring a dragon, the fact that you could is why DACFE will be terrified of you!" Arthur pointed at Lucy to emphasise this.

Lucy felt notably guilty more so under the heat of Arthur's rant. "There must be limits to this potential," Lucy reasoned shiftily not quite looking Arthur in the eye.

Arthur sighed for what sounded like the 50th time, "there are, but a non-supervised totally untrained, self-aware architect would not know them. DACFE to my knowledge has not made a school for architects, too much money, weirdly, hypnotism is much cheaper."

"I still feel like there is another way around this. Without me getting shot or hypnotised." Lucy pressed noticing the hint in Arthur's latest angry retort.

Arthur sighed for what seemed like a month. "There is," he admitted begrudgingly. "Although you better be thankful, you may come to hate it, but it is either that or turn yourself in or get shot. You're spoilt for choice really." He groaned, "I'm not a fan of it either, but I am not in the business of letting a young girl getting shot because she thought she was clever."

"What is it?" Lucy asked eagerly ignoring Arthur's insults and keen to not get shot.

"I extend my immunity to you. Immunity as in legal immunity. I have helped DACFE more than they care to admit as a leading expert in the field. In return I have free reign, no hypnotisms, no bullets, I am a free self-aware architect. That is on the proviso I keep my powers in check, which by the way I have done flawlessly for as long as I can remember."

"So, I control my powers and I get your immunity how?" Lucy asked blankly sensing a step was missing.

Arthur growled pacing up and down clearly not happy with this. He was muttering profanities for two minutes before stopping and facing Lucy. "You work for me," he said simply.

"Sorry?" Lucy blinked stupidly.

"I said you work for me. Keep close to me and work for me as I take you on as an apprentice of sorts. Though I fucking hate that apprentice training shit, so don't expect a good teacher or example. I work as a lecturer but also as a researcher into figments and architects, meaning you help me with my research." Lucy prepared to open her mouth exacting her displeasure of basically becoming his slave, but Arthur beat her to it. "Remember the alternative is being shot in the head or being hypnotised so forcefully you spend the rest of your days in a mental asylum."

Lucy ground her teeth not enjoying any of those options. Eventually she came to a decision. The only one she could make under the circumstances "I look forward to working with you Arthur Squire." Lucy tried her best to hide her displeasure, but it wasn't as convincing as it sounded in her head.

Arthur nodded looking sombre. "For now," he began scratching his neck awkwardly, "let's head back, I'm sure you, like me, have a lot process right now."

Lucy snorted, "understatement of the year." Lucy followed Arthur as he picked his newspaper and bag from the only switched on flood light. Switching it off Lucy meekly followed him outside the warehouse as he began closing the doors.

Despite all the heated exchanges they have had up until this point Lucy thought it best to lighten the mood, now things have calmed down. "So you know this basically means I have become your Padawan right?"

Arthur finished pad locking the door and gave her a peculiar look, "what's a Padawan?" he asked blankly.

Lucy stood there for a few seconds disbelieving what she just heard. "You know," she said as Arthur started walking away, "I reckon we are going to struggle you and I."

CHAPTER 10

"Phwoah! Now that is what I call a full English!" Brent exclaimed as the table order arrived. Being the smallest amongst the troupe he ironically ordered the largest meal.

Libby, Adam and Lucy all watched in bemusement at his glee when the waiter placed the plate in front of him.

"Are you hoping to grow taller with portions like that?" Libby mused eyeing the portion size with obvious jealousy.

Brent's happy face quickly contorted into a scowl, "my ma always said to grow big and strong you must eat a lot!" he managed through a mouthful of sausage.

"The eggs benedict?" the waiter asked.

"Mine," Adam said as he got a considerably smaller plate placed in front of him, he didn't look disappointed though.

"The sausage and bacon baguette?" a waitress turned up this time with the final two orders.

"That's mine thanks," Lucy said raising her hand like she was in class.

"And the smoked salmon and cream cheese bagel?"

"Mine," Libby said obviously as not as euthanistic as the rest.

After the staff had gone away Lucy looked around the table at her friends. The only other one who looked really awake was Brent, Libby and Adam still looked like zombies. It was her decision to ask them out for breakfast this Sunday morning, even calling it a treat as she would pay. After the best night's sleep she has ever had Lucy was practically skipping out of bed this morning. Brent only showed that enthusiasm after she said they would go for a fry up.

"You know, the English breakfast is one of the few good things I acknowledge came from the English," Brent mumbled through chunks of black pudding.

"Why are you looking at me when you said that?" Adam asked after tucking in his serviette like a bib.

"Because I consider you the living symbol of eight centuries of English oppression," Brent responded as if it was obvious.

Lucy began trying her hardest not to burst out laughing with food in her mouth.

Adam started stupidly blinking through his glasses clearly not expecting that response. "You are way too awake for a 10am Sunday hangover breakfast," is all he could say back. "Speaking of," Adam said keen to change topic, "how was your night Libby?"

Libby flinched when her name was mentioned. She had barely touched her bagel. Adam gave a knowing grin. "It was alright," she managed coughing slightly.

"I heard the flat door open at 6am, could it have been someone's morning jog?" Adam pressed pulling an even wider grin.

"If you're looking for revenge about the Mike shower incident, you gonna be disappointed Adam."

"Wait, what did Mike do in the shower?" Brent asked quizzically.

"Er nothing, nothing he didn't have any soap that's all!" Adam blurted out quickly.

Lucy and Libby gave knowing smirks to each other. But Lucy was not letting Libby get off the hook easily, "was this your first 6am jog Libby?" she asked sweetly, keen like Adam, to find out what happened.

Libby gave a furious glare at Lucy for the back stab as she nibbled her bagel clearly not having an appetite. "If you must know! I was out at a flat party, some guy from my course invited me."

"You were there all the way till 6am?" Brent asked sounding sceptical.

"She left at like 10pm she was definitely one of the first there," Adam added.

"Ugh you guys are so annoying!" she complained putting down her bagel. "Alright fine, if it gets you off my back I went to the party, got wasted by like 1am and was unable to get into the club."

"Because you were smashed?" Lucy clarified.

"Yeah duh, I was hugging the bouncer asking if he was single." After Brent, Adam and Lucy had finished sniggering she continued, "I had to find a way home and I didn't want to splash on a taxi by myself, so I took the Saturday night bus."

"And that took five hours?" Adam asked raising an eyebrow.

Libby sighed putting her head in her arms, "when your drunk and have no one to talk to, you kinda have a tendency to fall asleep... turns out I was asleep on the night bus for four hours until the new bus driver spotted me."

Adam, Lucy and Brent all roared with laughter upon hearing that. "What a bell end!" Adam said while laughing. Libby went scarlet.

"Brent remind me, when we get home I need to tell you a story. About Mike and the shower," Libby said calmly fixing Adam with a steely glare which quickly shut Adam up.

Brent looking clearly confused chirped, "why not now?"

"Because I have a feeling Lucy wants to tell us something, what with summoning us to the café at inhumane hours and paying for it all." Libby was always gifted at recognising people's intent before they even opened their mouths. Lucy smiled to herself, god have I found myself a good bunch she thought.

"Yeah I was hoping to talk to you all actually. If that is okay?" Lucy asked the floor as Adam nodded and Libby smiled encouragingly.

"Woooooo speech!!" Brent shouted childishly.

"Shut up Brent!" Adam and Libby said in unison. Before quickly turning back to Lucy. Brent shrugged and continued to gorge on his nearly finished full English.

"I have an apology and a confession to make. I know this sounds serious but bear with me." Lucy eyed her audience Libby looked curious, Adam puzzled and Brent amused. Before she could tempt another outburst from Brent she continued, "I feel like you have all tip-toed around me ever since my disastrous uni debut. What with me getting drunk and being a general problem to everyone."

"Don't worry we've all been there," Adam dismissed.

"Adam hush!" Libby snapped keen for Lucy to continue.

"Even if we have all been there and that was my first time being there, I still think it was unacceptable how angry I have been recently. I snapped at you all, shouted at you all and have been downright difficult to live with as a result." There were no interruptions this time, but Brent's facial expression changed from amusement to surprise. "I wanted to say sorry for that. I had my reasons, but it was unfair to be using you guys as an outlet of my frustration. I can't tell you how much I want you guys to be my friends. And I want you all to know that whatever was troubling me before it has gone now." Lucy pointed back at herself and didn't feel the need to force a smile "This is a new Lucy! So, what I'm trying to say is, um, this is embarrassing but, I want to start over. Press restart. And be the real me ages ago." Lucy gave a long enough pause to signify she was finished.

However, it was Brent who broke the silence first, "Jesus, is graduation tomorrow or something?" he remarked taking a sip out of his orange juice.

"Brent!" Libby and Adam again said at the same time.

"Sorry, couldn't help myself," he muttered rolling his eyes. Lucy didn't find it insensitive she merely smiled at Brent who cheeks were slightly red. Humour was his smokescreen for embarrassment. Despite being loud and grouchy Brent was usually nervous to make his own feelings known but little by little he was opening up.

"What I think our resident Scottish bell end is trying to tell you, is that you don't have to apologise Lucy," Libby said reaching out and gripping Lucy's hand gently.

Adam gave a knowing smile, "a toast," he said stupidly taking a piece of Brent's toast. Which made Lucy cackle a little too much and Brent try to take it back off Adam but to no avail. "To fellow flat mates, and my dearest friends. Here is to a year of continuing to be friends!" it was very like Adam to take charge of the situation. While self-proclaiming himself as the leader he was very charismatic and often unafraid to smooth things over by acting the fool.

Libby smiled raising her glass, "to friends!" she said rather excitedly. Libby was someone who like Lucy wants friends to call on and trust on. Her actions Lucy have seen in the group are generally selfless and seen as the social glue which bind them together. It will probably be Libby and not Lucy that will keep them together.

Lucy followed suit, "here's to this year," she agreed.

Brent who sat there with his arms folded said, "you know we have only known each other for four weeks right?" like that he brought it crashing to the earth.

"Oh, don't be such a grump Brent!" Libby exasperated still holding her glass up expectantly.

It was Lucy who spoke next, "c'mon, who is it who bought you a full English? Are you really going to let Adam keep these two hot babes to himself? We still have that chess game to play as well! You know you want to." Lucy gave a cheeky wink to an already in turmoil Brent. She hoped the triple whammy, of the bribe, his rivalry with Adam and his competitive drive in games to win him over.

"Alright fine!" Brent said raising his glass, "To… friends," he muttered sheepishly.

"Yes!" Lucy said happily as they all chinked glasses to celebrate a forged friendship.

"Can I now have my toast back?" Brent said turning on Adam.

"What toast?" Adam said as he was chewing.

"You bastard! That could have been another millimetre onto my height!!" Brent shouted as Adam smirked with puffed cheeks.

"I guess this is an appropriate time to tell you about the Mike story Brent," Libby interrupted slyly as Adam's eyes widened and all he could do is make muffled moans through the half-eaten toast. Brent eagerly turned his attention to Libby as she began recounting the tale.

Lucy laid back in her chair satisfied with her meal and the result in front of her. You see mum? Lucy thought. These lot aren't demons, they're friends, ones I intend to keep for life.

*   *   *

"Hey Lucy, you look well, something good happen?" April asked as Lucy sat down next to her.

"You could say that," Lucy bragged with a smile.

"Goddamn, you are like a different person. It's 9am and you look fine girl!" Lucy smiled again to the barrage of praise from April who also seemed very alert for a 9am lecture. Lucy couldn't also help but wonder how bad she must have looked a week before. "Do you think that arrogant lecturer will turn up again?" April whispered to Lucy, as Lucy started opening her notebook.

"Who knows? Do you want a mint?" Lucy asked holding out a packet.

"Damn yes! You're a life saver, I was in a rush I forgot to brush my teeth!" April quickly accepted the mint. "What a white girl assist!" she laughed raising her hand for a high five. Unlike last week's lecture Lucy saw herself keeping up with April's energy. Lucy smacked her palm with vigour, Lucy also felt being called a white girl by the black April all too telling of her easy-going nature.

The lecture hall died down as the door opened. To everyone's surprise a shuffling old man came through. It was Wentworth. Someone even gave a cheer.

Wentworth clearly startled by the whoop peered through his thick glasses up at the galley of students in front of him. "I didn't realise my presence was so sorely missed," he chuckled lightly as some students did the same. He placed his coat and bag on the chair and rolled up his sleeves. "Now before I begin, I want to clear up a misunderstanding which has spiralled out of control. Contrary to popular belief, I did not have a stroke, nor did I recently get diagnosed with cancer. Those of you, sweet as you are, who slotted sentimental cards under my office door were unfortunately fooled, I did however enjoy the chocolates," he laughed before continuing, "I only had a case of the flu which at my age can stop me from moving around as much as I would like. I am here to teach and promise you I will do so for the rest of this term."

There were more whoops from the ensemble of students who just two weeks earlier found him incredibly boring.

A student raised a hand to which Wentworth nodded for them to speak up "What of Arthur Squire and his assignment?" some students groaned at that.

Lucy was watching the crowd more so than Wentworth interested at the general consensus about Arthur. It didn't look at all positive.

"Ah yes, thank you for bringing that up," Wentworth encouraged licking his lips, "I'll get straight to it. The assignment is non-mandatory. Meaning you do not have to do it. Those of you have done it, well done but I'm afraid it is relatively pointless to this module." There were mixed reactions from the crowd of students upon hearing that. Those who were unhappy were probably the ones who wasted their time doing it.

April was beaming, "good thing I never did it!" she quipped happily.

"As for my fill in lecturer and associate Arthur Squire, his lecture was scheduled towards the end of this term. It was a guest lecture offering… er alternative perspectives on modern theory of social psychology. You won't in this module be lectured by him anymore. If you like his style, feel free to sign up to any of his modules which run for second years and above." Lucy realised Wentworth was being extremely professional about this despite his obvious distaste for the man. Wentworth gained some points from that speech with the crowd it would seem.

"Without further ado let's begin the lecture…"

*   *   *

Lucy left what was at no surprise to anyone. Another boring lecture. Wentworth may have won over the hearts and minds of first years who Arthur pissed off but that unfortunately did not excuse his teaching style. Arthur at least commanded a whole room of students and kept their attention for the whole hour.

Speaking of Arthur Lucy decided to swing by his office in her free hours. They obviously hadn't communicated since her agreeing to work for him and she hoped to have him answer a few of her questions at that. Albeit, Lucy expected it to be a challenge. As she entered the psychology department building she saw the receptionist Laura hard at work.

"Hey, do you know if Arthur is in his office right now?" Lucy asked putting her hands on the desk as Laura peered up from her computer.

"Well this is rare, a student actually wanting to see him. Are you here to complain?" she asked matter-of-factly.

"No, no nothing like that, just had a few questions is all."

"Hmm." Laura looked curious now. "Yeah he is in but don't be surprised if he doesn't want to talk to you. This is not his contact hour after all."

"Yeah of course, but it is worth a try! Thanks!" Lucy responded before making the same trek down the familiar blue, narrow corridor. Lucy passed Harkin's office and noticed the door had been left open, but no one was inside. Shrugging it off she continued down the corridor to Arthur's office.

As she reached the door and prepared to knock Lucy could hear voices from inside.

"And to top it all off! You knowingly instigated a rumour about Wentworth having a stroke when in fact we both knew he had a simple cold!!" That was unmistakeably the head of department Caitlin Harkin.

"He got a box of chocolates out of it, I was doing him a favour." That was unmistakeably Arthur.

"A favour?!! A favour?!!" Caitlin sounded almost hysterical, "in what world am I supposed to find a member of staff creating rumours about another member of staff's health! A favour?!"

"He got loads of cards, didn't he? A man his age never gets that much attention. The most they usually get is off the ten cats they own."

"Coincidental! I do not believe for a second you did it with that expected outcome!"

"Alright fine, but it was just a joke. It's not my fault millennials are gullible morons."

Lucy heard what sounded like a hand smack onto a table. "You are talking about our main source of income here Arthur," Caitlin growled, "they are expected to listen to you, to believe you. You are a lecturer!!"

"Your're sounding slightly too capitalist for them left wing views of yours Caitlin."

"ARTHUR!"

"Ugh! Fine! I'll clear up the misunderstanding and apologise to the fossil." Lucy could barely believe what she was hearing. Someone talking down Arthur and managing him. No wonder Caitlin was head of department with someone like him around.

"Hold on we are not done yet!"

"What! You serious?" Lucy felt like she was eavesdropping on a mother scolding her eldest son.

"There is the matter of the bogus assignment you set, plus calling a student an accident in front of the entire lecture hall!!"

"Wow you do have a backlog that was a week ago. First off, he asked for it. Second, the assignment wasn't bogus, if I remember correctly you encouraged a student to do it!"

"All because of the amount complaints I get about you pile up past my bloody head. And I only did that as I thought Wentworth had approved it as module convenor but look at that! I thought wrong!" Caitlin exasperated heavily before continuing in a considerably turned down voice, "am I here to continually pick up pieces of crap that you leave in your wake? Am I here to continually cover your fucking priceless arse while you smash it in to anything that can break?!"

There was an awkward silence. Lucy felt like it was now or never. She knocked.

There was flustered whispering before Arthur spoke up, "who is it?"

"Lucy Baxter, I was hoping to speak to you Arthur. Is now a bad time?"

"Er no, please come in."

Lucy opened the door to see a red faced but calming Caitlin standing over a seated Arthur. Lucy couldn't help but think it was like walking in on parents having an argument.

"Oh, hi Caitlin! Didn't realise it was you," Lucy lied, smiling.

Caitlin awkwardly smiled back, "ah Lucy, you look erm well. Better in fact!" She walked over to Lucy away from Arthur. She was considerably more glammed up than last time in a smart blue blazer and skirt. In her hands were a wad of forms which Lucy could only guess were Arthur complaint forms.

"Yeah, and I have to admit it was largely thanks to Arthur," Lucy said acting innocent.

"Oh," Caitlin said with surprise whirring back to glance at Arthur, "is that so?" She said the last part with more venom.

Arthur awkwardly rubbed his neck averting her dagger like eyes.

"So I take it your problem has been solved then?" Caitlin asked Lucy.

"Yes! And it is thanks to you as well for recommending him. Without him I don't know what I would have done!" Lucy was attempting to bail out Arthur not because she wanted him saved but because she wanted him to feel indebted to her.

"Well that's good news!" Caitlin said in a high-pitched voice but suddenly her voice went much lower, "are you sure he didn't pay you to say that?"

"I heard that," Arthur growled, "I have not gone that low."

"Tell that to Wentworth along with an apology!" Caitlin said pointing back at Arthur.

"I will," he replied plainly, "I am not apologising to the accident of the 20th century however."

Caitlin's eyes narrowed, "fine, I'll just tell them you have gone through a disciplinary procedure, which is not entirely inaccurate considering all this." She pointed to the office and to her red cheeks.

"You have made your point Caitlin," Arthur reassured her.

"Good, and you Lucy." Caitlin turned on Lucy who was taken aback. "You never saw or heard what you just heard and saw. Are we clear?" Lucy nodded immediately realising how strangely intimidating this woman can be. "Excellent, have a good day both." She started to head to the door but paused on the threshold before saying, "thank you Arthur for helping her. She was a mess when I found her." She turned to give Arthur a pleasant smile "I'm sure there are more that will need helping." With that she left.

Arthur got out of his chair to close the door Caitlin left open. "Lazy hag," he muttered.

"Wait does she know?" Lucy asked incredulously.

"Bits and bobs. She gets the gist and nothing more," Arthur replied curtly.

"Then how come she remembers?" Lucy challenged.

Arthur rolled his eyes as he returned to his seat, "because she is not an architect, hypnotism isn't really effective against normies. And she viewed some of my research before approving me as a member of staff."

"So, your research about figments and architects is available for public viewing then?" Lucy challenged further.

"No not really. She had to sign a state secrets form to view it. It's a long story. Can we cut to the chase? Why are you here?" he asked clearly grouchy as he had just been lectured by his boss.

"I have some questions," Lucy answered.

"So that's why you decided to bail me out? To get me on my good side?" Arthur snorted, "not half bad Lucy. I'm impressed. What is it you want to ask?"

Lucy smirked as her ploy had paid off sitting down on the familiar sofa chair. "I wanted to reflect on Saturday as well as ask about my new job."

"Figures," Arthur said aloud as he got a tooth pick out of his pocket and rammed it into his mouth. "Well ask away, I'm a busy man with a seminar in half an hour."

"Okay first things first, how much am I getting paid?" Lucy asked with a straight face.

Arthur looked at her for a second then started laughing. He roared with laughter. He carried on for a short while wiping a tear from his eye. He then finally glanced back at Lucy, "oh you were serious?"

"You knew damn well I was serious!" Lucy thundered as Arthur looked smug. You wouldn't believe it a minute ago that he was having his arse handed to him by Caitlin Lucy thought.

"Your memories intact and you live to believe in another day, that is your payment. Expenses will be covered by me however. You won't be paying a dime working with me. Anything else?"

Lucy ground her teeth to almost paste as she half expected this response. It was her feeling of being indebted to him that stopped her from pursuing the issue. "When are my working days? And for how long during those days?"

Arthur started chewing on the tooth pick absentmindedly. "When I want you to." he answered unhelpfully.

"Erm, I kind of need notice." Lucy pressed trying her best to keep it civil.

"Look Lucy," Arthur said losing his patience already, "this is not a 9-5 job. There is no rota, no minimum wage and no holidays. This is freelance. If you're working for me expect to be helping with my research. That means going on cases, searching for figments, pacifying architects, that sort of thing." With the last parts of the job entailed Lucy started sensing the adventure and excitement in it all. Finding more architects and figments? It does sound intriguing and somewhat fun. "Oh, and before I forget, there is no life insurance policy."

Lucy suddenly blinked back into reality, "why did you feel the need to say that?"

"I'll let you figure that one out by yourself."

"I'm truly honoured."

"I will allay one fear however. This will not get in the way of your uni life. At least for the most part. I'm first and foremost a lecturer meaning only on weekends and holidays do I get to do the exciting fieldwork. It'll be on those excursions you'll be tagging along on."

"So, I have basically done a deal with the devil that I sacrifice all my weekends in return for my life?" Lucy pondered sardonically.

Arthur merely smiled at that, not caring to answer.

"Another question then, what am I expecting? You said you encountered a dragon. A dragon! Am I going to encounter things like vampires or werewolves?" Lucy was a closet twilight fan.

Arthur gave her a curious look, "I have encountered both vampires and werewolves as well. If a non-aware architect believes in vampires, they will appear same as a self-aware architect could knowingly make a vampire into existence although they are not easy to imagine up. It goes without saying that despite being figments they are both exceptionally dangerous examples and I wouldn't recommend being around either of them."

"Are we like hunters or something?!" Lucy was now getting excited at the idea.

Arthur drew a scowl, "no we are academics. We study them. We don't hunt them and kill them. Although chances are we are more likely to be killed by them."

"Holy shit," Lucy whispered leaning back on her chair thoughtfully. "Being an architect is really powerful stuff isn't it?"

Arthur nodded, "and that is why DACFE has that attitude of keeping them on a leash wherever possible." He gave a stern look to Lucy as if to remind her of Saturday's events. "But, architects are not omnipotent. Just like the laws that govern the universe architects and figments are subject to constraints and rules like anything else. And that is what my study is interested in the most. Those rules and constraints."

"Erm, you have said it a lot but what does DACFE stand for?"

Arthur blew out some hot air which made a few hairs on his fringe raise briefly off his forehead, "Department for Architect Containment and Figment Extermination, civil servants really like their abbreviations."

"Should I be worried about them?" Lucy pressed conscious this could be a dangerous organisation to her.

"I think the average person should be nervous of centralised governments in general but in the sense of the immediate threat they have to you should be shielded by me. Remember I am extending my immunity to you. I have yet to do the paperwork and I'll notify them myself of what I have decided to do with you. They won't like it but I have enough of their agents' balls in a vice that it won't matter. Metaphorically of course." Arthur was seeking to reassure her, if in his own crass way.

"But there is a high chance I will encounter them?" said Lucy still not fully convinced.

Arthur snorted, "a high chance? You already have. Truman is one of their lackey's I nickname him the greyhound because he is becoming obsolete within the organisation. A shame but every dog has his day." He sniggered at his own joke. "Unfortunately, Lucy, we won't be escaping their influence they are simply too well-resourced. You heard about that arson attack on Aberstahl Manor?"

"I have only heard people mention it in passing. Not many are bothered by it, it was planned for demolition anyway right?"

Arthur snorted again louder this time, "100% DACFE were involved with that. It's their style to burn things to the ground. Or perhaps I'm being too harsh on them, it is the style of their best agent to burn shit to the ground." Arthur's face turned momentarily dark as if he was remembering something extremely unpleasant.

"Why would DACFE bother burning down some old manor?" Lucy felt like she was only asking questions around Arthur. There was so much to know about this new life she was going to experience.

"What does the last two letters in that abbreviation stand for again Lucy?" Arthur said like primary school teacher reminding a child what letter comes after P in the alphabet.

"Ok, ok. I get the idea!" Lucy said slightly annoyed with his tone. "I do have a serious question about architects now," Lucy continued conscious of time.

"Oh, good something I'm actually motivated to answer!" Arthur responded excitedly, Lucy decided to ignore what he just said.

"Is being an architect hereditary?"

Arthur leaned back in his chair at that, pondering that one for a good minute. "An interesting question for you to ask considering how many other things you could have asked. The answer is no. It is unfortunately entirely at random, there are no blood ties. It just develops in some people and that is simply that.

It can partially explain why architects have not been killed off, no one can predict who will be one." Lucy did not attempt to hide her visual disappointment at the answer. "Oh I see." Arthur had just got a brainwave. "you were hoping your mother was an architect and that could explain why she was so unstable. It's a good hypothesis but very unlikely."

"It was just a thought," Lucy said turning to stare out the window. Damn he's good Lucy thought to herself.

"Then let me ask you a question." Lucy turned back to look at Arthur "Throughout your whole backstory there is someone you seem to be forgetting." Lucy shrugged as if she did not know who, "your father."

Arthur dropped the bombshell as Lucy pretended to look indifferent "He ran away that's all that matters. He's a coward, nothing more."

"You don't intend to find him?"

"No, I don't."

"Why?"

"Because my mother told me to let it go. I'm moving on. He moved on ten years ago and I'm moving on now."

Arthur nodded thoughtfully at that answer either satisfied or deciding not to pursue it anymore.

"I have one final question however," Lucy asked hurriedly conscious of time.

Arthur glanced at his grandfather clock, "make it quick Lucy."

"As I am now a self-aware architect I can now bring my mother back whenever I want?"

Arthur gave Lucy a sad look. It was a not pitying look but one that understood. One that had been in that position before. "Your shadow Lucy, is an imitation of your mother. Nothing can bring back the dead. You may at any time chose to bring your shadow back, maybe even upgrade it to a familiar class, so it becomes an ally for you. You now know what power you have, it is up to you although I'd recommend against recklessly using it. I'll ask you now in fact, do you plan to bring her back?"

Lucy took her time, pondering, deciding and thinking. As Arthur was just preparing to leave he took a final glance at Lucy who smiled at him, "you know Arthur? I think I plan to let her rest now. She deserves that much."

The End

Printed in Great Britain
by Amazon